Six Years

SIX YEARS

HARLAN COBEN

THORNDIKE PRESS
A part of Gale, Cengage Learning

GALE
CENGAGE Learning®

Detroit • New York • San Francisco • New Haven, Conn • Waterville, Maine • London

LIBRARY OF CONGRESS CATALOGING-IN-PUBLICATION DATA

Coben, Harlan, 1962-
 Six years / by Harlan Coben.
  pages ; cm. — (Thorndike Press large print core)
 ISBN-13: 978-1-4104-5606-9 (hardcover)
 ISBN-10: 1-4104-5606-4 (hardcover)
 1. Large type books. I. Title.
PS3553.O225S58 2013
813'.54—dc23   2013003302

Published in 2013 by arrangement with Dutton, a member of Penguin Group (USA) Inc.

Printed in the United States of America
1 2 3 4 5 6 7 17 16 15 14 13

To Brad Bradbeer
Without you, dear friend,
there'd be no Win

CHAPTER 1

I sat in the back pew and watched the only woman I would ever love marry another man.

Natalie wore white, of course, looking extra mock-me-forever gorgeous. There had always been both a fragility and quiet strength to her beauty, and up there, Natalie looked ethereal, almost otherworldly.

She bit down on her lower lip. I flashed back to those lazy mornings when we would make love and then she'd throw on my blue dress shirt and we'd head downstairs. We would sit in the breakfast nook and read the paper and eventually she'd take out her pad and start sketching. As she drew me, she would bite down on her lip just like this.

Two hands reached into my chest, grabbed my brittle heart on either side, and snapped it in two.

Why had I come?

Do you believe in love at first sight?

Neither do I. I do, however, believe in major, more-than-just-physical attraction at first sight. I believe that every once in a while — once, maybe twice in a lifetime — you are drawn to someone so deeply, so primordially, so immediately — a stronger-than-magnetic pull. That was how it was with Natalie. Sometimes that is all there is. Sometimes it grows and gathers heat and turns into a glorious inferno that you know is real and meant to last forever.

And sometimes you just get fooled into thinking the first is the second.

I had naively thought that we were forever. I, who had never really believed in commitment and had done all I could to escape its shackles, knew right away — well, within a week anyway — that this was the woman I was going to wake up next to every single day. This was the woman I'd lay my life down to protect. This was the woman — yes, I know how corny this sounds — whom I could do nothing without, who would make even the mundane something poignant.

Gag me with a spoon, right?

A minister with a cleanly shaven head was talking, but the rush of blood in my ears made it impossible to make out his words. I stared at Natalie. I wanted her to be happy.

That wasn't just lip service, the lie we often tell ourselves because, in truth, if our lover doesn't want us, then we want her miserable, don't we? But here I really meant it. If I truly believed that Natalie would be happier without me, then I would let her go, no matter how crushing. But I didn't believe that she would be happier, despite what she had said or done. Or maybe that is yet another self-rationalization, another lie, we tell ourselves.

Natalie did not so much as glance at me, but I could see something tighten around her mouth. She knew that I was in the room. She kept her eyes on her husband-to-be. His name, I had recently found out, was Todd. I hate the name Todd. Todd. They probably called him Toddy or the Todd-Man or the Toddster.

Todd's hair was too long, and he sported that four-day-stubble beard some people found hip and others, like me, found punchworthy. His eyes smoothly and smugly skimmed the guests before getting snagged on, well, me. They stayed there a second, sizing me up before deciding that I wasn't worth the time.

Why had Natalie gone back to him?

The maid of honor was Natalie's sister, Julie. She stood on the dais with a bouquet in both hands and a lifeless, robotic smile on her lips. We'd never met, but I'd seen pictures and heard them talk on the phone. Julie, too, looked stunned by this development. I tried to meet her eye, but she was working that thousand-yard stare.

I looked back at Natalie's face, and it was as if small explosives detonated in my chest. Just boom, boom, boom. Man, this had been a bad idea. When the best man brought out the rings, my lungs started shutting down. It was hard to breathe.

Enough.

I had come here to see it for myself, I guess. I had learned the hard way that I needed that. My father died of a massive coronary five months ago. He had never had a heart problem before and was by all accounts in good shape. I remembered sitting in that waiting room, being called into the doctor's office, being told the devastating news — and then being asked, both there and at the funeral home, if I wanted to see his body. I passed. I figured that I didn't want to remember him lying on a gurney or in a casket. I would remember him as he was.

But as time went on, I started having trouble accepting his death. He had been so vibrant, so alive. Two days before his death, we had gone to a New York Rangers hockey game — Dad had season tickets — and the game had gone into overtime and we screamed and cheered and, well, how could he be dead? Part of me started wondering if somehow there had been a mistake made or if it was all a great big con and that my dad was maybe somehow still alive. I know that makes no sense, but desperation can toy with you and if you give desperation any wiggle room, it will find alternative answers.

Part of me was haunted by the fact that I never saw my father's body. I didn't want to make the same mistake here. But, to keep within this lame metaphor, I had now seen the dead body. There was no reason to check the pulse or poke at it or hang around it longer than necessary.

I tried to make my departure as inconspicuous as I could. This is no easy feat when you're six-five and are built, to use Natalie's phrase, "like a lumberjack." I have big hands. Natalie had loved them. She would hold them in her own and trace the lines on my palm. She said they were real hands, a man's hands. She had drawn them too because, she said, they told my story — my blue-collar up-bringing, my working my way through Lanford College as a bouncer at a local nightclub, and also, somehow, the fact that I was now the youngest professor in their political science department.

I stumbled out of the small white chapel and into the warm summer air. Summer. Was that all this had been in the end? A summer fling? Instead of two randy kids seeking activity at camp, we were two adults seeking solitude on retreat — she to do her art, me to write my poly-sci dissertation — who met and fell hard and now that it was nearing September, well, all good things come to an end. Our whole relationship did have that unreal quality to it, both of us away from our regular lives and all the mundanity that goes along with that. Maybe that was what made it so awesome. Maybe the fact that we only spent time in this reality-free bubble made our relationship better and more intense. Maybe I was full of crap.

From behind the church door I heard cheers, applause. That snapped me out of my stupor. The service was over. Todd and Natalie were now Mr. and Mrs. Stubble Face. They'd be coming down the aisle soon. I wondered whether they'd get rice thrown at them. Todd probably wouldn't like that. It'd mess up his hair and get stuck in the stubble.

Again I didn't need to see more.

I headed behind the white chapel, getting

out of sight just as the chapel doors flew open. I stared out at the clearing. Nothing there, just, well, clearing. There were trees in the distance. The cabins were on the other side of the hill. The chapel was part of the artist retreat where Natalie was staying. Mine was down the road at a retreat for writers. Both retreats were old Vermont farms that still grew a bit of the organic.

"Hello, Jake."

I turned toward the familiar voice. There, standing no more than ten yards away from me, was Natalie. I quickly looked toward her left ring finger. As if reading my thoughts, she raised the hand to show me the new wedding band.

"Congratulations," I said. "I'm very happy for you."

She ignored that comment. "I can't believe you're here."

I spread my arms. "I heard there would be great passed hors d'oeuvres. It's hard to keep me away from those."

"Funny."

I shrugged while my heart turned into dust and blew away.

"Everyone said you'd never show," Natalie said. "But I knew you would."

"I still love you," I said.

"I know."

"And you still love me."

"I don't, Jake. See?"

She waved the ring in my face.

"Honey?" Todd and his facial hair came around the corner. He spotted me and frowned. "Who is this?"

But it was clear that he knew.

"Jake Fisher," I said. "Congratulations on the nuptials."

"Where have I seen you before?"

I let Natalie handle that one. She put a comforting hand on his shoulder and said, "Jake has been modeling for a lot of us. You probably recognize him from some of our pieces."

He still frowned. Natalie got in front of him and said, "If you could just give us a second, okay? I'll be right there."

Todd glanced over at me. I didn't move. I didn't back up. I didn't look away.

Grudgingly he said, "Okay. But don't be long."

He gave me one more hard look and started back around the chapel. Natalie looked over at me. I pointed toward where Todd had vanished.

"He seems fun," I said.

"Why are you here?"

"I needed to tell you that I love you," I said. "I needed to tell you that I always will."

"It's over, Jake. You'll move on. You'll be fine."

I said nothing.

"Jake?"

"What?"

She tilted her head a little. She knew what that head tilt did to me. "Promise me you'll leave us alone."

I just stood there.

"Promise me you won't follow us or call or even e-mail."

The pain in my chest grew. It became something sharp and heavy.

"Promise me, Jake. Promise me you'll leave us alone."

Her eyes locked on to mine.

"Okay," I said. "I promise."

Without another word, Natalie walked away, back to the front of that chapel toward the man she had just married. I stood there a moment, trying to catch my breath. I tried to get angry, tried to make light of it, tried to shrug it off and tell her it was her loss. I tried all that, and then I even tried to be mature about it, but I still knew that this was all a stall technique, so I wouldn't have to face the fact that I would be forever brokenhearted.

I stayed there behind the chapel until I figured everyone was gone. Then I came back around. The minister with the cleanly shaven head was outside on the steps. So was Natalie's sister, Julie. She put a hand on my arm. "Are you okay?"

"I'm super," I said to her.

The minister smiled at me. "A lovely day for a wedding, don't you think?"

I blinked into the sunlight. "I guess it is," I said, and then I walked away.

I would do as Natalie asked. I would leave her alone. I would think about her every day, but I'd never call or reach out or even look her up online. I would keep my promise.

For six years.

CHAPTER 2

Six years later

The biggest change in my life, though I couldn't know it at the time, would arrive sometime between 3:29 P.M. and 3:30 P.M.

My freshman class on the politics of moral reasoning had just ended. I was heading out of Bard Hall. The day was campus-ready. The sun shone brightly on this crisp Massachusetts afternoon. There was an Ultimate Frisbee game on the quad. Students lay strewn all over the place, as though scattered by some giant hand. Music blasted. It was as if the dream campus brochure had come to life.

I love days like this, but then again, who doesn't?

"Professor Fisher?"

I turned to the voice. Seven students were sitting in a semicircle in the grass. The girl who spoke was in the middle.

"Would you like to join us?" she asked.

I waved them off with a smile. "Thanks, but I have office hours."

I kept walking. I wouldn't have stayed anyway, though I would have loved to sit with them on such a glorious day — who wouldn't? There were fine lines between teacher and student, and, sorry, uncharitable as this might sound, I didn't want to be *that* teacher, if you know what I mean, the teacher who hangs out a little too much with the student body and attends the occasional frat party and maybe offers up a beer at the football game tailgate. A professor should be supportive and approachable, but a professor should be neither buddy nor parent.

When I got to Clark House, Mrs. Dinsmore greeted me with a familiar scowl. Mrs. Dinsmore, a classic battle-axe, had been the political science department receptionist here since, I believe, the Hoover administration. She was at least two hundred years old but was only as impatient and nasty as someone half that age.

"Good afternoon, sexy," I said to her. "Any messages?"

"On your desk," Mrs. Dinsmore said. Even her voice scowled. "And there's the usual line of coeds outside your door."

"Okay, thanks."

"Looks like a Rockettes audition back there."

"Got it."

"Your predecessor was never this accessible."

"Oh, come now, Mrs. Dinsmore. I visited him here all the time when I was a student."

"Yeah, but at least your shorts were an appropriate length."

"And that disappointed you a little, didn't it?"

Mrs. Dinsmore did her best not to smile at me. "Just get out of my face, will you?"

"Just admit it."

"You want a kick in the pants? Get out of here."

I blew her a kiss and took the back entrance so as to avoid the line of students who signed up for Friday office hours. I have two hours of "unscheduled" office time every Friday from 3:00 to 5:00 P.M. It was open time, nine minutes per student, no schedule, no early sign-up. You just show up — first come, first served. We keep strictly on the clock. You have nine minutes. No more, no less, and then one minute to leave and let the next student settle in and have their turn. If you need more time or if I'm your thesis adviser or what have you, Mrs. Dinsmore will schedule you for a longer ap-

19

pointment.

At exactly 3:00 P.M., I let in the first student. She wanted to discuss theories on Locke and Rousseau, two political scientists better known now by their *Lost* TV show reincarnations than their philosophical theories. The second student had no real reason to be here other than to — and I am being blunt here — suck up. Sometimes I wanted to hold up a hand and say, "Bake me some cookies instead," but I get it. The third student was into grade groveling; that is, she thought that her B+ paper should have been an A−, when in fact it probably should have been a B.

This was how it was. Some came to my office to learn, some came to impress, some came to grovel, some came to chat — that was all okay. I don't make judgments based on these visits. That would be wrong. I treat every student who walks through those doors the same because we are here to *teach,* if not political science, maybe a little something about critical thinking or even — gasp! — life. If students came to us fully formed and without insecurities, what would be the point?

"It stays a B plus," I said when she finished her pitch. "But I bet you'll be able to get the grade up with the next essay."

The buzzer on the clock sounded. Yes, as I said, I keep the times in here strict. It was now exactly 3:29. That was how, when I looked back at all that would happen, I knew exactly when it all first began — between 3:29 P.M. and 3:30 P.M.

"Thank you, Professor," she said, standing to leave. I stood with her.

My office hadn't been changed one iota since I became department head four years ago, taking over this room from my predecessor and mentor, Professor Malcolm Hume, secretary of state for one administration, chief of staff for another. There was still the wonderful nostalgic essence of academic disarray — antique globes, oversize books, yellowing manuscripts, posters peeling off the wall, framed portraits of men with beards. There was no desk in the room, just a big oak table that could seat twelve, the exact number in my senior thesis class.

There was clutter everywhere. I hadn't bothered redecorating, not so much because I wanted to honor my mentor as most believed but because, one, I was lazy and really couldn't be bothered; two, I didn't really have a personal style or family photographs to put up and didn't really care for that "the office is a reflection of the man" nonsense or if I did, then this indeed was

21

the man; and three, I always found clutter to be conducive to individual expression. There is something about sterility and organization that inhibits spontaneity in a student. Clutter seems to welcome free expression from my students — the environment is already muddled and messed, they seem to think, so what further harm could my ridiculous ideas do to it?

But mostly it was because I was lazy and couldn't be bothered.

We both stood from the big oak table and shook hands. She held mine a second longer than she had to so I disengaged intentionally fast. No, this doesn't happen all the time. But it does happen. I'm thirty-five now, but when I first started here — the young professor in his twenties — it happened more often. Do you remember that scene in *Raiders of the Lost Ark* where one student wrote "LOVE YOU" on her eyelids? Something like that happened to me in my first semester. Except the first word wasn't "LOVE" and the second word had been switched from "YOU" to "ME." I don't flatter myself about it. We professors are in a position of fairly immense power. The men who fall for this or believe that they are somehow worthy of such attention (not to be sexist, but it was almost always men) are usually more insecure and needy than any daddy-issued coed one might happen upon.

As I sat down and waited for the next student to arrive, I glanced at the computer on the right side of the table. The college's home screen was up. The page was typically collegiate, I guess. On the left, there was a slideshow of college life, students of all races, creeds, religions, and genders having a studiously good time, interacting with one another, with professors, extracurricular activities, you get the idea. The banner on the top featured the school's logo and most recognizable buildings, including prestigious Johnson Chapel, a large-scale version of the chapel where I had watched Natalie get married.

On the right part of the screen, there was a college newsfeed and now, as Barry Watkins, the next student on the sign-up sheet, entered the room and said, "Yo, Prof, how's it hanging?" I spotted an obituary in the feed that made me pause.

"Hey, Barry," I said, eyes still on the screen. "Take a seat."

He did so, throwing his feet up on the table. He knew that I didn't care. Barry came every week. We talked about everything and nothing. His visits were more watered-down therapy than anything in the realm of academia, but again that was perfectly okay with me.

I took a closer look at the monitor. What had made me pause was the stamp-size photograph of the deceased. I didn't recognize him — not at that distance — but he looked young. In a way, that was not unusual for the obituaries. Many times the college, rather than securing a more recent photograph, would scan in the deceased's yearbook photograph, but here, even at a quick glance, I could see that this was not the case. The hairstyle wasn't something from, say, the sixties or seventies. The photograph wasn't in black-and-white either, something the yearbook had been up until 1989.

Still we are a small college, four hundred or so students per class. Death was not uncommon, but maybe because of the size of the school or my close affiliation as both a student and member of the faculty I always felt somewhat personally involved when someone from here died.

"Yo, Teach?"

"One second, Barry."

I was now infringing on his clock time. I use a portable scoreboard timer, the kind you see in basketball gyms all over this country, with giant red digital numbers. A

24

friend had given it to me as a gift, assuming because of my size that I must have played hoops. I hadn't, but I loved the clock. Since it was set to automatically count down from nine minutes, I could see now that we were on 8:49.

I clicked on the small photograph. When the larger one came up, I managed to hold back the gasp.

The name of the deceased was Todd Sanderson.

I had blocked Todd's last name from my memory — the wedding invite had just said "Todd and Natalie's Nuptials!" — but, man, I knew the face. Gone was the hip stubble. He was clean-shaven here, his hair closer to a buzz cut. I wondered whether that was Natalie's influence — she had always complained that my stubble irritated her skin — and then I wondered why I would be thinking about something so asinine.

"The clock is ticking, Teach."

"One second, Barry. And don't call me Teach."

Todd's age was listed as forty-two. That was a little older than I expected. Natalie was thirty-four, just a year younger than me. I had figured that Todd would be closer to our age. According to the obituary, Todd

25

had been an all-league tight end on the football team and a Rhodes Scholar finalist. Impressive. He had graduated summa cum laude from the history department, had founded a charity called Fresh Start, and during his senior year, he had been president of Psi U, my fraternity.

Todd was not only an alumnus of my school but we had both pledged the same fraternity. How had I not known any of that?

There was more, a lot more, but I skipped down to the last line:

Funeral services are Sunday in Palmetto Bluff, South Carolina, near Savannah, Georgia. Mr. Sanderson is survived by his wife and two children.

Two children?

"Professor Fisher?"

There was something funny in Barry's voice. "Sorry, I was just —"

"No, man, don't be. You okay though?"

"Yes, I'm fine."

"You sure? You look pale, man." Barry dropped his sneakers to the floor and put his hands on the desk. "Look, I can come back another time."

"No," I said.

I turned away from the monitor. It would

26

have to wait. Natalie's husband had died young. That was sad, yes, tragic even, but it had nothing to do with me. It was not a reason to cancel work or inconvenience my students. It had thrown me for a loop, of course — not only Todd dying but the fact that he had gone to my alma mater. That was a somewhat bizarre coincidence, I guess, but not exactly an earth-shattering revelation.

Maybe Natalie simply liked Lanford men.

"So what's up?" I asked Barry.

"Do you know Professor Byrner?"

"Sure."

"He's a total tool."

He was, but I wouldn't say that. "What seems to be the issue?"

I hadn't seen a cause of death in the obituary. The campus ones often didn't have one. I would look again later. If it wasn't in there, maybe I could find a more complete obituary online.

Then again, why would I want to learn more? What difference did it make?

Best to stay away from this.

Either way it would have to wait for office hours to end. I finished up with Barry and kept going. I tried to push thoughts of the obituary aside and focus on my remaining students. I was off my game, but the students were oblivious. Students cannot imagine that professors have real lives in the same way they can't imagine their parents having sex. On one level, that was fine. On another, I constantly remind them to look past themselves. Part of the human condition is that we all think that we are uniquely complex while everyone else is somewhat simpler to read. That is not true, of course. We all have our own dreams and hopes and wants and lust and heartaches. We all have our own brand of crazy.

My mind drifted. I watched the clock trudge slowly forward as if I were the most bored student in the most boring class. When five o'clock came I headed back to the computer monitor. I brought up Todd Sanderson's obituary in full.

Nope, no cause of death was given.

Curious. Sometimes there was a hint in the suggested donation area. It will say in lieu of flowers please make a donation to the American Cancer Society or something like that. But nothing was listed. There was also no mention of Todd's occupation, but again, so what?

My office door flew open, and Benedict Edwards, a professor in the humanities department and my closest friend, entered. He didn't bother knocking, but he never had or felt the need to. We often met on Fridays at five o'clock and visited a bar where as a student I worked as a bouncer. Back then it was new and shiny and hip and trendy. Now it was old and broken-down and about as hip and trendy as Betamax.

Benedict was pretty much my physical opposite — tiny, small-boned, and African American. His eyes were magnified by giant Ant-Man glasses that looked like the safety goggles in the chemistry department. Apollo Creed had to be the inspiration behind his too big mustache and too poufy Afro. He had the slender fingers of a female pianist, feet that a ballerina would envy, and he wouldn't be mistaken for a lumberjack by a blind man.

Despite this — or maybe because of it — Benedict was also a total "playah" and picked up more women than a rapper with a radio hit.

"What's wrong?" Benedict asked.

I skipped the "Nothing" or "How do you know something's wrong?" and went straight to it: "Have you ever heard of a guy named Todd Sanderson?"

"Don't think so. Who is he?"

"An alum. His obituary is online."

I turned the screen toward him. Benedict adjusted the goggle-glasses. "Don't recognize him. Why?"

"Remember Natalie?"

A shadow crossed his face. "I haven't heard you say her name in —"

"Yeah, yeah. Anyway, this is — or was — her husband."

"The guy she dumped you for?"

"Yes."

"And now he's dead."

"Apparently."

"So," Benedict said, arching an eyebrow, "she's single again."

"Sensitive."

"I'm worried. You're my best wingman. I have the rap the ladies love, sure, but you have the good looks. I don't want to lose you."

"Sensitive," I said again.

"You going to call her?"

"Who?" I asked.

"Condoleezza Rice. Who do you think I mean? Natalie."

"Yeah, sure. Say something like 'Hey, the guy you dumped me for is dead. Want to catch a movie?'"

Benedict was reading the obituary. "Wait."

"What?"

"Says here she has two kids."

"So?"

"That makes it more complicated."

"Will you stop?"

"I mean two kids. She could be fat now." Benedict looked over at me with his magnified eyes. "So what does Natalie look like now? I mean, two kids. She's probably chunky, right?"

"How would I know?"

"Uh, the same way everyone would — Google, Facebook, that kinda thing."

I shook my head. "Haven't done that."

"What? Everyone does that. Heck, I do that with all my former loves."

"And the Internet can handle that kind of traffic?"

Benedict grinned. "I do need my own server."

"Man, I hope that's not a euphemism."

But I saw something sad behind his grin. I remembered one time at a bar when Benedict had gotten particularly wasted, I caught him staring at a well-worn photograph he kept hidden in his wallet. I asked him who it was. "The only girl I'll ever love," he told me in a slurry voice. Then Benedict tucked the photograph back behind his credit card and despite hints from me, he has never said another word about it.

He'd had that same sad grin on then.

"I promised Natalie," I said.

"Promised her what?"

"That I'd leave them alone. That I'd never look them up or bother them."

Benedict considered that. "It seems you kept that promise, Jake."

I said nothing. Benedict had lied earlier. He didn't check the Facebook page of old girlfriends or if he did, he didn't do it with much enthusiasm. But once when I burst into his office — like him, I never knocked — I saw him using Facebook. I caught a quick glance and saw that the page he had up belonged to that same woman whose picture he carried in his wallet. Benedict quickly shut the browser down, but I bet that he checked that page a lot. Every day, even. I bet that he looked at every new photograph of the only woman he ever loved. I bet that he looked at her life now, her family maybe, the man who shared her bed, and that he stared at them the same way he stared at the photograph in his wallet. I don't have proof of any of this, just a feeling, but I don't think I'm too far off.

Like I said before, we all have our own brand of crazy.

"What are you trying to say?" I asked him.

"I'm just telling you that that whole 'them' stuff is over now."

"Natalie hasn't been a part of my life in a long time."

"You really believe that?" Benedict asked. "Did she make you promise to forget how you felt too?"

"I thought you were afraid of losing your best wingman."

"You're not that good-looking."

"Cruel bastard."

He rose. "We humanities professors know all."

Benedict left me alone then. I stood and walked over to the window. I looked out on the commons. I watched the students walk by and, as I often did when confronted with a life situation, I wondered what I'd advise one of them if they were in my shoes. Suddenly, without warning, it all came rushing in at once — that white chapel, the way she wore her hair, the way she held up her ring finger, all the pain, the want, the emotions, the love, the hurt. My knees buckled. I thought that I had stopped carrying a torch for her. She had crushed me, but I had picked up the pieces, put myself back together, and moved on with my life.

How stupid to have such thoughts now. How selfish. How inappropriate. The woman had just lost her husband, and prick that I am, I was worried about the ramifications for me. Let it go, I told myself. Forget it and her. Move on.

But I couldn't. I was simply not built that way.

I had last seen Natalie at a wedding. Now I would see her at a funeral. Some people would find irony in that — I was not one of them.

I headed back to the computer and booked a flight to Savannah.

CHAPTER 3

The first sign something was off occurred during the eulogy.

Palmetto Bluff was not so much a town as a gigantic gated community. The newly built "village" was beautiful, clean, nicely maintained, historically accurate — all of which gave the place a sterile, Disney-Epcot faux feel. Everything seemed a little too perfect. The sparkly white chapel — yep, another one — sat on a bluff so picturesque it appeared to be, well, a picture. The heat, however, was all too real — a living, breathing thing with humidity thick enough to double as a beaded curtain.

Another fleeting moment of reason questioned why I had come down here, but I swatted it away. I was here now, thus making the question moot. The Inn at Palmetto Bluff looked like a movie facade. I stepped into its cute bar and ordered a scotch straight up from a cute barmaid.

"You here for the funeral?" she asked me.

"Yep."

"Tragic."

I nodded and stared down at my drink. The cute barmaid picked up the hint and said no more.

I pride myself on being an enlightened man. I do not believe in fate or destiny or any of that superstitious nonsense, yet here I was, justifying my impulsive behavior in just such a manner. I am *supposed* to be here, I told myself. Compelled to board that flight. I didn't know why. I had seen with my own two eyes Natalie marry another man, and yet even now, I still couldn't quite accept it. There was still an innate need for closure. Six years ago, Natalie had dumped me with a note telling me she was marrying her old beau. The next day, I got an invitation to their wedding. No wonder it all still felt . . . incomplete. Now I was here in the hopes of finding, if not closure, completion.

Amazing what we can self-rationalize when we really want something.

But what exactly did I want here?

I finished my drink, thanked the cute barmaid, and carefully started toward the chapel. I kept my distance, of course. I might be horrible and callous and self-involved, but not so much as to intrude on a widow burying her husband. I stayed behind a large tree — a palmetto, what else? — not daring to so much as sneak a look at the mourners.

When I heard the opening hymn, I figured that the coast was as clear as it was going to be. A quick glance confirmed it. Everyone was inside the chapel now. I started toward it. I could hear a gospel choir singing. They were, in a word, magnificent. Not sure what exactly to do, I tried the chapel door, found it unlocked (well, duh), and pushed inside. I lowered my head as I entered, putting a hand to my face as though scratching an itch.

Talk about a poor man's disguise.

There was no need. The chapel was packed. I stood in the back with other late-arriving mourners who couldn't find a seat. The choir finished the spirited hymn, and a man — I don't know if he was a minister or priest or what — took to the pulpit. He began to talk about Todd as a "caring physician, good neighbor, generous friend, and wonderful family man." Physician. I hadn't known that. The man waxed eloquent on Todd's strengths — his charity work, his winning personality, his generosity of spirit, his ability to make every person feel special, his willingness to roll up his sleeves and pitch in whenever anyone, stranger or friend, needed a hand. I naturally wrote this off as familiar funeral narrative — we have a natural habit of overpraising the deceased — but I could see the tears in the eyes of the mourners, the way they nodded along with the words, as though it was a song only they could hear.

From my perch in the back I tried to glance up front for a glimpse of Natalie, but there were too many heads in the way. I didn't want to make myself conspicuous, so I stopped. Besides, I had come into the chapel and looked around and even listened to words of praise for the deceased. Wasn't that enough? What else was there to do here?

It was time to leave.

"Our first eulogy," the man at the pulpit said, "comes from Eric Sanderson."

A pale teen — I would guess that he was around sixteen — rose and moved to the pulpit. My first thought was that Eric must be Todd Sanderson's (and by extension, Natalie's) nephew, but that thought was quickly shot down by the boy's opening sentence.

"My father was my hero . . ."

Father?

It took me a few seconds. Minds have a habit of going on certain tracks and not being able to hop off. When I was a child, my father told me an old riddle that he thought would fool me. "A father and son get in a car accident. The father dies. The boy is rushed to the hospital. The surgeon says, 'I can't operate on this boy. He's my son.' How can that be?" This was what I mean about tracks. For my father's generation, this riddle was, I guess, mildly difficult to figure, but for people my age, the answer — the surgeon was his mother — was so obvious, I remember laughing out loud. "What next, Dad? Are you going to start using your eight-track player?"

Here was something similar. How, I wondered, could a man who has only been married to Natalie six years have a teenage son? Answer: Eric was Todd's son, not Natalie's. Either Todd had been married previously or at the very least had a child with another woman.

I tried again to see Natalie in the front row. I craned my neck, but the woman standing next to me gave me an exasperated sigh for invading her space. Up on the podium, Todd's son, Eric, was killing it. He spoke beautifully and movingly. There wasn't a dry eye in the chapel except, well, mine.

So now what? Just stand here? Pay my

respects to the widow and, what, confuse her or disrupt her day of mourning? And what about selfish ol' me? Did I really want to see her face again, see her crying over the loss of the love of her life?

I didn't think so. I checked my watch. I had booked my flight out tonight. Yep, quick in and out. No muss, no fuss, no overnight, no hotel cost. Closure on the cheap.

There were those who would state the obvious about Natalie and me — that is, I had idealized our time together out of all rational proportion. I understand that. Objectively I see where that argument has validity. But the heart isn't objective. I, who worshipped the great thinkers, theorists, and philosophers of our time, would never stoop so low as to use an axiom as trite as, *I just know.* But I *do know.* I know what Natalie and I were. I can see it through clear eyes, nothing even slightly tinted, and because of that, I cannot compute what we've become.

In sum, I still don't get what happened to us.

As Eric finished up and took his seat, the sounds of sniffles and gentle sobs echoed through the sparkly white chapel. The clergyman who'd been running the funeral moved back to the pulpit and used the universal "please rise" hand gesture. When

40

the congregation began to stand, I used the diversion to slip back outside. I moved across the way, back to the cover of the palmetto tree. I leaned against the trunk, staying out of sight of the chapel.

"Are you okay?"

I turned and saw the cute barmaid. "I'm fine, thanks."

"Great man, the doc."

"Yeah," I said.

"Were you close?"

I didn't answer. A few minutes later, the chapel doors opened. The coffin was rolled into the blazing sun. When it got near the hearse, the pallbearers, one of whom was his son, Eric, surrounded the casket. A woman with a big black hat came out next. She had one arm around a girl of maybe fourteen. A tall man stood next to her. She leaned on him. The man looked a bit like Todd. I guessed this was his brother and sister, but it was only a guess. The pallbearers lifted the coffin and slid it into the back of the hearse. The woman with the black hat and the girl were escorted to the first limousine. The tall maybe-brother opened the door for them. Eric got in after them. I watched the rest of the mourners start coming out.

No sign of Natalie yet.

I found that only mildly odd. I had seen it work both ways. Sometimes the wife was the first person to depart, trailing the coffin, sometimes resting a hand on it. And sometimes she was the last, waiting for the entire chapel to empty out before braving the walk up the aisle. I remembered my own mother hadn't wanted to deal with anyone at my father's funeral. She went so far as to slip out a side door to avoid the crush of family and friends.

I watched mourners exit. Their grief, like the southern heat, had become a living, breathing thing. It was genuine and palpable. These people were not here out of mere courtesy. They cared for this man. They were rocked by his death, but then again, what had I expected? Did I think Natalie would dump me for a loser? Wasn't it better to have lost out to this beloved healer instead of a swarthy douchebag?

Good question.

The barmaid was still standing next to me. "How did he die?" I whispered.

"You don't know?"

I shook my head. Silence. I turned toward her.

"Murdered," she said.

The word hung in the humid air, refusing to go away. I repeated it. "Murdered?"

"Yes."

I opened my mouth, closed it, tried again. "How? Who?"

"He was shot, I think. I'm not sure about that part. The police don't know who. They think it was a robbery gone wrong. You know, a guy broke in and didn't know someone was home."

Numbness crept in now. The flow of people had stopped coming out of the chapel. I stared at the door and waited now for Natalie to make her appearance.

But she didn't.

The man who'd led the service came out, closing the doors behind him. He got into the front of the hearse. The hearse started rolling out. The first limousine followed.

"Is there a side exit?" I asked.

"What?"

"To the chapel. Is there another door?"

She frowned. "No," she said. "There's only that one door."

The procession was under way now. Where the hell was Natalie?

"Aren't you going to the graveyard?" the barmaid asked me.

"No," I said.

She put a hand on my forearm. "You look like you could use a drink."

It was hard to argue with that. I half

stumbled behind her toward the bar and half collapsed onto the same stool as before. She poured me another scotch. I kept my eyes on the procession, on the chapel door, on the little town square.

No Natalie.

"My name is Tess, by the way."

"Jake," I said.

"So how did you know Dr. Sanderson?"

"We went to the same college."

"Really?"

"Yes. Why?"

"You look younger."

"I am. It was an alumni connection."

"Oh, okay, that makes sense."

"Tess?"

"Yes?"

"Do you know Dr. Sanderson's family at all?"

"His son, Eric, used to date my niece. Good kid."

"How old is he?"

"Sixteen, maybe seventeen. Such a tragedy. He and his father were so close."

I didn't know how to broach the subject so I just asked: "Do you know Dr. Sanderson's wife?"

Tess cocked her head. "You don't?"

"No," I lied. "I never met her. We just knew each other through a few college events. He'd come alone."

"You seem awfully emotional for a guy who only knew him through a few college events."

I didn't know how to answer that one, so I stalled by taking a deep sip. Then I said, "It's just that, well, I didn't see her at the funeral."

"How would you know?"

"What?"

"You just said you never met her. How would you know?"

Man, I was really not good at this, was I? "I've seen photographs."

"They must not have been good ones."

"What do you mean?"

"She was right there. Came out right after the coffin with Katie."

"Katie?"

"Their daughter. Eric was one of the pallbearers. Then Dr. Sanderson's brother came out with Katie and Delia."

I remembered them, of course. "Delia?"

"Dr. Sanderson's wife."

My head started spinning. "I thought her name was Natalie."

She crossed her arms and frowned at me. "Natalie? No. Her name is Delia. She and Dr. Sanderson were high school sweethearts. Grew up right down the road here.

45

They've been married for ages."

I just stared at her.

"Jake?"

"What?" I said.

"Are you sure you're even at the right funeral?"

CHAPTER 4

I headed back to the airport and took the next flight home. What else could I do? I guess I could have approached the grieving widow graveside and asked her why her dearly departed husband married the love of my life six years ago, but just then, that felt somewhat inappropriate. I'm sensitive like that.

So with a nonrefundable ticket on a professor's salary, plus classes tomorrow and students to see, I reluctantly ducked into one of those "express" jets that are too small for guys my size, folding my legs up so that my knees felt as though they were under my chin, and flew back to Lanford. I live in personality-imperiled campus housing made of washed-out brick. The décor might generously be dubbed "functional." It was clean and comfortable, I guess, with one of those couch-loveseat combos you see advertised in highway stores for $699. The overall effect is, I think, more apathetic than downright bad, but that also may just be what I tell myself. The small kitchen had a microwave and toaster oven — it had a real oven too, but I don't think I've ever used it — and the dishwasher breaks a lot. As you may have guessed, I don't entertain here too often.

This is not to say that I don't date or even have meaningful relationships. I do, though most of these relationships carry a three-month expiration date. Some might find insight in the fact that Natalie and I lasted a little over three months, but I wouldn't be one of them. No, I don't live in heartache. I don't cry myself to sleep or any of that. I am, I tell myself, over it. But I do feel a void, icky as that sounds. And — like it or not — I still think about her every single day.

Now what?

The man who had married the woman of my dreams was, it seemed, married to another woman — not to mention that he was, well, deceased. To put it another way, Natalie was not at the funeral of her husband. That seemed to warrant some kind of response on my part, didn't it?

I remembered my six-year-old promise. Natalie had said, "Promise me you'll leave us alone." Us. Not him or her. Us. At the risk of sounding cold and perhaps overly literal, there was no "us" anymore. Todd was dead. That meant, I firmly believed, that the promise, if it even could still exist because the "us" no longer existed, should be declared null and void.

I booted up the computer — yes, it was old — and typed Natalie Avery into the search engine. A list of links came up. I started going through them, but quickly got discouraged. Her old gallery page still had some of her paintings up. Nothing had been added in, well, six years. I found a few articles on art openings and the like, but again all of them were old. I clicked the button for more current links. There were two hits on white pages, but one woman named Natalie Avery was seventy-nine years old and married to a man named Harrison. The other was sixty-six and married to a Thomas. There were the other routine mentions you would find for pretty much any name — genealogy sites, high school and college alumni pages, that kind of thing.

But really, in the end, nothing appeared relevant.

So what happened to my Natalie?

I decided to try googling Todd Sanderson, see what I could find there. He was indeed a physician — more specifically, a surgeon.

Impressive. His office was in Savannah, Georgia, and he was affiliated with Memorial University Medical Center. His specialty was cosmetic surgery. I didn't know if that meant serious cleft palates or boob jobs. I didn't know how that could possibly be relevant either. Dr. Sanderson was not big on social networking. He had no Facebook account or LinkedIn or Twitter, none of that.

There were a few mentions of Todd Sanderson and his wife, Delia, at various functions for a charity called Fresh Start, but for the most part there was very little to learn here. I tried throwing in his name with Natalie's. I got bupkis. I sat back and thought a moment. Then I leaned forward and tried their son, Eric Sanderson. He was only a kid, so I didn't think there'd be much, but I figured that he'd probably have a Facebook profile. I started there. Parents often choose not to have a Facebook page, but I've yet to meet a student who didn't have one.

A few minutes later, I hit bingo. Eric Sanderson, Savannah, Georgia.

The profile picture was, poignantly enough, a photograph of Eric and his late father, Todd. They both had wide smiles, trying to hold up a big fish of some kind, happily struggling with the weight. A father-son fishing trip, I figured with the pang of a man who wants to be a father. The sun was setting behind them, their faces in shadow, but you could feel the contentment radiate through my computer monitor. I was struck by a strange thought.

Todd Sanderson was a good man.

Yes, it was only a photograph and, yes, I was aware of how people could fake smiles or entire life scenarios, but I sensed good-ness here.

I checked out the rest of Eric's photo-graphs. Most were of Eric and his friends — hey, he was a teenager — at school, at parties, at sporting events, you know the drill. Why does everyone make pouty lips or hand gestures in photographs nowadays? What's up with that? Dumb thought but the mind goes where it goes.

There was an album simply titled FAM-ILY. The photos ran through a gamut of years. Eric was a baby in some. Then his sister joined. Then there was the trip to Dis-ney World, other fishing vacations, family dinners, church confirmation, soccer games. I checked them all.

Todd never had long hair — not in any of them. He was never anything but clean-shaven.

So what did that mean?

Not a clue.

I clicked on Eric's wall or whatever you call that opening page. There were dozens of condolence messages.

"Your dad was the best, I'm so sorry."

"If there is anything I can do."

"RIP, Dr. S. You rocked."

"I'll never forget the time your dad helped out with my sister."

Then I saw one that made me pause:

"Such a senseless tragedy. I will never understand the cruelty of human beings."

I clicked for "older posts" to come up. There, six more down, I found another that caught my eye:

"I hope they catch the a&&hole who did this and fry him."

I brought up a news search engine and tried to find out more. It didn't take long to stumble across an article:

HOMICIDE IN SAVANNAH

Local Surgeon Murdered

Popular local surgeon and humanitarian Dr. Todd Sanderson was killed in his home last night in what police believe may have been a robbery gone wrong.

Someone tried my front door, but it was locked. I heard the rustling of the doormat — in a fit of originality, I hide my spare key beneath it — and then the key was in the lock and the door opened. Benedict came in.

"Hey," he said. "Surfing porn?"

I frowned. "No one uses the term 'surfing' anymore."

"I'm old-school." Benedict headed to the fridge and grabbed a beer. "How was your trip?"

"Surprising," I said.

"Do tell."

I did. Benedict was a great listener. He was one of those guys who actually listened to every single word and remained focused on you and only you and didn't talk over you. This isn't faked either, and he doesn't just save this for his closest friends. People fascinate him. I would list that as Benedict's greatest strength as a teacher but it would probably be more apropos to list it as his greatest strength as a Don Juan. Single women can fight off a lot of pickup routines, but a guy who genuinely cares about what they say? Gigolo wannabes, take note.

When I finished, Benedict took a swig of his beer. "Wow. I mean . . . wow. That's all I can say."

"Wow?"

"Yeah."

"Are you sure you're not an English professor?"

"You do know," he said slowly, "that there is probably a logical explanation for all this, right?"

"Such as?"

He rubbed his chin. "Maybe Todd is one of those guys with several families, but they don't know about each other."

"Huh?"

"Lotharios who have lots of wives and kids and one lives in, say, Denver, and the other lives in Seattle, and he divides his time between them and they don't know. You see it on *Dateline* all the time. They're bigamists. Or polygamists. And they can get away with it for years."

I made a face. "If that's your logical explanation, I'd love to hear your far-fetched one."

"Fair point. So how about I give you the most obvious one?"

"The most obvious explanation?"

"Yes."

"Go for it."

Benedict spread his hands. "It's not the same Todd."

I said nothing.

"You don't remember the guy's last name, right?"

"Right."

"So are you sure that it's the same guy? Todd isn't the most uncommon name in the world. Think about it, Jake. You see a picture six years later, your mind plays a few tricks with you, and voilà, you think it's your archenemy."

"He isn't my archenemy."

"*Wasn't* your archenemy. Dead, remember? That puts him in the past tense. But seriously, you want the most obvious explanation?" He leaned forward. "It's all a simple case of mistaken identity."

I had, of course, already considered this. I had even considered Benedict's conning bigamist explanation. Both made more sense than . . . than what? What else was there, really? What other possible — obvious, logical, far-fetched — explanation was there?

"Well?" Benedict said.

"It makes sense."

"See?"

"This Todd — Todd Sanderson, MD — looked different from Natalie's Todd. His hair is shorter. His face is freshly shaven."

"So there you go."

I glanced away.

"What?"

"I'm not sure I buy it."

"Why not?"

"For one thing, the man was murdered."

"So? If anything, that backs my polygamist theory. He crossed the wrong gal and kapow."

"Come on, you don't really think that's the answer."

Benedict sat back. He started plucking at his lower lip with two fingers. "She left you for another man."

I waited for him to say more. When he didn't, I said, "Uh, yeah, Captain Obvious, I know."

"That was hard for you." He sounded sad now, wistful. "I get it. I get it more than you know." I thought now about the photograph, about the love he lost, about how many of us go around with some kind of heartache

56

and never show it. "You two were in love. So you can't accept it — how could she dump you for another man?"

I frowned again, but I could feel the twang in my chest. "Are you sure you're not a psychology professor?"

"You want this so badly — this second chance, this chance at real redemption — that you can't see the truth."

"What truth is that, Benedict?"

"She's gone," he said, simple as that. "She dumped you. None of this changes that."

I swallowed, tried to swim through that crystal-clear reality. "I think there is more to it."

"Like what?"

"I don't know," I admitted.

Benedict considered that for a moment. "But you won't stop trying to find out, will you?"

"I will," I said. "But not today. And probably not tomorrow."

Benedict shrugged, rose, grabbed another beer. "So let's have it. What's our next step?"

CHAPTER 5

I had no answer to that one, and it was getting late. Benedict suggested a bar and some late-night carousing. I thought that it might be an excellent distraction but I had essays to grade, so I begged off. I managed to get through about three of them before realizing that my mind wasn't there and grading papers now wouldn't be fair to my students.

I made a sandwich and tried looking up Natalie's name again, this time doing an "image" search. I saw an old bio picture of her. The image struck me hard in the chest so I clicked it off. I found some of her old paintings. Several of them were of my hands and torso. Painful memories didn't just ease back in — they shoved the door open hard, all of them and all at once. The way she tilted her head, the way the sunlight burst through the skylight of her studio, that look of concentration on her face, the playful smile when she took a break. The memories almost made me double over in pain. I missed her that much. I missed her with an ache that was physical and something beyond. I had blocked it on and off for six years, but suddenly the longing had flooded back, as strong as the day we last made love in that cabin at the retreat.

Screw it.

I wanted to see her and be damned the consequences. If Natalie could look me in the eye a second time and dismiss me, well, I would deal with it then. But not now. Not tonight. Right now, I simply needed to find her.

Okay, slow down. Let me think this through. What do I need to do here? First, I have to figure out if Todd Sanderson is Natalie's Todd. There was plenty of evidence to suggest, as Benedict had clearly explained, that this was simply a case of mistaken identity.

How should I go about proving it one way or the other?

I needed to know more about him. For example, what would Dr. Todd Sanderson, happily married father of two living in Savannah, be doing at an artist retreat in Vermont six years earlier? I needed to see more pictures of him. I needed to do more background, starting . . .

Starting here. At Lanford.

That was it. The school still maintains every student file, though they can only be viewed by the student or with the student's permission. I looked at my own a few years back. For the most part, there was nothing remarkable, but my professor in freshman year Spanish, a class I ended up dropping, suspected that I had "adjustment" problems and perhaps could benefit from seeing the school psychologist. That was crap, of course. I was terrible at Spanish — foreign languages are my academic Achilles' heel — and you're allowed a freshman drop to maintain your GPA. The note had been in the professor's own handwriting, and that somehow made it worse.

The point?

There could be something in Todd's file, if I could figure a way to finagle it, that would tell me something about him. You might ask, "Like what?" I might reply, "I have no friggin' idea." It still felt like a place to start.

So what else?

The obvious: Check in on Natalie. If I found her still happily married to her Todd, I would be able to drop this immediately. That was the most direct route here, wasn't it? The question was, how?

I continued an online search, hoping to stumble across an address or a clue, but there was absolutely nothing. I know that we supposedly live our entire lives online nowadays, but I have found this not to be the case. If a person wanted to stay in the shadows, they could. It took effort, but you really could remain off the grid.

The question might be, why would you expend the effort?

I debated calling her sister, if I could find the number, but what exactly would I say? "Hi, uh, this is Jake Fisher, your sister's old, uh, fling. Um, did Natalie's husband die?"

That might be a tough approach.

I remembered listening to a phone conversation between the two sisters where Natalie gushingly told Julie, "Oh man, wait till you meet my wonderful boyfriend . . ." And, yep, we did eventually meet. Sort of. At Natalie's wedding to another man.

Her father was dead. Her mom, well, that would be the same problem as with the sister. Friends of Natalie's . . . that was an issue too. Natalie and I had spent our time together in retreats in Kraftboro, Vermont. I was at one to write my political science dissertation, Natalie was doing her art at the neighboring farm-cum-retreat. I was supposed to stay six weeks. I stayed double that because, one, I met Natalie, and two, I lost focus on my writing after I met Natalie. I had never visited her hometown in northern New Jersey, and she had only come to campus for one brief visit. Our relationship had stayed in that Vermont bubble.

I can almost see the head nods now. Ah, you think, that explains it. It was a summer romance, built in an unreal world of no responsibilities or reality. Under those conditions, it is easy for love and obsession to bloom without taking root, only to wither and die when the cold of September rolled around. Natalie, being the more insightful of us, saw and accepted that truth. I did not.

I understand that sentiment. I can only say that it is wrong.

Natalie's sister's name was Julie Pottham. Six years ago, Julie had been married with an infant son. I looked her up online. This time, it didn't take long. Julie lived in Ramsey, New Jersey. I wrote down the phone number on a slip of paper — like Benedict, I can be old-school — and stared at it. Outside my window I could hear students laughing. It was midnight. Too late to call. It might be best to sleep on this decision anyway. In the meantime, there were papers I needed to correct. There was a

She sat back and crossed her arms. "Didn't I just read his obituary on the alumni page?"

"You did."

Mrs. Dinsmore studied my face. My smile was gone. A few seconds later, she slipped her reading glasses back on and said, "I'll see what I can do."

"Thank you."

I headed into my office and closed the door. No more excuses. It was nearly 10:00 A.M. now. I took out the piece of paper and looked at the number I'd jotted down last night. I picked up the phone, hit the button for an outside line, and dialed.

I had rehearsed what I would say, but nothing had sounded sane, so I figured that I would play it by ear. The phone rang two times, then three. Julie probably wouldn't answer. No one answered home phones anymore, especially when they came from an unfamiliar number. The caller ID would show Lanford College. I didn't know if that would encourage or discourage answering.

On the fourth ring, the phone was picked up. I gripped the receiver tighter and waited. A woman said a tentative "Hello?"

"Julie?"

"Who is this please?"

"It's Jake Fisher."

class tomorrow I had to prepare for. There was a life I had to lead.

There was no point in trying to sleep. I focused on the student essays. Most were numbingly tedious and expected, written as though to fit a high school teacher's rote specifications. These were top-level students who knew how to write "A+" high school papers, what with their opening paragraph, introductory sentences, supportive body, all that stuff that makes an essay solid and ridiculously boring. As I mentioned earlier, my job is to get them to think critically. That was always more important to me than having them remember the specific philosophies of, say, Hobbes or Locke. You could always look those up and be reminded of what they were. Rather, what I really hoped was my students would learn to both respect and piss all over Hobbes and Locke. I wanted them to not only think outside the box, but to get to that outside by smashing the box into little pieces.

Some were getting that. Most were not as of yet. But, hey, if they all got it right away, what would be the point of my job?

At around four in the morning I headed to bed to pretend that sleep would find me. It didn't. By 7:00 A.M., I had made up my mind: I would call Natalie's sister. I remembered the robotic smile in the white chapel, the pale face, the way Julie asked me if I was okay, as if she truly understood. She might be an ally.

Either way, what did I have to lose?

It had been too late to call last night. It was too early now. I showered and got ready for my 8:00 A.M. Rule of Law class over in Vitale Hall. I would call Natalie's sister as soon as class ended.

I expected to sleepwalk through the class. I was obviously distracted and, let's face it, 8:00 A.M. was too early for most college students. But not today. Today the class was beyond lively, with hands shooting up, points and counterpoints worded strongly but with no animosity. I took no sides, of course. I moderated and marveled. The class was in the zone. Usually with the early class, the clock's minute hand moved as though bathed in syrup. Today I wanted to reach up and grab that stupid hand and stop it from flying forward. I loved every moment. The ninety minutes passed in a blur, and I realized yet again how lucky I was to have this job.

Lucky in occupation, unlucky in love. Or something like that.

I headed to my office at Clark House to make the phone call. I stopped at Mrs. Dinsmore's desk and awarded her my best charm-yer-pants-off smile. She frowned and said, "That work with single women nowadays?"

"What, the charming smile?"

"Yeah."

"Sometimes," I said.

She shook her head. "And they say not to worry about the future." Mrs. Dinsmore sighed and straightened out some papers. "Okay, pretend you got me all hot and bothered. What do you want?"

I tried to shake away the hot-and-bothered image. It wasn't easy. "I need to get ahold of a student file."

"Do you have the student's permission?"

"No."

"Ergo the charming smile."

"Right."

"Is this one of your current students?"

I reloaded the smile. "No. He was never a student of mine."

She arched an eyebrow.

"In fact, he graduated twenty years ago."

"You're kidding, right?"

"Do I look like I'm kidding?"

"Actually, with that smile, you look kind of constipated. What's the student's name?"

"Todd Sanderson."

Nothing.

"I dated your sister."

"What's your name again?"

"Jake Fisher."

"Have we met?"

"Sort of. I mean, we were both at Natalie's wedding —"

"I don't understand. Who are you exactly?"

"Before Natalie married Todd, she and I were, uh, seeing each other."

Silence.

"Hello?" I said.

"Is this a joke?"

"What? No. In Vermont. Your sister and I —"

"I don't know who you are."

"You used to talk to your sister on the phone a lot. I even heard you two talking about me, in fact. After the wedding, you put your hand on my arm and asked me if I was okay."

"I have no idea what you're talking about."

I was gripping the receiver so tight I feared it might shatter. "Like I said, Natalie and I dated —"

"What do you want? Why are you calling me?"

Wow, that was a good question. "I wanted to talk to Natalie."

"What?"

"I just wanted to make sure that she was okay. I saw an obituary for Todd, and I thought that maybe I should reach out and just, I don't know, offer my condolences."

More silence. I let it last as long as I could.

"Julie?"

"I don't know who you are or what you're talking about, but never call here again. Do you understand? Never."

She hung up the phone.

CHAPTER 6

I tried calling back, but Julie didn't answer.

I didn't understand. Had she really forgotten who I was? That seemed doubtful. Had I scared her with my call-out-of-the-blue? I didn't know. The whole conversation had been surreal and spooky. It would have been one thing to tell me that Natalie didn't want to hear from me or that I was wrong, Todd was still alive. Whatever. But she didn't even know who I was.

How was that possible?

So now what? Calm down, for one. Deep breaths. I needed to continue my two-prong attack: Figure out what the deal was with the late Todd Sanderson, and find Natalie. The second would, of course, negate the first. Once I found Natalie, I would know all. I wondered how to do that exactly. I had looked her up online and found nothing. Her sister, too, seemed to be a dead end. So where to go? I didn't know, but in this day and age, how hard would it be to get an address on her?

An idea came to me. I signed on to the campus website and checked the teaching schedules. Professor Shanta Newlin had a class in an hour.

I buzzed Mrs. Dinsmore.

"What, you expect me to have the file that fast?"

"No, it isn't that. I'm wondering if you know where Professor Newlin is."

"Well, well. This day gets more and more interesting. You know she's engaged, right?"

I should have known better. "Mrs. Dinsmore . . ."

"Don't get your panties in a bunch. She's having breakfast with her thesis students in Valentine."

Valentine was the campus cafeteria. I hurried across the quad toward it. It was an odd thing. A college professor always has to be on. You have to keep your head up. You have to smile or wave at every student. You have to remember every name. There was a strange sort of celebrity to walking around campus. I would claim that it didn't matter to me, but I confess that I liked the attention and took it pretty seriously. So even now, rushed and anxious and distracted as I was, I made sure that no student felt blown off.

I avoided the two main dining rooms. These were for students. The professors who sometimes chose to join them once again felt a little desperate to me. There were lines, and I admit that they are sometimes fuzzy and flimsy and arbitrary, but I still drew them and kept on my side of them. Professor Newlin, a class act all the way, would do likewise, which was why I was confident she'd be tucked away in one of the back private dining halls, reserved for such faculty-student interaction.

She was in Bradbeer dining hall. On campus, every building, room, chair, table, shelf, and tile is named after someone who gave money. Some people bristle at this. I like it. This ivy-covered institution is isolated enough, as it should be. There is no harm in letting a little real-world, cold-cash reality in every once in a while.

I peeked in through the window. Shanta Newlin caught my eye and held up a finger signaling one minute. I nodded and waited. Five minutes later the door opened and the students streamed out. Shanta stood in the doorway. When the students were gone, she said, "Walk with me. I have to be somewhere."

I did. Shanta Newlin had one of the most impressive résumés I'd ever seen. She graduated Stanford as a Rhodes Scholar and attended Columbia Law School. She then worked for both the CIA and FBI before serving in the last administration as an undersecretary of state.

"So what's up?"

Her manner was, as always, brusque. When she first came to campus we had dinner. It wasn't a date. It was a "let's see if we want to" date. There is a subtle difference. After that date, she chose not to pursue it, and I was okay with that.

"I need a favor," I said.

Shanta nodded, inviting me to make my request.

"I'm looking for someone. An old friend. I've tried all the usual methods — Google, calling the family, whatever. I can't get an address."

"And you figured that with my old contacts, I'd be able to help."

"Something like that," I said. "Well, yes, exactly like that."

"Her name?"

"I didn't say it was a she."

Shanta frowned. "Name?"

"Natalie Avery."

"When was the last time you saw her or

had an address?"

"Six years ago."

Shanta kept walking, military style, ramrod back, very fast. "Was she the one, Jake?"

"Pardon?"

A small smile came to her lips. "Do you know why I never followed up on our first date?"

"It wasn't really a date," I said. "It was more a 'let's see if we want to' date."

"What?"

"Never mind. I figured that you didn't follow up because you had no interest."

"Uh, that would be a no. Here is what I saw that night: You're a great guy, you're funny, you're smart, you have a full-time job, and you have blue eyes to die for. Do you know how many single straight guys I'd met with that criteria?"

I wasn't sure what to say, so I stayed quiet.

"But I could sense it. That's part of being a trained detective, maybe. I study body language. I look for the little things."

"Sense what?"

"You're damaged goods."

"Gee, thanks."

She shrugged. "Some men carry torches for old loves, and then some guys — not many, but some — get completely consumed by the torch's flames. It makes them nothing but long-term trouble for the follow-ups."

I said nothing.

"So this Natalie Avery that you're suddenly desperate to find," Shanta said. "Is she that flame?"

What would be the point in lying? "Yes."

She stopped and looked way up at me. "And it hurt bad?"

"You have no idea."

Shanta Newlin nodded and started walking away, leaving me behind. "I'll have her address for you by the end of the day."

CHAPTER 7

On television, the detective always goes back to the scene of the crime. Or, come to think of it, maybe it's the criminal who does that. Whatever. I was at a dead end, so I figured that I'd go back to where it all happened.

The retreats in Vermont.

Lanford was only about forty-five minutes from the Vermont border, but then you had another two hours plus to get up to where Natalie and I first met. Northern Vermont is rural. I grew up in Philadelphia and Natalie was from northern New Jersey. We didn't know rural like this. Yes, an objective observer might again point out that in such a secluded venue, love would flourish in an unrealistic way. I might agree or I might point out that in the absence of other distractions — like, say, anything — love might suffocate under the weight of too much togetherness, thus making this proof of something far deeper than a summer fling.

The sun was starting to weaken by the time I passed my old retreat on Route 14. The six-acre "subsistence farm" was run by writer-in-residence Darly Wanatick, who offered critiques of the retreatees' work. For those who don't know, subsistence farming is farming that provides the basic needs for the farmer and his family without surpluses for marketing. In short, you grow it, you eat it, you don't sell it. For those who don't know what a writer in residence is or what qualifies him or her to critique your writing, it meant that Darly owned the property and wrote a weekly shopping column in the free local paper, the *Kraftboro Grocer*. The retreat housed six writers at a time. Each writer had a bedroom in the main house and a shack or "work cottage" in which to write. We all met up for dinner at night. That was it. There was no Internet, no TV, no phones, yes lights, but no motorcar, not a single luxury. Cows, sheep, and chickens meandered around the property. It started out soothing and relaxing and I enjoyed that unplugged, unconnected solitude for about, oh, three days and then my brain cells began to rust and corrode. The theory seemed to be if you make an author feel this numbingly bored, he or she will flock to the salvation of his legal pad or laptop and produce pages. It worked for a while and then it felt as though I'd been placed in solitary confinement. I spent one entire afternoon watching a colony of ants carry a bread crumb across the "writer cottage" floor. So enamored was I with this bit of entertainment I strategically placed more bread crumbs in various corners in order to create insect relay races.

Dinner with my fellow retreat scribes was not much of a reprieve. They were all precious pseudo-intellectuals writing the next great American novel, and when the subject of my nonfiction dissertation was tossed up, it landed upon the old kitchen table with the thud of a heaping pile of donkey dung. Sometimes these great American novelists did dramatic readings of their own work. The works were pretentious, tedious, self-involved crap written in a prose style one might best describe as "Look at me! *Please* look at me!" I never said any of this out loud, of course. When they read, I sat with my most studiously enraptured expression frozen to my face, nodding at regular intervals to appear wise and engaged and also to prevent myself from actually nodding off. One guy named Lars was writing a six-hundred-page poem on Hitler's last days in the bunker, written from the viewpoint of Eva Braun's dog. His first reading consisted of ten minutes of barking.

"It sets the mood," he explained, and he was correct if that mood was to punch him hard in the face.

Natalie's artist retreat was different. It was called the Creative Recharge Colony and had a decidedly more crunchy-granola, hemp, hippie-esque, "Kumbaya" commune feel to it. They took breaks by working in a garden that grew organic (and I am not just talking about food here). They gathered around a fire at night and sang songs of peace and harmony that would make Joan Baez gag. They were, interestingly enough, wary of strangers (perhaps because of what they "grew organic") and there was a guarded, cultish edge to some of the staff. The property was more than a hundred acres with a main house, true cottages with fireplaces and private decks, a swimming pool designed to look like a pond, a cafeteria with fantastic coffee and a wide variety of sandwiches that all tasted like sprouts covered in wood shavings — and on the border with the actual town of Kraftboro, a white chapel where one could, if they so desired, get married.

The first thing I noticed was that the entrance was now unmarked. Gone was the brightly painted CREATIVE RECHARGE sign, like something you'd see advertising a kids' summer camp. A thick chain blocked my car from heading up the drive. I pulled over, turned off the ignition, and got out of the car. There were several NO TRESPASSING signs, but those had always been there. With the new chain and without the Creative Recharge welcome, the no trespassing signs took on a more ominous tone.

I wasn't sure what to do.

I knew that the main house was about a quarter mile up the drive. I could leave my car here and walk it. See what's what. But what would be the point? I hadn't been up here in six years. The retreat probably sold the land, and the new owner probably craved privacy. That might explain all this.

Still it didn't feel right.

What would be the harm, I thought, in going up and knocking on the door of the main house? Then again, the thick chain and no trespassing signs were not exactly welcome mats. I was still trying to decide what to do when a Kraftboro police cruiser pulled up next to me. Two officers got out. One was short and stocky with bloated gym muscles. The other was tall and thin with slicked-back hair and the small mustache of a guy in a silent movie. Both wore aviator sunglasses, so you couldn't see their eyes.

Short and Stocky hitched up his pants a bit and said, "Can I help you?"

They both gave me hard stares. Or at least I think they were hard stares. I mean, I couldn't see their eyes.

"I was interested in visiting the Creative Recharge retreat."

"The what?" Stocky asked. "What for?"

"Because I need to creatively recharge."

"You being a smart mouth with me?"

His voice had a little too much snap in it. I didn't like the attitude. I didn't understand the attitude either, except for the fact that they were cops in a small town and I was probably the first guy they could hassle for something other than underage drinking.

"No, Officer," I said.

Stocky looked at Thin Man. Thin Man remained silent. "You must have the wrong address."

"I'm pretty sure this is the place," I said.

"There is no Creative Recharge retreat here. It closed down."

"So which is it?" I asked.

"Pardon me?"

"Is this the wrong address," I said, "or did the Creative Recharge retreat close down?"

Stocky didn't like that answer. He whipped off his sunglasses and used them to point at me. "Are you being a wiseass with me?"

"I'm trying to find my retreat."

"I don't know anything about any retreat. This land has been owned by the Drachman family for, what, Jerry, fifty years?"

"At least," Thin Man said.

"I was here six years ago," I said.

"I don't know nothing about that," Stocky said. "I only know that you're on private property and if you don't get off it, I'm going to bring you in."

I looked down at my feet. I wasn't on the driveway or any private property. I was on the road.

Stocky moved closer to me, getting into my personal space. I confess that I was scared, but I had learned something in my years of bouncing at bars. You never show fear. That was something you always heard about when it came to the animal kingdom, and trust me, there are no wilder animals than human beings "unwinding" at late-night bars. So even though I didn't like what was happening, even though I had no leverage and was trying to figure a safe way out of this, I didn't back away when Stocky got all up on me. He didn't like that. I held my ground and looked down at him. Way down. He really didn't like that.

"Let me see some ID, hotshot."

"Why?" I asked.

Stocky looked at Thin Man. "Jerry, go run the license plate through the system."

Jerry nodded and headed back to the squad car.

"For what?" I asked. "I don't understand. I'm just here for a retreat."

"You got two choices," Stocky said to me. "One" — he held up a pudgy finger — "you show me your identification without any more back talk. Two" — yep, another chubby digit — "I arrest you for trespassing."

None of this felt right. I glanced behind me at a tree and saw what looked like a security camera pointed down at us. I didn't like this. I didn't like this at all, but there was nothing to be gained by antagonizing a cop. I needed to keep my big mouth shut.

I started to reach into my pocket to get my wallet when Stocky held up a hand and said, "Steady. Slow down."

"What?"

"Reach into your pocket, but make no sudden moves."

"You're kidding, right?"

So much for keeping my big mouth shut.

"Do I look like I'm kidding? Use two fingers. Your thumb and your index finger. Move slowly."

My wallet was deep down in my front pocket. Extracting it with two fingers took longer than it should.

"I'm waiting," he said.

"Give me a second."

I finally got ahold of the wallet and handed it to him. He started to look through it, as though on a scavenger hunt. He stopped at my Lanford College ID, looked at the photograph, looked at me, then he frowned.

"This you?"

"Yes."

"Jacob Fisher."

"Everyone calls me Jake."

He frowned down at my photograph.

"I know," I said. "It is hard to capture my raw animal magnetism in photography."

"You have a college ID in here."

I didn't hear a question so I didn't answer one.

"You look kind of old to be a student."

"I'm not a student. I'm a professor. See where it says 'staff'?"

Thin Man came back from the car. He shook his head. I guessed that meant the license plate check came back negative.

"Why would a big-time professor be coming up to our little town?"

I remembered something that I saw on television once. "I need to reach into my pocket again. That okay?"

"What for?"

"You'll see."

I pulled out my smartphone.

"What do you need that for?" Stocky asked.

I pointed it at him and hit the video record button. "This is on a live feed to my home computer, Officer." That was a lie. It was only recording on my phone, but what the heck. "Everything you say and do can be seen by my colleagues." More lies, but good ones. "I'd very much like to know why you need to see my identification and are asking so many questions about me."

Stocky put the sunglasses back on as though that would mask the rage. He closed his lips so tight that they were quaking. He handed me back my wallet and said, "We had a complaint that you were trespassing. Despite finding you on a private property and listening to some story about a retreat that doesn't exist, we decided to let you off with just a warning. Please leave these premises. Have a nice day."

Stocky and Thin Man headed back to their squad car. They sat in the front and waited until I was back in mine. There was no other play here. I got into my car and drove away.

CHAPTER 8

I didn't go far.

I drove to the village of Kraftboro. If it had a big, sudden influx of new construction and cash, it might raise itself to the level of small-town America. It looked like something out of an old movie. I half expected to see a barbershop quartet in straw hats. There was a general store (the sign actually said GENERAL STORE), an old "stone mill" with an unmanned "visitor's center," a gas station that also housed a one-chair barbershop, and a bookstore café. Natalie and I had spent a lot of time in that bookstore café. It was small, so there wasn't much browsing, but there was a corner table and Natalie and I would sit there and read the paper and sip coffee. Cookie, a baker who'd escaped the big city, used to run the place with her partner, Denise. She always played *Redemption's Son* by Joseph Arthur or Damien Rice's *O,* and after a while, Natalie and I started thinking of those — gag alert — as "our" albums. I wondered whether Cookie was still there. Cookie baked what Natalie considered the greatest scones in the history of the world. Then again, Natalie loved all scones. I, on the other hand, still have trouble differentiating scones from dry, rock-hard bread.

See? We had our differences.

I parked down the road and started journeying up the same path I had stumbled down six years earlier. The wooded trail ran for about a hundred yards. In the clearing I spotted the familiar white chapel on the edge of the property I had just been booted off. Some service or meeting was letting out. I watched the congregants blink their way back into the lowering sun. The chapel was, as far as I knew, nondenominational. It seemed more utilitarian, if you will, than Unitarian, a gathering place more than any sort of house of deeply religious worship.

I waited, smiling like I belonged, nodding like Mr. Friendly as about a dozen people walked past me and down the path. I checked the faces, but there was no one that I recognized from six years ago. No surprise really.

A tall woman with a severe hair bun waited by the chapel steps. I made my way over, maintaining the Mr. Friendly smile.

"May I help you?" she asked.

Good question. What did I hope to find here? It wasn't as though I had a plan.

"Are you looking for Reverend Kelly?" she asked. "Because he's not around right now."

"Do you work here?" I asked.

"Sort of. I'm Lucy Cutting, the registrar. It's a volunteer position."

I stood there.

"Is there something I can help you with?"

"I don't know how to put this . . . ," I began. And then: "Six years ago I attended a wedding here. I knew the bride, but not the groom."

Her eyes narrowed a bit, more curious than wary. I pushed ahead.

"Anyway, I recently saw an obituary for a man named Todd. That was the groom's name. Todd."

"Todd is a fairly common name," she said.

"Yes, of course, but there was also a photograph of the deceased. It looked like, I know how this sounds, but it looked like the same man I saw marry my friend. The problem is, I never learned Todd's last name so I don't know if it is him or not. And if it is, well, I'd like to pay my respects."

Lucy Cutting scratched her cheek. "Can't you just call?"

"I wish I could, but no." I was going with honesty here. It felt good. "For one thing I don't know where Natalie — that's the bride's name — I don't know where she lives now. She changed her last name to his, I think. So I can't find them. And also, to be completely up-front, I had a past with this woman."

"I see."

"So if the man I saw in the obituary wasn't her husband —"

"Your communication might be un-wanted," she finished for me.

"Exactly."

She thought about that. "And if it was her husband?"

I shrugged. She scratched her cheek some more. I tried to look nonthreatening, even demure, which really doesn't play on a guy my size. I almost batted my eyelashes.

"I wasn't here six years ago," she said.

"Oh."

"But we can check the schedule books. They've always kept immaculate records — every wedding, baptism, communion, bris, whatever."

Bris? "That would be great."

She led me down the steps. "Do you remember the date of the wedding?"

I did, of course. I gave her the exact date.

We reached a small office. Lucy Cutting opened a file cabinet, thumbed through it, and pulled out one of those accounting books. As she flipped through it, I could see that she was right. The records were immaculate. There was a column for the date, type of event, participants, start and end times — all written in handwriting that could double as calligraphy.

"Let's see what we can find here . . ."

She made a production of putting on her reading glasses. She licked her index finger schoolmarm-like, flipped a few more pages, and found the one she wanted. The same finger started tracing down the page. When she frowned, I thought to myself, Uh-oh . . .

"Are you sure about the date?" she asked me.

"Positive."

"I don't see any wedding that day. There was one two days earlier. Larry Rosen married Heidi Fleisher."

"That's not it," I said.

"Can I help you?"

The voice startled us both.

Lucy Cutting said, "Oh, hello, Reverend. I didn't expect you back so soon."

I turned, saw the man, and nearly hugged him with joy. Pay dirt. It was the same minister with the shaved head who'd presided over Natalie's wedding. He reached out his hand to shake mine, a practiced smile at the ready, but when he saw my face, I saw the smile flicker.

"Hello," he said to me. "I'm Reverend Kelly."

"Jake Fisher. We've met before."

He made a skeptical face and turned back to Lucy Cutting. "What's going on, Lucy?"

"I was looking up a record for this gentleman," she began to explain. He listened patiently. I studied his face, but I wasn't sure what I was seeing, just that he was trying to control his emotions somehow. When she was done, he turned to me and raised both palms to the sky. "If it isn't in the records . . ."

"You were there," I said.

"Excuse me?"

"You presided over the wedding. That's where we met."

"I don't recall that. So many events. You understand."

"After the wedding, you were in front of the chapel with the bride's sister. A woman named Julie Pottham. When I walked by, you said it was a lovely day for a wedding."

He arched an eyebrow. "How could I have possibly forgotten that?"

Sarcasm does not normally wear well on

men of the cloth, but it fit Reverend Kelly as though hand tailored. I pressed on. "The bride was named Natalie Avery. She was a painter at the Creative Recharge retreat."

"The what?"

"Creative Recharge. They own this land, right?"

"What are you talking about? The town owns this land."

I didn't want to argue deeds and boundaries right now. I tried another avenue. "The wedding. It was last-minute. Maybe that's why it isn't in the records."

"I'm sorry. Mr. . . . ?"

"Fisher. Jake Fisher."

"Mr. Fisher, first off, even if it was a last-minute wedding, it would certainly be recorded. Second, well, I'm confused what exactly you're looking for."

Lucy Cutting answered for me. "The groom's last name."

He gave her a quick glare. "We aren't in the information business, Miss Cutting."

She looked down, properly chastised.

"You have to remember the wedding," I said.

"I'm sorry I don't."

I stepped closer, looking down on him. "You do. I know you do."

I heard the desperation in my own voice,

and didn't like it. Reverend Kelly tried to meet my eye, but he couldn't quite do it. "Are you calling me a liar?"

"You remember," I said. "Why won't you help me?"

"I don't remember," he said. "But why are you so anxious to find the wife of another man or, if your story is true, a recent widow?"

"To pay my respects," I said.

My hollow words hung in the air like thick humidity. No one moved. No one spoke. Finally Reverend Kelly broke the silence.

"Whatever your motive for finding this woman, we have no interest in being party to it." He stepped away and showed me the door. "I think it'd be best if you left immediately."

Once again, dazed by betrayal and heartbreak, I stumbled back down the path toward the village center. I could almost get the reverend's behavior. If he did remember the wedding — and I suspect he did — he wouldn't want to give Natalie's dumped boyfriend any information said boyfriend didn't already have. It seemed an extreme hypothesis on my part, but at least it kind of made sense. What I couldn't make sense of, what I couldn't figure out in any way, shape, or form, was why Lucy Cutting had found nothing in the neat-to-the-point-of-anal records on Natalie and Todd's nuptials. And why the hell had no one heard of the Creative Recharge retreat?

I couldn't get that to mesh.

So now what? I had come here in hopes of . . . of what? Of learning Todd's last name for one thing. That could end this pretty quickly. If not, perhaps someone here still kept in touch with Natalie. That could end this all pretty quickly too.

"Promise me, Jake. Promise me you'll leave us alone."

Those were the last words the love of my life said to me. The very last. And here I was, six years later, going back to where it all began, to break my word. I waited to find irony in that, but irony would not come.

As I hit the town center, the gentle aroma of fresh pastries made me pull up. The Kraftboro Bookstore Café. Natalie's favorite scones. I thought about it and decided that it was worth a try.

When I opened the door, a little bell rang, but that sound was quickly forgotten. Elton John was singing that the child's name was Levon, and he'd be a good man. I felt a rush and a shiver. Both tables were taken, including, of course, our old favorite. I stared at it, just standing there like a big goof, and for a moment I swore I could hear Natalie's laugh. A man with a maroon baseball cap came in behind me. I was still blocking the door.

"Uh, excuse me," he said.

I moved to the side to let him pass. My eyes found the coffee bar. A woman with wildly curly hair wearing, yep, a purple tie-dyed shirt had her back to me. No doubt about it. It was Cookie. My heart picked up a step. She turned, saw me, and smiled. "Can I get you something?"

"Hi, Cookie."

"Hey."

Silence.

"Do you remember me?" I asked.

She was wiping frosting off her hands with a hand towel. "I'm bad with faces, but even worse with names. What can I get you?"

"I used to come in here," I said. "Six years ago. My girlfriend's name was Natalie Avery. We used to sit at the corner table."

She nodded but not like she remembered. She nodded like she wanted to appease the lunatic. "Lots of customers in and out. Coffee? Doughnut?"

"Natalie loved your scones."

"A scone it is. Blueberry?"

"I'm Jake Fisher. I was writing my dissertation on the rule of law. You used to ask me about it. Natalie was an artist from the retreat. She'd break out her sketchpad right in that corner." I gestured toward it, as though that mattered. "Six years ago. Over the summer. Heck, you were the one to point her out to me."

"Uh-huh," she said, her fingers toying with her necklace as though they were prayer beads. "See, that's the good part of being called Cookie. You don't forget a name like Cookie. It sticks in the mind. But the bad part is, since everyone remembers your name, they think you should do the same. You know what I mean?"

"I do," I said. Then: "You really don't remember?"

She didn't bother replying. I looked around the café. People at the tables were starting to stare. The guy with the maroon baseball cap was over by the magazines, pretending he wasn't hearing a thing. I turned back to Cookie.

"Small coffee, please."

"No scones?"

"No thanks."

She grabbed a cup and started to fill it.

"Are you still with Denise?" I asked.

Her body stiffened.

"She used to work at the retreat up the

hill too," I said. "That's how I knew her."

I saw Cookie swallow. "We never worked at the retreat."

"Sure you did. The Creative Recharge, right up the path. Denise would bring in the coffee and your scones."

She finished pouring the coffee and put it on the counter in front of me. "Look, mister, I have work to do."

I leaned closer to her. "Natalie loved your scones."

"So you said."

"You two used to talk about them all the time."

"I talk to a lot of people about my scones, okay? I'm sorry I don't remember you. I probably should have been polite and faked it and been all, 'Oh sure, you and your scone-loving girlfriend, how you guys doing?' But I didn't. Here's your coffee. Can I get you something else?"

I took out my card with all my phone numbers on it. "If you remember any-thing . . ."

"Can I get you something else?" she asked, more bite in her voice now.

"No."

"Then that's a buck fifty. Have a nice day."

CHAPTER 9

I now understand when someone says they feel as though they're being followed.

How did I know? Intuition maybe. My lizard brain could sense it. I could feel it in almost a physical way. That, plus the same car — a gray Chevy van with a Vermont license plate — had been behind me since I left the town of Kraftboro.

I couldn't swear to it, but I thought that maybe the driver was wearing a maroon baseball cap.

I wasn't sure what to do about this. I tried to make out the license plate number, but it was too dark now. If I slowed down, he'd slow down. If I picked up speed, well, you get the drift. An idea came to me. I pulled over at a rest stop to see what the tail would do. I saw the van slow and then drive on. From that point on, I didn't see the van again.

So maybe he wasn't following me.

I was about ten minutes away from Lanford when my cell phone rang. I had the phone set up to go through the car Bluetooth — something it took me much too long to figure out — so I could see on the radio screen that it was Shanta Newlin. She had promised to get back to me by the end of the day with Natalie's address. I answered the call with a press of a button on the steering wheel.

"It's Shanta," she said.

"Yeah, I know. I got that caller ID thing up."

"And I think my years at the FBI make me special," she said. "Where are you?"

"I'm driving back to Lanford."

"Back from where?"

"It's a long story," I said. "Did you find her address?"

"That's why I called," Shanta said. I could hear something in the background — a man's voice maybe. "I don't have it yet."

"Oh?" I said, because what else was I going to say to that. "Is there a problem?"

"I need you to give me until the morning, okay?"

"Sure," I said. Then I repeated: "Is there a problem?"

There was a pause that lasted a beat too

99

long. "Just give me till morning." She hung up.

What the hell?

I hadn't liked the tone. I hadn't liked the fact that a woman with enormous contacts in the FBI needed until morning to find the address of a random woman. My smartphone dinged, signaling that I was getting a new e-mail. I ignored it. I am not a goody-goody or any of that, but I never text or e-mail and drive. Two years ago, a student at Lanford had been seriously injured while texting and driving. The eighteen-year-old woman in the passenger seat, a freshman in my Rule of Law class, died in the crash. Even before that, even before the wealth of obvious information about the downright stupidity if not criminal negligence in texting while driving, I was not a fan. I like driving. I like the solitude and the music. In spite of my earlier misgivings about techno-logical seclusion, we all need to disconnect more often. I realize that I sound like a grumpy old man, complaining that when-ever I see a table of college "friends" sitting together they are inevitably texting with unseen others, searching, always searching, I guess, for something that might be better, a perpetual life hunt for digital greener grass, an attempt to smell roses that are elsewhere at the expense of the ones in front of you, but there are few times that I feel more at peace, more in tune, more Zen, if you will, than when I force myself to unplug.

Right now I was flipping stations, settling on one that played 1st Wave music from the eighties. General Public asked, where is the tenderness? I wondered that too. Where is the tenderness? For that matter, where is Natalie?

I was getting loopy.

I parked in front of my housing — I didn't call it my house or my apartment because it was and felt like campus housing. Night had fallen, but because we are a college campus, there was plenty of artificial illumination. I checked the new e-mail and saw it was from Mrs. Dinsmore. The subject read:

Here's the student file you requested

Good work, you sexy beast, I thought. I clicked on the message. It read in its entirety:

How much elaboration do you need on "Here's the student file you requested"?

Clearly the answer was, none.

My phone's screen was too small to see

the attached file, so I hurried up the walk in order to view it on my laptop. I put my key in the lock, opened the front door, and flipped on the lights. For some reason I expected, I don't know, to find the place in shambles, as though someone had ransacked the joint, as they say. I had seen too many movies. My apartment remained, at kindest, nondescript.

I rushed over to my computer and jumped on the e-mail. I opened the one from Mrs. Dinsmore and downloaded the attachment. As I mentioned earlier, I saw my student file years ago. It was, I thought, a tad disturbing, reading professors' comments that had not been shared with me. I guess at some point the school decided that it was too much to store all these old records so they'd scanned them into digital forms.

I started with Todd's freshman year. There was nothing particularly spectacular there except that Todd was, well, spectacular. Straight A+'s across the board. No freshman got straight A+'s. Professor Charles Powell noted that Todd was "an exceptional student." Professor Ruth Kugelmass raved, "A special kid." Even Professor Malcolm Hume, never one easy with praise, commented: "Todd Sanderson is almost supernaturally gifted." Wow. I found this strange.

I had been a good student here, and the only note I'd found in my file was negative. The only ones I'd ever written were negative. If all was okay, the professor just left it alone and let the grade suffice. The rule of thumb in student files seemed to be, "If you have nothing negative to say, don't say anything at all."

But not with good ol' Todd.

First-semester sophomore year followed the same pattern — incredible grades — but then things changed abruptly. Next to second semester was a big "LOA."

Leave of Absence.

Hmm. I checked for a reason and it only said, "Personal." That was bizarre. We rarely, if ever, leave it at just that — "Personal" in a student file — because the file is closed and confidential. Or supposed to be. We write openly in here.

So why be so circumspect about Todd's LOA?

Usually the "personal" reason involves some kind of financial hardship or an illness, either the student's or a close family member's, either physical or mental. But those reasons are always listed in the private student files. None was listed here.

Interesting.

Or not. For one thing they were probably

more discreet about personal issues twenty years ago. But second . . . well, who cared? What on earth could Todd's taking time off as a sophomore have to do with his marrying Natalie and then dying and leaving behind a different wife?

When Todd came back to school, there were now more professor comments — not the ones a student would long for. One professor described him as "distracted." Another said that Todd was "clearly bitter" and "not the same." Another suggested that Todd should take more time off to deal with "the situation." No one mentioned what the situation was.

I clicked to the next page. Todd had been brought up to the disciplinary board. Some schools have students deal with disciplinary issues, but we have a three-professor rotating panel. I did it for a two-month stint last year. Most of the cases that came before us dealt with two campus epidemics: underage drinking and cheating. The rest were a smattering of thefts or threats of violence or some variety of sexual assault or aggression that didn't meet the standard for law enforcement.

The case that came before the disciplinarian board involved an altercation between Todd and another student named Ryan

McCarthy. McCarthy ended up hospital-ized with contusions and a broken nose. The school was calling for a heavy suspension or even expulsion, but the three-professor panel gave Todd a total pass. That surprised me. There were no details or minutes on the actual hearing or the subsequent delib-erations. That surprised me too.

The handwritten decision had been scanned into the file:

Todd Sanderson, a superior member of the Lanford College community, has had a tough blow in his life, but we think he is on the way back. He has recently worked with a faculty member to create a charity to make amends for his recent actions. He understands the ramifica-tions of what he has done, and due to the highly unusual extenuating circum-stances in this case, we have agreed that Todd Sanderson should not face expul-sion.

My eyes traveled down to the bottom of the page to see the professor who had signed the panel's opinion. I made a face. Professor Eban Trainor. I should have known. I knew Trainor well enough. We were not what one would call friendly.

If I wanted to learn more about this "tough blow" or indeed this decision, I would need to talk to Eban. I wasn't looking forward to that.

It was late, but I wasn't worried about waking Benedict. He only used a cell phone and turned it off when sleeping. He answered on the third ring.

"What?"

"Eban Trainor," I said.

"What about him?"

"He still hate my guts?"

"I would assume so. Why?"

"I need to ask him about my buddy Todd Sanderson. Do you think you can smooth it out?"

"Smooth it out? Sure. Why do you think they call me the Sandman?"

"Because you put your students to sleep?"

"You really know how to butter a guy up when you're asking for a favor. I'll call you in the morning."

We hung up. I sat back, unsure what to do next, when my monitor dinged that I had received a new e-mail. I was going to ignore it. Like most people I knew, I got too many irrelevant e-mails during all hours of the day. This would undoubtedly be yet another.

Then I saw the sender's e-mail address:

RSbyJA@ymail.com

I stared at it until my eyes watered. There was a rushing in my ears. Everything around me was silent and too still. I kept staring, but the letters didn't change.

RSbyJA.

It took me no time to see what those letters meant: *Redemption's Son* by Joseph Arthur — the album Natalie and I listened to in the café.

The subject was empty. My hand found the mouse. I tried to get the cursor over the e-mail so I could open it, but first I had to control my shake. I took a deep breath and willed my hand still. The room remained a hushed quiet, almost expectantly so. I moved the cursor over the e-mail and clicked on it.

The e-mail stopped my heart.

There, on my screen, were four words. That was all, just four words, but those four words sliced through my chest like a reaper's scythe, making it nearly impossible to breathe. I collapsed back on the chair, lost, as the four words on the screen stared back at me:

You made a promise.

CHAPTER 10

The e-mail wasn't signed. Didn't matter.

I quickly hit the reply button and typed:

Natalie? Are you okay? Please just let me know that.

I hit send.

I would explain to you how time slowed to a crawl as I waited for her next e-mail, but that wasn't really what happened. There was no time for it, I guess. Three seconds later, my new-e-mail-ding sounded. My heart raced until I saw the sender's name:

MAILDAEMON

I clicked open but I already knew what I would find:

This e-mail address doesn't exist . . .

I almost smacked the computer in frustration, as if it were a candy machine that wouldn't dispense the Milky Way. I actually shouted "No way!" out loud. I didn't know what to do. I sat there and I started drowning. I felt as though I were sinking and couldn't even flail my way back to the surface.

I went back to googling. I tried the e-mail and different variations, but it was just a waste of time. I read her e-mail again:

You made a promise.

I had, hadn't I? And when you stopped and thought about it, why did I break that promise? A man had died. Maybe it was her husband. Maybe it wasn't. Still, was that a reason to go back on my promise to her? Maybe. Maybe it was at first. But now she had made it clear. That was the purpose of the e-mail. Natalie was calling me on it. She was reminding me of the promise because she knew that I don't make promises idly.

It was why she had made me promise to stay away in the first place.

I thought about that now. I thought about the funeral and the visit to Vermont and this student file. What did it all add up to? I don't know. If it had originally warranted going back on my word, I now had proof that I could no longer justify it. Natalie's message couldn't have been clearer.

You made a promise.

With a tentative finger, I touched the words on the screen. My heart crumbled anew. Too bad, tough guy. So okay, heartbreak notwithstanding, I would let it go. I would back off. I would keep my word.

I headed to bed and fell asleep almost immediately. I know. I was surprised by that too, but I think all the blows since reading that obituary, the swirl of memory and emotion, of heartbreak and confusion, wore me down like a boxer taking body shots for twelve solid rounds. Eventually, I just folded.

Unlike Benedict, I often forget to turn my cell phone off. His call at 8:00 A.M. woke me up.

"Eban has reluctantly agreed to meet with you."

"Did you tell him what it's about?"

"You didn't tell me what it's about."

"Oh. Right."

"You got a nine A.M. class. He'll be waiting for you at his house when you're done."

I felt the pang deep in my chest. "His house?"

"Yeah, I didn't think you'd like that. He insisted."

"Douchebag move."

"He isn't so bad."

"He's a lecherous creep."

"And that's bad because?"

"You don't do what he does."

"You don't know what he does. Go. Be nice. Get what you need."

Benedict hung up. I checked my e-mail and texts. Nothing. This whole strange episode in my life had taken on a surreal, dream-like quality. I worked hard to dismiss it. I did indeed have a 9:00 A.M. class on Law and the Constitution. That was my priority again. Yep, I'd put it behind me. I actually sang in the shower. I dressed and walked across campus with my smile wide and my head high. There was a little hop in my step. The sun bathed the campus in a warm, celestial beacon. I kept smiling. I smiled at the brick buildings longing for ivy. I smiled at the trees, at the lush grass, at the statues of famous alumni, at the view of the athletic fields down the hill. When students said hello to me, I greeted them with a level of enthusiasm that made one fear I was suddenly into religious conversion.

When class started, I stood in the front of the room and shouted "Good morning, everyone!" like a born-again cheerleader on too much Red Bull. The students gave me curious looks. I was starting to scare myself, so I tried to dial it back.

You made a promise.

And what about you, Natalie? Wasn't there at least an implied promise to me in your words and actions? How do you just capture a heart and crush it like that? Yes, I'm a big boy. I get the risks of falling in love. But we said things. We felt things. They weren't lies. And yet. You dumped me. You invited me to your wedding. Why? Why would anyone be that cruel, or were you trying to hammer home the fact that it was time for me to move on?

I did move on. You reached into my chest, plucked out my heart, tore it up, and walked away, but I picked up the shreds and moved on.

I shook my head. Picked up the shreds? Sheesh, that was horrible. That's the problem with falling in love. It makes you start talking like a bad country song.

Natalie had e-mailed me. Or at least, I thought it was Natalie. Who else could it be? But either way, even though she was telling me to stay away, it was communication. It was her reaching out to me. Reaching? Sure. But she had used that e-mail address. RSbyJA. She had remembered it. It had meant something to her, something that still resonated, and that gave me — I don't know — hope. Hope is cruel. Hope reminds me of what almost was. Hope makes the physical ache return.

I called on Eileen Sinagra, one of my brightest students. She began to explain one of the finer points of Madison and *The Federalist Papers.* I nodded, encouraging her to continue, when I saw something out of the corner of my eye. I moved closer to the window for a better look. I stopped.

"Professor Fisher?"

In the parking lot was a gray Chevy van. I checked the license plates. I couldn't make out the numbers from here, but I could see the color and pattern.

Vermont plates.

I didn't think twice. I didn't consider that it probably meant absolutely nothing, that gray Chevy vans are hardly rare, that there are plenty of Vermont license plates in western Massachusetts. None of that made any difference.

I was already sprinting toward the door when I shouted, "I'll be right back, stay here." I started down the corridor. The floor had just been mopped. I skidded around the WET sign and slammed open the door. The parking lot was across the commons. I hurdled a bush and ran full speed across the grass. My students must have thought that I'd gone off the deep end. I didn't really care.

"Go, Professor Fisher! I'll hit you!"

A student, mistaking my running for desire to participate, actually threw me a Frisbee. I let it land and kept running.

"Dude, you gotta work on your catches."

I ignored the voice. I was getting closer to the Chevy van when I saw its lights go on.

The driver had started up the van.

I ran even faster. That bright beacon of sun shone off the front windshield, blocking my view of the driver. I lowered my head and pumped my legs, but the Chevy van was backing out of the space now. I was too far away. I wasn't going to make it.

The van shifted into drive.

I pulled up and tried to get a look at the driver. No go. Too much glare, but I thought I saw . . .

A maroon baseball cap?

There was no way to be sure. I did, however, memorize the license plate — like that would help, like that would do any good — and then I stood, panting, as the van sped away.

CHAPTER 11

Professor Eban Trainor sat on the lemonade porch in front of a gorgeous Second-Empire Victorian. I knew the house well. For half a century it had been home to Professor Malcolm Hume, my mentor. A lot of good times had been had in this house. Poly-sci wine tastings, staff parties, late-night cognac, philosophical arguments, literary discussions — all things academia. But, alas, God has an interesting sense of humor. Professor Hume's wife passed away after forty-eight years of marriage, and his health followed. Eventually he could not take care of this great old house by himself. He now resided in a gated community in Vero Beach, Florida, while Professor Eban Trainor, the closest thing I had to an enemy on campus, had purchased this beloved dwelling, making himself the new lord of the manor.

I felt my phone buzz in my pocket. It was

a text from Shanta:

JUDIE'S. 1:00 P.M.

Quite the wordsmith, but I knew what she meant. We should meet at Judie's Restaurant on Main Avenue at 1:00 P.M. Okay, fine. I put the phone away and started up the porch steps.

Eban rose and offered me a condescending smile. "Jacob. So good to see you."

His handshake felt greasy. His fingernails were manicured. Women found him handsome in an aging-playboy sort of way, what with the long unruly hair and big green eyes. His skin was waxy, as though his face were either melting or still recovering from some kind of skin treatment. I suspected Botox. He wore slacks a size too tight and a dress shirt that could have used one more closed button. His cologne smelled like too many European businessmen jammed into a morning elevator.

"Do you mind sitting on the porch?" he asked. "It's so beautiful out."

I readily agreed. I didn't want to go inside and see what he'd done with the place. I knew the work had been extensive. Gone, I was sure, were the dark woods, the cognac and cigar feel, traded in for blond wood and couches in colors like "eggshell" and "churned butter" and gatherings that only served white wine and Sprite because they wouldn't stain the upholstery.

On cue, he offered me white wine. I politely declined. He had his in hand. It wasn't even noon. We both sat on wicker chairs with big pillows.

"So what can I do for you, Jacob?" he asked.

I had taken a class with him sophomore year on Mid-Twentieth-Century Drama. He wasn't a bad teacher. He was both effective and affected, the kind of teacher who loves nothing more than the sound of his voice and while he is rarely boring — the kiss of death in any class — the lessons are all a tad professor-centric. He spent one week reading Genet's *The Maids* in its entirety out loud, taking on each character, reveling in his own performance, not to mention the S&M scenes. The performance was good, no doubt, but, alas, it was all him.

"I wanted to ask you about a student," I said

Eban raised both eyebrows as though my words were both intriguing and surprising. "Oh?"

"Todd Sanderson."

"Oh?"

I saw him stiffen. He didn't want me to see it. But I did. He looked off and stroked his chin.

"You remember him," I said.

Eban Trainor stroked his chin some more. "The name rings a bell, but . . ." A few more strokes and then Eban shrugged in surrender. "I'm sorry. So many years, so many students."

Why didn't I believe him?

"You didn't have him in class," I said.

"Oh?"

Again with the oh.

"He came up before the discipline committee when you were in charge. This would have been about twenty years ago."

"And you expect me to still remember?"

"You helped keep him on campus after an altercation. Here, let me show you." I pulled out my laptop and brought up the scan of his handwritten decision. I held out the laptop. Eban hesitated as though it might contain explosives. He took out his reading glasses and examined the letter.

"Wait, where did you get this?"

"It's important, Eban."

"This is from a student's confidential file." A small smile crossed his lips. "Isn't reading this file breaking the rules, Jacob? Wouldn't you say you were crossing boundaries?"

119

So there it was. Six years ago, just a scant few weeks before I headed up to that retreat in Vermont, Professor Eban Trainor hosted a graduation party at his then-house. Trainor frequently hosted parties at his house. In fact, he was somewhat legendary for both throwing and attending them. When I was a sophomore, there had been a rather famous incident at Jones College, the nearby all-women institution, during which a fire alarm went off at three in the morning, forcing a dorm to evacuate, and there stood Professor Trainor, half-dressed. True, the coed he'd been seeing that particular night was of legal age and not one of his students. But this was typical Trainor. He was a letch and a drunk, and I didn't like him.

The graduation party six years ago was mostly attended by students, many of whom were underclassmen and thus underage. Alcohol had been served. A lot of it. Campus police were called. Two students were taken to the hospital for alcohol poisoning, something that happens with increasing frequency on college campuses. Or maybe that's what I tell myself because I like to think that it was not as bad in "my day."

Professor Trainor was brought up before the administration for his actions. There

120

were calls for his resignation. He refused. He claimed that, yes, he had offered alcohol to the attendees but only seniors who were over twenty-one years old were invited. If underclassmen crashed the party, he should not be held responsible. He also suggested that much of the alcohol had been consumed before his party began, at a nearby fraternity kegger.

The professors on campus govern themselves. We rarely do more than slap one another on the wrist. Like with the student discipline committee, professors rotate through. As luck would have it, I was on the committee when this incident occurred. Trainor had tenure and couldn't be fired, but I firmly believed that he deserved some sort of disciplinary action. We took a vote to have Trainor removed as chairman of the English department. I argued in favor of the punishment. There were simply too many incidents of this kind of behavior in his past. Interestingly enough, my beloved mentor, Malcolm Hume, did not agree.

"Are you really going to blame Eban for students drinking too much?" he had asked me.

"There are reasons why we have rules about fraternizing with students when alcohol is served."

"The extenuating circumstances don't mean anything to you?"

They might have, I guessed, if I hadn't already seen Eban's pattern of obvious bad behavior and poor choices. This wasn't a court of law or a question of rights; this was a great job and a privilege. In my view, his actions warranted termination — we expel students for far less and with far less evidence — but at the very least, he deserved a demotion. Despite my mentor's urging, I voted in favor of taking away his chairmanship, but I was outvoted by a wide margin.

Those hearings might be long over, but the resentment lasts. I had used those exact terms — "broken rules," "crossed boundaries" — during the supposedly closed debates. Nice to have my own words thrown back at my face, but maybe that was fair.

"This particular student," I said, "is dead."

"So his confidential file is now fair game?"

"I'm not here to argue legal minutiae with you."

"No, no, Jacob, you're a big-picture guy, aren't you?"

This was a waste of time. "I don't really understand your reticence."

"That surprises me, Jacob. You're usually such a rules follower. The information you're asking for is confidential. I'm protecting Mr. Sanderson's privacy."

"But again," I said, "he's dead."

I did not want to sit here, on this lemonade porch where my beloved mentor spent so many wonderful hours, another moment. I rose and reached for my laptop. He did not hand it back to me. He started doing the chin rub again.

"Sit," he said.

I did.

"Would you tell me why a case this old would have relevance to you now?"

"It would be very hard to explain," I said.

"But it is clearly very important to you."

"Yes."

"How did Todd Sanderson die?"

"He was murdered."

Eban closed his eyes as though that revelation made it all so much worse. "By whom?"

"The police don't know yet."

"Ironic," he said.

"How so?"

"That he would die by violence. I remember the case. Todd Sanderson injured a fellow student in a violent altercation. Well, that's not really an adequate way of stating it. In truth, Todd Sanderson nearly killed a fellow student."

Eban Trainor looked off again and took a gulp of wine. I waited for him to say more.

It took some time, but eventually he continued. "It happened at a Thursday night kegger at Chi Psi."

Chi Psi sponsored a kegger every Thursday night for as long as anyone could remember. The powers that be tried to stop it twelve years ago, but a wealthy alum simply bought a house off campus specifically for their use. He could have donated the money to a worthy cause. Instead he bought a party house for his younger frat brothers to imbibe in. Go figure.

"Naturally both participants were drunk," Eban said. "Words were exchanged, but there was little doubt that Todd Sanderson turned this verbal altercation into something horribly physical. When all is said, the other student — I'm sorry, I don't remember his name, it may have been McCarthy or McCaffrey, something like that — had to be hospitalized. He had a broken nose and a crushed cheekbone. But that wasn't the worst part."

He stopped again. I picked up the hint.

"What was the worst part?" I asked.

"Todd Sanderson nearly choked the other student to death. It took five people to pull him off. The other student was unconscious. He had to be resuscitated."

"Wow," I said.

Eban Trainor shut his eyes for a moment. "I can't see how this matters anymore. We should let him rest in peace."

"I'm not asking out of some kind of prurient interest."

The thin smile crossed his lips again. "Oh, I know, Jacob. You are, if nothing else, a righteous man. I'm sure your interest here is nothing but the healthiest and most well-meaning."

I let that pass.

"So why was Sanderson let off?" I asked.

"You read my decision."

"I did," I said. "Something about 'highly unusual extenuating circumstances.' "

"That's correct."

I waited again, figuring my follow-up question was obvious. When Trainor didn't say anything, I gave the proper prompt: "What were the extenuating circumstances?"

"The other student — McCarthy. That was his name. I remember now." Trainor took a deep breath. "Mr. McCarthy made derogatory comments about a certain incident. When Sanderson heard the comments, he more or less — yet understandably — lost control." Eban held a hand up in my face as though I were about to object, which I wasn't about to do at all. "Yes, Jacob, I

125

know that we do not excuse violence under any circumstances. That would be your stand, I am certain. But we looked at this unusual case from every level. We heard from several Todd Sanderson supporters. One, in particular, defended him with great gusto."

I met his eyes and saw something mocking in them. "Who would that be, Eban?"

"Hint: He used to own this house."

That surprised me. "Professor Hume defended Todd Sanderson?"

"What's the word attorneys always use?" He rubbed his chin again. "*Vigorously.* He even helped him set up a charity when the case was over."

I tried to put it together. Hume detested violence in all forms. He was one of those people who felt too much. Cruelty on any level made him cringe. If you hurt, he hurt.

"I confess," Eban continued, "that I was surprised too, but your mentor has always understood extenuating circumstances, hasn't he?"

We weren't talking about Todd Sanderson anymore, so I brought the topic back to him.

"And what were the extenuating circumstances in this case?"

"Well, for one thing, Todd Sanderson had just come back from a long leave. He had

serve any time?"

"No. He was found innocent."

"Oh?" I said.

"The outcome didn't really get much press. That's part of our process. The accusation gets page one. The retraction not so much."

"So he was found not guilty?"

"That's correct."

"Big difference though between not guilty and innocent."

"True," Eban said, "but not in this case. During the first week of trial, it came to light that a vindictive parent made it up because Todd's father wouldn't let his son pitch. The lie just snowballed. But in the end Todd's father was cleared of all charges."

"And Todd returned to school?"

"Yes."

"And I assume the derogatory comment had something to do with the accusations against Todd's father?"

Eban raised an unsteady hand in mock toast. "You are correct, sir. You see, despite the new evidence, many believed, as you did, that where there was smoke there was fire. Mr. Sanderson must have done *something*. Maybe not this. But something.

129

missed the prior semester for personal reasons."

I had just about had enough. "Eban?"

"Yes?"

"Could we stop dancing around here? What happened to Todd Sanderson? Why did he leave campus? What were the extenuating circumstances that would cause a man as anti-violence as Malcolm Hume to defend such an extreme assault?"

"It's not in the file?"

"You know it's not. Everything but the decision was kept off the record. So what happened to him?"

"Not to him," Trainor said. "To his father."

He reached behind him for a glass and handed it to me. He didn't ask; he just handed me the glass. I took it and let him pour the wine into it. It was still not yet noon, but I figured that this would be the wrong time to comment on morning drinking. I accepted it and hoped that it would loosen his tongue.

Eban Trainor sat back and crossed his legs. He stared into his wineglass as though it were a crystal ball. "Do you remember the Martindale Little League incident?"

Now it was my turn to look at the wine. I took a sip. "The pedophilia scandal?"

"Yes."

come back. He saw it as abandoning his father in his hour of most need. Todd flat-out refused to return until the situation at home got better. But of course, as we know all too well, situations like this don't get better. So Todd's father did the only thing he thought he could to end his own pain and free his son to continue his studies."

Our eyes met. His were wet now.

"Oh no," I said.

"Oh yes."

"How . . . ?"

"His father broke into the school where he used to work and shot himself in the head. See, he didn't want his son to be the one who found his body."

Chapter 12

Three weeks before Natalie dumped me, when we were madly in love, we sneaked down from our retreats in Kraftboro to visit Lanford. "I want to see this place that means so much to you," she said.

I remember the way her eyes lit up when she walked with me on that campus. We held hands. Natalie wore a big straw hat, which was both endearing and odd, and sunglasses. She looked a bit like a movie star in disguise.

"When you were a student here," she asked me, "where did you take the hot coeds?"

"Straight to bed."

Natalie playfully slapped my arm. "I'm serious. And hungry."

So we headed to Judie's Restaurant on Main Avenue. Judie made a wonderful popover and apple butter. Natalie loved it. I watched her take it all in — the artwork, the décor, the young waitstaff, the menu, everything. "So this is where you took your ladies?"

"The classy ones," I said.

"Wait, where did you take the, uh, class-less ones?"

"Barsolotti's. The dive bar next door." I smiled.

"What?"

"We used to play condom roulette."

"Excuse me?"

"Not with girls. I was kidding about that. I'd go there with friends. There was a condom dispenser in the men's room."

"A condom dispenser?"

"Yep."

"Like a condom vending machine."

"Exactly," I said.

Natalie nodded. "Classy."

"I know, right?"

"So what are the rules of condom roulette?"

"It's silly."

"Oh, you're not getting off that easy. I want to hear."

There was that smile that knocked me back a step.

"Okay," I said. "You play with four guys . . . this is so stupid."

"Please? I love it. Come on. You play with

four guys . . ." She gestured for me to continue.

"The condoms come in four colors," I explained. "Midnight Black, Cherry Red, Lemon Yellow, Orange Orange."

"You're making up those last two."

"Something like that. The point is, they came in four colors, but you never knew which one you'd get. So see, we'd each put three bucks in the pot and choose a color. Then one of us would go to the dispenser and bring back the wrapped condom. Again, you didn't know the color until you actually open the wrapper. Someone would do a drumroll. Another guy would do the play-by-play like it was an Olympic event. Finally, the package was opened, and whoever picked the right color got the money."

"Oh, that's too awesome."

"Yeah, well," I said. "Of course, the winner had to buy the next pitcher of beer, so there wasn't much of a financial windfall. Eventually Barsy — that's the guy who owned the place — made it a full-fledged game with rules and league play and a leader board."

She took my hand. "Could we play?"

"What, now? No."

"Please."

"No way."

"After the game," Natalie whispered, giving me a look that singed my eyebrows, "we could use the condom."

"I call Midnight Black," I said.

She laughed. I could still hear that sound as I entered Judie's, as if her laugh were still here, still echoing, still mocking me. I hadn't been back to Judie's in, well, six years. I looked over at the table where we'd sat. It was empty.

"Jake?"

I spun toward my right. Shanta Newlin sat at a quiet table over by the bay windows. She didn't wave or nod. Her body language, usually fully loaded with confidence, seemed all wrong. I sat across from her. She barely looked up.

"Hi," I said.

Still staring at the table, Shanta said, "Tell me the whole story, Jake."

"Why? What's going on?"

Her eyes came up, pinning me interrogator-style. I could see the FBI agent now. "Is she really an old girlfriend?"

"What? Yes, of course."

"And why do you all of a sudden want to find her?"

I hesitated.

"Jake?"

The e-mail came back to me:

You made a promise.

"I asked you a favor," I said.

"I know."

"So you can either let me know what you found or we can just forget it. I'm not sure I get why you need to know more."

The young waitress — Judie always hired college kids — gave us menus and asked if we would like drinks. We both ordered iced teas. When she left, Shanta turned the hard eyes back on me.

"I'm trying to help you, Jake."

"Maybe we should just let it go."

"You're kidding, right?"

"No," I said. "She asked me to leave her alone. I should probably have listened."

"When?"

"When what?"

"When did she ask you to leave her alone?" Shanta asked.

"What difference does that make?"

"Just tell me, okay? It could be important."

"How?" Then, figuring, what was the harm, I added: "Six years ago."

"You said that you were in love with her."

"Yes."

"So was this when you broke up?"

I shook my head. "It was at her wedding to another man."

That made her blink. My words diffused the hard glare, at least for the moment. "Just so I'm clear on this, you went to her wedding — were you still in love with her? Dumb question. Of course you were. You still are. So you went to her wedding, and while you were there, Natalie told you to leave her alone?"

"Something like that, yes."

"That must have been some scene."

"It wasn't like it sounds. We had just broken up. She ended up choosing another guy over me. An old boyfriend. They got married a few days later." I tried to shrug it off. "It happens."

"You think?" Shanta said with the confused head tilt of a freshman. "Go on."

"Go on with what? I went to the wedding. Natalie asked me to accept her choice and leave them be. I said I would."

"I see. Have you had any contact with her during the past six years?"

"No."

"None at all?"

I realized now how good Shanta was at this. I had taken the position that I wouldn't talk, and now you pretty much couldn't get me to shut up. "Right, none at all."

"And you're sure her name is Natalie Avery?"

"That's not the kind of thing you make a mistake about. Enough questions. What did you find, Shanta?"

"Nothing."

"Nothing?"

The waitress came back with a big smile and our iced teas. "Here are some of Judie's fresh popovers." Her voice was the happy song of youth. The popover scent rose from the table and took me back to my last visit here, yep, six years ago.

"Any questions about the menu?" the perky waitress asked.

I couldn't answer.

"Jake?" Shanta said.

I swallowed. "No questions."

Shanta ordered a grilled portobello mushroom sandwich. I went with the turkey BLT on rye. When the waitress was gone, I leaned across the table. "What do you mean you found nothing?"

"What part of 'nothing' is confusing you, Jake? I found nothing on your ex — zippo, *nada,* zilch. No address, no tax returns, no bank account, no credit card statement. Not-a-thing, no thing, nothing. There is not one shred of evidence that your Natalie Avery even exists anymore."

I tried to take this in.

Shanta put her hands on the table. "Do

you know how hard it is to live off the grid like that?"

"Not really, no."

"In this day and age with computers and all the technology? It's pretty close to impossible."

"Maybe there's a reasonable explanation," I said.

"Like what?"

"Maybe she moved overseas."

"Then there's no record of her going there. No passport issued. No entry or exit in the computer. Like I said before —"

"Nothing," I finished for her.

Shanta nodded.

"She's a person, Shanta. She exists."

"Well, she existed. Six years ago. That was the last time we had an address on her. She has a sister named Julie Pottham. Her mother, Sylvia Avery, is in a nursing home. Do you know all this?"

"Yes."

"Who did she marry?"

Should I answer that one? I saw little harm. "Todd Sanderson."

She jotted the name down. "And why did you want to look her up now?"

You made a promise.

"It doesn't matter," I said. "I should just let it be."

"Are you serious?"

"I am. It was a whim. I mean, it's been six years. She married another man and made me promise to leave her alone. So what exactly am I looking for anyway?"

"But that's what makes me curious, Jake."

"What does?"

"You kept this promise for six years. Why did you suddenly break it?"

I didn't want to answer that, and something else was starting to gnaw at me. "Why are you so interested?"

She didn't reply.

"I asked you to look a person up. You could have just told me that you didn't find anything. Why are you asking me all these questions about her?"

Shanta seemed taken aback. "I was just trying to help."

"You're not telling me something."

"Neither are you," Shanta said. "Why now, Jake? Why are you looking for your old love now?"

I stared down at the popover. I thought about that day in this restaurant six years ago, the way Natalie tore off small pieces of her popover, the look of concentration as she buttered it, the way she simply enjoyed everything. When we were together, even the smallest thing took on significance. Every touch brought pleasure.

You made a promise.

Even now, even after all that had happened, I couldn't betray her. Stupid? Yep. Naive? Oh, several steps south of that. But I couldn't do it.

"Talk to me, Jake."

I shook my head. "No."

"Why the hell not?"

"Who ordered turkey BLT?"

It was another waitress, this one less perky and more harried. I raised my hand.

"And the grilled portobello sandwich?"

"Wrap it for me," Shanta said, rising. "I lost my appetite."

CHAPTER 13

The first time I met Natalie she was wearing sunglasses indoors. To make matters worse, it was nighttime.

I rolled my eyes, thinking it was for effect. I figured that she fancied herself an Artiste with a capital *A*. We were attending a mixer of sorts, the art colony and the writers' retreat, sharing one another's work. This was my first time attending, but I soon learned that it was a weekly gathering. The art was displayed in the back of Darly Wanatick's barn. Chairs were set up for the readings.

The woman in the sunglasses — I hadn't met her yet — sat in the last row, her arms crossed. A bearded man with dark curly hair sat next to her. I wondered whether they were together. Remember the blowhard named Lars who was writing poetry from the perspective of Hitler's dog? He began to read. He read for a long time. I began to fidget. The woman in the sunglasses remained still.

When I could listen no longer, rude or not, I wandered toward the back of the barn and started to check out the various art on display. Most of it, well, I will be kind. I didn't "get it." There was an installation piece called *Breakfast in America* that featured spilled boxes of cold cereal on a kitchen table. That was it. There were boxes of Cap'n Crunch, Cap'n Crunch with Peanut Butter (one person actually muttered, "Notice there is no Cap'n Crunch with Crunch Berries — why? — what is the artist saying?"), Lucky Charms, Cocoa Puffs, Sugar Smacks, even my old favorite, Quisp. I looked at the spilled cereal coating the table. It did not speak to me, though my stomach grumbled a little.

When one person asked, "What do you think?" I was tempted to say that it needed a little milk.

As I kept walking, only one artist's work gave me real pause. I stopped at a painting of a small cottage on top of a hill. There was a soft morning glow hitting the side — the pinkness that comes with the first light of day. I couldn't tell you why but it choked me up. Maybe it was the dark windows, as though the cottage had once been warm but it was abandoned now. I don't know. But I stood in front of the painting and felt lost and moved. I stepped slowly from one painting to the next. They all delivered a blow of some kind. Some made me melancholy. Some made me nostalgic, whimsical, passionate. None left me indifferent.

I will spare you the "big reveal" that the paintings were done by Natalie.

A woman was smiling at my reaction. "Do you like them?"

"Very much," I said. "Are you the artist?"

"Heavens no. I run the bakery and coffee shop in town." She offered me her hand. "They call me Cookie."

I shook it. "Wait. Cookie runs a bakery?"

"Yeah, I know. Too precious, right?"

"Maybe a tad."

"The artist is Natalie Avery. She's right over there."

Cookie pointed to the woman with the sunglasses.

"Oh," I said.

"Oh what?"

With the sunglasses-indoors look, I had her pegged as the creator of *Breakfast in America*. Lars had just finished his reading. The crowd gave him a small golf-clap, but Lars, sporting an ascot, bowed as though it were a thunderous standing ovation.

Everyone quickly rose except for Natalie. The man with the beard and curly hair whispered something to her as he stood, but still she didn't move. She stayed with her arms crossed, still lost, it seemed, in the essence of Hitler's dog.

I approached her. She looked right through me.

"The cottage in your painting. Where is it?"

"Huh?" she said, startled. "Nowhere. What painting?"

I frowned. "Aren't you Natalie Avery?"

"Me?" She seemed befuddled by the question. "Yeah, why?"

"The painting of the cottage. I really loved it. It . . . I don't know. It moved me."

"Cottage?" She sat up, took off the sunglasses, and rubbed her eyes. "Sure, right, a cottage."

I frowned again. I was not sure what reaction I expected, but something a bit more demonstrative than this. I looked down at her. Sometimes I am not the sharpest knife in the drawer but when she rubbed her eyes again, the realization hit me.

"You were sleeping!" I said.

"What?" she said. "No."

But she rubbed her eyes some more.

"Holy crap," I said. "That's why you're

wearing the sunglasses. So no one can tell."

"Shh."

"You were sleeping this whole time!"

"Keep it down."

She finally looked up at me and I remembered thinking that she had a beautiful, sweet face. I would soon learn that Natalie had what I'd call a slow beauty, the kind you don't really notice at first and then it knocks you back and grows on you and she gets more beautiful every time you see her and then you can't believe that you ever thought that she was anything less than completely stunning. Whenever I saw her, my entire body reacted, as though it were the first time or better.

"Was I that obvious?" she asked in a whisper.

"Not at all," I said. "I just thought you were being a pretentious ass."

She arched an eyebrow. "What better disguise to blend in with this crowd?"

I shook my head. "And I thought you were a genius when I saw your paintings."

"Really?" She seemed caught off guard by the compliment.

"Really."

She cleared her throat. "And now that you see how deceptive I can be?"

"I think you're a *diabolical* genius."

146

Natalie liked that. "You can't fault me. That Lars guy is like human Ambien. He opens his mouth, I'm out."

"I'm Jake Fisher."

"Natalie Avery."

"So do you want to grab a cup of coffee, Natalie Avery? Looks like you could use one."

She hesitated, studying my face to the point where I think I started to redden. She tucked a ringlet of black hair behind her ear and stood. She moved closer to me, and I remember thinking that she was wonderfully petite, smaller than I had imagined when she'd been sitting. She looked way up at me, and a smile slowly came to her face. It was, I must say, a great smile. "Sure, why not?"

That image of that smile held in my brain for a beat before it mercifully dissolved away.

I was out at the Library Bar with Benedict. The Library Bar was pretty much exactly that — an old, dark-wood campus library that had recently been converted into a retro-trendy drinking establishment. The owners were clever enough to change very little of the old library. The books were still on the oak shelves, sorted in alphabetical order or the Dewey Decimal System or whatever the librarians had used. The "bar" was the old circulation desk. The coasters were old card files that had been laminated. The lights were green library lamps.

The young female bartenders wore their hair in severe buns and sported fitted conservative clothes and, of course, horn-rimmed glasses. Yep, the fantasy librarian hottie. Once an hour, a loud librarian *shush* would play over the loudspeaker and the bartenders would rip off their glasses, let loose their bun, and unbutton the top of their blouse.

Cheesy but it worked.

Benedict and I were getting properly oiled. I threw my arm loosely around him and leaned in close. "You know what we should do?" I asked him.

Benedict made a face. "Sober up?"

"Ha! Good one. No, no. We should set up a rousing tournament of condom roulette. Single elimination. I'm thinking sixty-four teams. Like our own March Madness."

"We aren't in Barsolotti's, Jake. This place doesn't have a condom vending machine."

"It doesn't?"

"No."

"Shame."

"Yeah," Benedict said. Then he whispered, "Pair of red-hot spank-worthy honeys at three o'clock."

I was about to turn to my left, then to my right, and suddenly the concept of three o'clock made no sense to me. "Wait," I said, "where's my twelve o'clock again?"

Benedict sighed. "You're facing twelve o'clock."

"So three o'clock would be . . . ?"

"Just turn to your right, Jake."

You may have guessed that I do not handle spirits well. This surprises people. When they see someone my size, they expect me to drink smaller folks under the table. I can't. I hold my liquor about as well as a freshman coed at her first mixer.

"Well?"

I knew the type before my eyes even had a chance to settle on them. There sat two blondes who looked good-to-great in low Library Bar light and ordinary-to-frightful in the light of the morning sun. Benedict slid toward them and started chatting them up. Benedict could chat up a file cabinet. The two women looked past him and at me. Benedict signaled for me to join them.

Why the hell not?

You made a promise.

Damn straight I did. Thanks for the

reminder. Might as well keep it and try to score me a honey, right? I weaved my way toward them.

"Ladies, meet the legendary Professor Jacob Fisher."

"Wow," one of the blondes said, "he's a big boy," and — because Benedict couldn't help but be obvious — he winked and said, "You got no idea, sweetheart."

I bit back the sigh, said hello, and sat. Benedict "macked" on them with pickup lines, specifically handpicked for this bar: "It's a library so it's perfectly okay to check you out." "Will I be fined if I keep you out late?" The blondes loved it. I tried to join in, but I have never been great with superficial banter. Natalie's face kept appearing. I kept pushing it away. We ordered more drinks. And more.

After a while we all stumbled to couches near the former children's section. My head lolled back, and I may have passed out for a bit. When I woke up, one of the blondes started talking to me. I introduced myself.

"My name is Windy," she said.

"Wendy?"

"No, Windy. With an *i* instead of an *e*." She said this as though she had said it a million times before, which, I guessed, she had.

"Like the song?" I asked.

She looked surprised. "You know the song? You don't look old enough."

" 'Everyone knows it's Windy,' " I sang. Then: "My dad loved the Association."

"Wow. My dad too. That's how I got the name."

It turned into, surprisingly enough, a real conversation. Windy was thirty-one years old and worked as a bank teller, but she was getting her degree in pediatric nursing, her dream job, at the community college down the road. She took care of her handicapped brother.

"Alex has cerebral palsy," Windy said, showing me the picture of her brother in a wheelchair. The boy's face was radiant. I stared at it, as if somehow the goodness could come out of the picture and be a part of me. Windy saw it, nodded, and said in the softest voice: "He's the light of my life."

An hour passed. Maybe two. Windy and I chatted. During nights like these, there is always a time when you know if you are going to, ahem, close the sale (or, to stay within the library metaphors, if you are going to get your library card punched) or not. We were at that time now, and it was clear that the answer was yes.

The ladies left to powder their noses. I

felt overly mellow from drink. Part of me wondered whether I'd be able to perform. Most of me didn't really care.

"You know what I like about both of them?" Benedict pointed to a shelf of books. "They're stacked. Get it? Library, books, stacked?"

I groaned out loud. "I think I'm going to be sick."

"Amusing," Benedict said. "By the way, where were you last night?"

"I didn't tell you?"

"No."

"I went up to Vermont," I said. "To Natalie's old retreat."

He turned toward me. "Whatever for?"

It was an odd thing, but when Benedict talked after drinking too much, a hint of a British accent came through. I assumed that it was from his prep school days. The more he drank, the more pronounced the accent.

"To get answers," I said.

"And did you get any?"

"Yep."

"Do tell."

"One" — I stuck a finger in the air — "no one knows who Natalie is. Two" — another finger — "no one knows who I am. Three" — you get the point with the fingers — "there is no record at the chapel Natalie ever got married. Four, the minister I saw conducting the wedding swears it never happened. Five, the lady who owned the coffee shop we used to go to and who first pointed Natalie out to me had no idea who I was and didn't remember either Natalie or me."

I put my hand down.

"Oh, and Natalie's art retreat?" I said. "The Creative Recharge Colony? It's not there and everyone swears it never existed and that it's always been a family-run farm. In short, I think I'm losing my mind."

Benedict turned away and started sipping his beer.

"What?" I said.

"Nothing."

I gave him a little shove. "No, come on. What is it?"

Benedict kept his head lowered. "Six years ago, when you went up to that retreat, you were in pretty bad shape."

"Maybe a little. So?"

"Your father had died. You felt alone. Your dissertation wasn't going well. You were upset and on edge. You were angry about Trainor getting off with nary a slap."

"What's your point?"

"Nothing," he said. "Forget it."

"Don't give me that. What?"

My head was really swimming now. I

153

should have stopped several glasses ago. I remembered once when I had too much to drink my freshman year and I started walking back to my dorm. I never quite arrived. When I woke up, I was lying on top of a bush. I remembered staring up at the stars in the night sky and wondering why the ground felt so prickly. I had that sway now, like I was on a boat in a rough sea.

"Natalie," Benedict said.

"What about her?"

He turned those glass-magnified eyes toward me. "How come I never met her?"

My vision was getting a little fuzzy. "What?"

"Natalie. How come I never met her?"

"Because we were in Vermont the whole time."

"You never came to campus?"

"Just once. We went to Judie's."

"So how come you didn't bring her by to meet me?"

I shrugged with a little too much gusto. "I don't know. Maybe you were away?"

"I was here all that summer."

Silence. I tried to remember. Had I tried to introduce her to Benedict?

"I'm your best friend, right?" he said.

"Right."

"And if you married her, I would have

been the best man."

"You know it."

"So don't you find it bizarre that I never met her?" he asked.

"When you put it that way . . ." I frowned. "Wait, are you trying to make a point here?"

"No," he said quietly. "It's just odd is all."

"Odd how?"

He said nothing.

"Odd like I-made-her-up odd? Is that what you mean?"

"No. I'm just saying."

"Saying what?"

"That summer. You needed something to hold on to."

"And I found it. And lost it."

"Okay, fine, drop it."

But, no, that would not do. Not right now. Not with my anger and the drink talking. "And speaking of which," I said, "how come I never met the love of your life?"

"What are you talking about?"

Oh man, I was drunk. "The picture in your wallet. How come I never met her?"

It looked as though I'd slapped him across the face. "Leave it alone, Jake."

"I'm just saying."

"Leave. It. Alone."

I opened my mouth, closed it. The ladies reappeared. Benedict gave his head a shake

155

and suddenly the smile was back on it.

"Which one do you want?" Benedict asked me.

I looked at him. "For real?"

"Yes."

"Windy," I said.

"Which one is that?"

"Seriously?"

"I'm not good with names," Benedict said.

"Windy is the one I've been talking to all night."

"In other words," Benedict said, "you want the hotter one. Fine, whatever."

I went back to Windy's place. We took it slow until we took it fast. It wasn't full-on bliss, but it was awfully sweet. It was around 3:00 A.M. when Windy walked me to the door.

Not sure what to say, I stupidly went with "Uh, thank you."

"Uh, you're welcome?"

We kissed lightly on the lips. It wasn't something that would last, we both knew that, but it was a small, quick delight, and sometimes in this world, there was nothing wrong with that.

I stumbled back across campus. There were students still out. I tried to stay in the shadows, but Barry, the student who visits my office weekly, spotted me and cried out,

"Taking the walk of shame, Teach?"

Caught.

I gave him a good-hearted wave and continued serpentine-style to my humble abode.

A sudden head rush hit me as I entered. I stayed still, waiting for my legs to come back to me. When the dizziness receded, I headed into the kitchen and grabbed a glass of ice water. I drank it in big gulps and poured another. I would be hurting tomorrow, no question about it.

Exhaustion weighed down my bones. I stepped into my bedroom and flicked on the light. There, sitting on the edge of my bed, was the man with the maroon baseball cap. I jumped back, startled.

The man gave me a friendly wave. "Hey, Jake. Sheesh, look at you. Have you been out carousing?"

For a second, no more, I just stood there. The man smiled at me as though this were the most natural encounter in the history of the world. He even touched the front of his cap at me, as though he were a professional golfer acknowledging the gallery.

"Who the hell are you?" I asked.

"That's not really relevant, Jake."

"Like hell it isn't. Who are you?"

The man sighed, let down, it seemed, by

my seemingly irrational insistence on knowing his identity. "Let's just say I'm a friend."

"You were in the café. In Vermont."

"Guilty."

"And you followed me back here. You
were in that van."

"Guilty again. Man, you smell like cheap
booze and cheaper sex. Not that there's
anything wrong with that."

I tried to keep from swaying. "What do
you want?"

"I want us to take a ride."

"Where?"

"Where?" He arched an eyebrow. "Let's
not play games here, Jake. You know where."

"I don't have the slightest idea what
you're talking about," I said. "How did you
get in here anyway?"

The man almost rolled his eyes at that
one. "Oh, right, Jake, that's what we want
to waste time discussing — how I managed
to get past that piece-of-crap excuse for a
lock on your back door. You'd be better off
sealing it closed with Scotch tape."

I opened my mouth, closed it, tried again.
"Who the hell are you?"

"Bob. Okay, Jake? Since you don't seem
to be able to get past this name issue, my
name is Bob. You're Jake, I'm Bob. Now can
we get moving, please?"

The man stood. I braced myself, ready to relive my bouncer days. There was no way I was letting this guy out of here without an explanation. If the man was intimidated, he was doing a pretty good job of hiding it.

"Are we ready to go now," he asked me, "or do you want to waste more time?"

"Go where?"

Bob frowned as though I were putting him on. "Come on, Jake. Where do you think?" He gestured toward the door behind me. "To see Natalie, of course. We better hurry."

CHAPTER 14

The van was parked in the faculty lot behind Moore dormitory.

The campus was still now. The music had ceased, replaced by the incessant chirping of crickets. I could see the silhouettes of a few students in the distance, but for the most part, 3:00 A.M. seemed to be the witching hour.

Bob and I walked side by side, two buddies out for a night stroll. The drink was still canoodling with certain brain synapses, but the combination of night air and surprise visitor was sobering me up pretty rapidly. As we neared the now-familiar Chevy van, the back door slid open. A man stepped out.

I didn't like this.

The man was tall and thin with cheekbones that could dice tomatoes and perfectly coiffed hair. He looked like a male model, right down to that vaguely knowing

160

scowl. During my years as a bouncer, I developed something of a sixth sense for trouble. It just happens after you work a job like that long enough. A man walks by you and the danger comes off in hot waves, like those squiggly lines in a cartoon. This guy gave off hot danger-waves like an exploding supernova.

I pulled up. "Who's this?"

"Again with the names?" Bob said. Then, with a dramatic sigh, he added, "Otto. Jake, meet my friend Otto."

"Otto and Bob," I said.

"Yes."

"Two palindromes."

"You college professors and your fancy words." We had reached the van. Otto stepped to the side to let me in, but I didn't move. "Get in," Bob said.

I shook my head. "My mommy told me not to get in cars with strangers."

"Yo, Teach!"

My eyes flew open as I turned toward the voice. Barry was semi-running toward us. He had clearly imbibed, and so the steps made him look like a marionette with twisted strings. "Yo, Teach, a quick question if I — ?"

Barry never finished his sentence. Without warning or hesitation, Otto stepped forward, reared back, and punched Barry square in the face. I stood there for a moment, shocked by the suddenness of it. Barry went horizontal in the air. He landed on the asphalt with a hard thud, his head lolling back. His eyes were closed. Blood streamed from his nose.

I dropped to one knee. "Barry?"

He didn't move.

Otto took out a gun.

I positioned my body to the left a bit, so I could shield Barry from Otto's gun.

"Otto won't shoot you," Bob said in the same calm voice. "He'll just start shooting students until you get in the van."

I cradled Barry's head. I could see that he was breathing. I was about to check his pulse when I heard a voice cry out.

"Barry?" It was another student. "Where are you, bro?"

Fear seized me as Otto raised his gun. I debated making a move, but as though reading my mind, Otto took a step farther away from me.

Another student yelled, "I think he's over there — by that van. Barry?"

Otto aimed the gun toward the voice. Bob looked at me and gave a half shrug.

"Okay!" I whisper-shouted. "I'm going! Don't shoot anyone."

I quickly rolled into the back of the van. The seats had all been cleared out. There was a bench against one side — that was it for seating. Otto lowered the gun and slid in next to me. Bob took the driver's seat. Barry was still out cold. The students were getting closer as we pulled away. I heard one cry out, "What the . . . oh my God! Barry?"

If Bob and Otto were worried about someone spotting the license plate, they didn't show it. Bob drove the van at an aggravatingly slow speed. I didn't want that. I wanted Bob to hit the gas. I wanted him to hurry. I wanted to get Otto and Bob as far away from the students as possible.

I turned to Otto. "Why the hell did you hit him like that?"

Otto looked back at me with eyes that sent a chill straight through my heart. They were lifeless eyes, not the slightest hint of light behind them. It was as though I were looking into the eyes of an inanimate object — the eyes of an end table, maybe, or a cardboard box.

From the front seat, Bob said, "Toss your wallet and phone into the front passenger seat, please."

I did as he asked. I took a quick inventory of the back of the van and didn't like what I saw. The carpeting had been ripped out, revealing a bare metal floor. There was a rusty toolbox by Otto's feet. I had no idea what was in it. There was a bar welded into the van wall across from me. I swallowed hard when I saw the handcuffs. One loop of the handcuff was fastened to the bar. The other handcuff loop was open, waiting perhaps for a wrist.

Otto kept the gun on me.

When we hit the highway, Bob began to steer casually with his palms, like my father used to when we'd head to the hardware store for a weekend home project. "Jake?" Bob called to me.

"Yes."

"Where to?"

"Huh?" I said.

"It's simple, Jake," Bob said. "You're going to tell us where Natalie is."

"Me?"

"Yep."

"I don't have the slightest idea where she is. I thought you said —"

That was when Otto sucker punched me deep in the gut. The air rushed from my lungs. I folded at the waist like a suitcase. My knees dropped hard to the metal floor of the van. If you have ever had the wind knocked out of you, you know how it completely paralyzes you. You feel as though you're going to suffocate. All you can do is curl up in a ball and pray for oxygen to return.

Bob's voice: "Where is she?"

I couldn't give an answer, even if I had one. My breath was gone. I tried to ride it out, tried to remember that if I didn't struggle, the air would return, but it was as though someone was holding my head underwater and I was supposed to trust that he would eventually let me go.

Bob's voice again: "Jake?"

Otto kicked me hard in the side of the head. I rolled onto my back and saw stars. My chest started hitching, my breaths finally coming in small, grateful sips. Otto kicked my head again. Blackness seeped into my edges. My eyes rolled back. My stomach roiled. I thought that I might be sick and, because the mind works weirdly, I actually thought that it was a good thing that they had pulled out the carpet so the mess would be easier to clean.

"Where is she?" Bob asked again.

Scuttle-crawling to the far side of the van, I managed to spit out, "I don't know, I swear!"

I pressed my back against the van wall. That bar with the handcuff was above my left shoulder. Otto kept the gun on me. I didn't move. I was trying to buy time, catch my breath, recover, think straight. The booze was still there, still making everything a bit of a haze, but pain was an efficient way to bring clarity and focus back into your life.

I pulled my knees in to my chest. As I did, I felt something small and jagged against my leg. A small shard of glass, I figured, or maybe a rough pebble. I looked down at the ground, and with mounting dread, I saw that it was neither.

It was a tooth.

My breath caught in my throat. I looked across and saw a hint of a smile on Otto's model face. He opened the box, revealing a set of rusted tools. I saw a set of pliers, a hacksaw, a box cutter — and then I stopped looking.

Bob: "Where is she?"

"I already told you. I don't know."

"That answer," Bob said. I could see the back of his head shaking. "It's very disappointing."

Otto remained impassive. He kept the gun aimed at me, but his gaze kept sneaking a loving look at his tools. The dead eyes would light up when they landed on the pliers, the hacksaw, the box cutter.

Bob again: "Jake?"

"What?"

"Otto is going to cuff you now. You won't do anything stupid. He has a gun, and hey, we can always drive back to campus and use your students for target practice. You understand me?"

I swallowed again, my mind whirling. "I don't know anything."

Bob gave an overdramatic sigh. "I didn't ask you if you knew anything, Jake. Well, I mean, yes, I asked you that before, but right now, I'm asking if you understand what I said — about the handcuffs and the student target practice. Did you understand all that, Jake?"

"Yes."

"Okay, so stay still." Bob used his blinker and slid into the left lane. We were still on the highway. "Go ahead, Otto."

I didn't have much time. I knew that. Seconds maybe. Once the handcuff was in place — once I was fastened to the van wall — I was finished. I looked down at the tooth.

A good reminder of what was about to come.

Otto came at me from near the back door. He still held the gun. I could rush him, I guess, but he'd be expecting that. I considered trying to open the side door and roll out, take my chances with this van moving more than sixty miles per hour on a highway. But the door locks were down. I'd never get one open in time.

Otto finally spoke: "Grab the bar next to the cuff with your left hand. Use all your fingers to hold on."

I got why. I'd have one hand occupied. Only one to watch. Not that it would matter. It would take him a mere second to snap the cuff into place, and then, well, game over. I gripped the bar — and an idea came to me.

It was a long shot, maybe even an impossibility, but once the cuff snapped down and I was locked into place and Otto went to work on me with his little toolbox . . .

I had no choice.

Otto was prepared for me to rush at him. What he wasn't prepared for was my going in the other direction.

I tried to relax. Timing was everything here. I was tall. Without that, I didn't have a chance. I was also counting on the fact that Otto wouldn't want to shoot me, that they truly did want me — as Bob had implied with his threat about shooting students instead of me — alive.

I would have a second. Less. Tenths of a

second maybe.

Otto reached toward the cuff. When his fingers found it, I made my move.

Using the hand gripping the bar for leverage, I swung my legs up — but not to kick Otto. That would be pointless and expected. Instead, I pushed off, making my long body horizontal. I wasn't exactly flying across the van like some veteran martial artist, but with my height and all those damn core exercises I'd been doing, I was able to snap my leg around like a whip.

I aimed the heel of my shoe for the side of Bob's head.

Otto reacted fast. At the exact moment my heel hit pay dirt, Otto tackled me in midair, dropping me hard to the ground. He grabbed me around the neck and started to squeeze.

But he was too late.

My kick had landed on Bob's skull with force, jerking his head to the side. Bob's hands instinctively leapt off the steering wheel. The car veered sharply, sending Otto and me — and the gun — into a rolling heap.

It was on.

Otto still had his arm around my neck, but without the gun, it was just man against man. He was a good, experienced fighter. I was a good, experienced fighter. He was probably six feet tall and 180 pounds. I'm nearly six-six and weigh 230.

Advantage: Me.

I smashed him hard against the back of the van. His grip on my neck loosened. I smashed him again. He let go. My eyes searched the van floor for the gun.

I couldn't see it.

The van was still veering right, then left, as Bob tried to regain control.

I stumbled forward, landing on my knees. I heard a skittering noise, and there, in the corner in front of me, I saw the gun. I crawled toward it, but Otto grabbed me by the leg and pulled me back. We had a brief tug-of-war, me trying to get closer to the gun, him pulling me back. I tried to stomp on his face, but I missed.

Then Otto lowered his head and bit hard into my leg.

I let out a howl of pain.

He held on to the meaty part of my calf by the teeth. Panicked, I kicked out harder. He held on. The pain was making my vision grow cloudy again. The van mercifully swerved again. Otto flew to the right. I rolled to the left. He landed near the tool chest. His fingers disappeared inside of it.

Where the hell was that gun?

I couldn't find it.

From the front, Bob said, "Give up now and we won't hurt more students."

But I wasn't listening to that crap. I looked left and right. No sign of the gun.

Otto pulled his hand back into view. He had the box cutter now. He hit the button with his thumb. The blade popped out.

Suddenly my size advantage was irrelevant.

He started toward me, leading with the sharp edge. I was cornered and trapped. No sign of the gun. No real chance of jumping him without getting sliced up good. That left me with only one option.

When in doubt, go with what has already worked.

I turned and punched Bob in the back of the head.

Once again the van swerved, sending both Otto and me airborne. When I landed, I saw an opening. I lowered my head and dived at him. Otto still had the box cutter. He lashed out at me, but I grabbed his wrist. Once again I tried to use my weight advantage.

Up front, Bob was having a tougher time controlling the car.

Otto and I started rolling. I kept one hand on his wrist. I wrapped my legs around his body. I jammed my free forearm into the crook of Otto's neck, trying to get at his windpipe. He lowered his chin to block. Still I had my forearm against his neck. If I could just worm my arm in a little deeper . . .

That was when it happened.

Bob slammed on the brakes. The van stopped short. The momentum lifted Otto and me into the air and sent us crashing hard against the floor. The thing was, my forearm stayed pinned against his throat throughout. Think about it. My weight plus the velocity of the car and the sudden stop — it all turned my forearm into a pile driver.

I heard a horrible crinkling sound, like dozens of damp twigs snapping. Otto's windpipe gave way like wet papier-mâché. My arm hit something hard — I could actually feel the floor of the van through the skin and cartilage of his neck. Otto's entire body went slack. I looked down at the pretty-boy face. The eyes were open, and now they did not just appear lifeless — they genuinely were.

I almost hoped for a blink. There was none.

Otto was dead.

I rolled off him.

"Otto?"

It was Bob. From the driver's seat, I saw him reach into his pocket. I wondered whether he was reaching for a gun, but I was not in the mood to hang around and find out. I grabbed the lock on the back door of the van and pulled it up. I pulled the handle and took one last look back as the back door opened.

Yep, Bob had a gun, and it was aimed right at me.

I ducked as the bullet landed above my head. So much for not wanting me dead. I rolled out of the back of the van and landed hard on my right shoulder. I saw headlights heading toward me. My eyes widened. A car was headed directly for me.

I ducked and rolled yet again. Tires screeched. The car passed so close to me I felt the dirt kick up into my face. Horns began to honk. Someone cursed.

Bob's van began to move. The feeling of relief flooded my veins. I clawed my way to the relative safety of the left shoulder. With all the cars flying by, I figured Bob would drive away.

He didn't.

The van was now on the same shoulder, maybe twenty yards from where I lay sprawled.

With the gun still in his hand, Bob jumped out of the driver's-side door. I was spent. I didn't think I could move, but here's the thing: When someone has a gun, stuff like pain and exhaustion become, at best, secondary.

Again I had only one option.

I leapt straight into the bush off the side of the road. I didn't look first. I didn't test it out. I just leapt. In the darkness I hadn't seen the incline. I tumbled down through the brush, letting gravity take me farther away from the road. I expected to reach the bottom soon, but it seemed to take a long time.

I tumbled long and hard. My head smacked against a rock. My legs hit a tree. My ribs hit . . . I don't even know what. I kept rolling. I tumbled through the thicket, tumbled and tumbled until my eyes began to close and the world turned black and still.

CHAPTER 15

When I saw the headlights, I let out a gasp and tried yet again to roll away. The headlights followed me.

"Sir?"

I lay flat on my back, staring straight up in the air. That was curious. How could a car be approaching me head-on if I was facing the sky? I raised my arm to block the light. A thunderbolt of pain ripped down my shoulder socket.

"Sir, are you okay?"

I shielded my eyes and squinted. The two headlights merged into one flashlight. The person pointing it moved the beam away from my eyes. I blinked up and saw a cop standing over me. I sat up slowly, my entire body crying out in protest.

"Where am I?" I asked.

"You don't know where you are?"

I shook my head, trying to clear it. It was pitch-dark. I was lying in shrubbery of some kind. For a moment I flashed back to my freshman year of college, that time I ended up in a bush after a night of too much inexperienced drinking.

"What's your name, sir?" the cop asked.

"Jake Fisher."

"Mr. Fisher, have you been drinking tonight?"

"I was attacked," I said.

"Attacked?"

"Two men with guns."

"Mr. Fisher?"

"Yes?"

The cop had that condescending-patient-cop tone. "Have you been drinking tonight?"

"I was. Much earlier."

"Mr. Fisher, I'm State Trooper John Ong. You appear to have some injuries. Would you like us to take you to a hospital?"

I was trying hard to focus. Every brain wave seemed to travel through some kind of shower-door distortion. "I'm not sure."

"We will call for an ambulance," he said.

"I don't think that's necessary." I looked around. "Where am I?"

"Mr. Fisher, may I see some identification, please?"

"Sure." I reached into my back pocket, but then I remembered that I had tossed my wallet and phone into the front passenger seat next to Bob. "They stole it."

"Who?"

"The two men who attacked me."

"The guys with the guns?"

"Yes."

"So it was a robbery?"

"No."

The images flashed across my eyes — my forearm against Otto's neck, the box cutter in his hand, the tool chest, the handcuff, that naked, horrible, paralyzing fear, the sudden stop, the squelching sound as his windpipe collapsed like a twig. I closed my eyes and tried to make them go away.

Then, almost more to myself than State Trooper Ong, "I killed one of them."

"Excuse me?"

There were tears in my eyes now. I did not know what to do. I had killed a man, but it had been both an accident and in self-defense. I needed to explain that. I couldn't just keep that to myself. I knew better. Many of the students who majored in political science were also pre-law. Most of my fellow professors had even gotten their JDs and passed the bar. I knew a lot about the Constitution and rights and how our legal system worked. In short, you need to be careful about what you say. You cannot "unring" that bell. I wanted to talk. I needed to talk. But I couldn't just blurt out admissions of murder.

I heard sirens and saw the ambulance pull up.

State Trooper John Ong shone the light back in my eyes. That couldn't have been an accident. "Mr. Fisher?"

"I'd like to call my attorney," I said.

I don't have an attorney.

I am a single college professor with no criminal record and very few resources. What would I need an attorney for?

"Okay, I have good news and bad news," Benedict said.

I had instead called Benedict. Benedict wasn't a member of the bar, but he had gotten a law degree at Stanford. I sat on one of those gurneys covered with what seemed to be butcher paper. I was in the ER of a small hospital. The doctor on duty — who looked almost as exhausted as I felt — had told me that I had probably suffered a concussion. My head ached like it. I also had various contusions, cuts, and maybe a sprain. He didn't know what to make of the teeth marks. With the adrenaline spikes ebbing away, the pain was gaining ground and confidence. He promised to prescribe some

Percocet for me.

"I'm listening," I said.

"The good news is, the cops think you've gone completely nuts and don't believe a word of what you say."

"And the bad news?"

"I tend to agree with them, though I add the strong possibility of an alcohol-induced hallucination."

"I was attacked."

"Yes, I get that," Benedict said. "Two men, guns, a van, something about power tools."

"Tools. No one said anything about power."

"Right, whatever. You also drank a lot and then you got some strange."

I pulled up my calf to reveal the bite mark. "How do you explain that?"

"Wendy must have been wild."

"Windy," I corrected him. This was pointless. "So what now?"

"I don't like to brag," Benedict said, "but I have some top-drawer legal advice for you, if you'd like to hear it."

"I do."

"Stop confessing to killing another human being."

"Wow," I said, "and you didn't want to brag."

"It's also in a lot of the law books," Benedict said. "Look, the license plate number you gave? It doesn't exist. There is no body or signs of violence or a crime — only a minor misdemeanor because you, admittedly drunk, trespassed into a man's backyard by falling down a hill. The cops are willing to let you go with just a ticket. Let's just get home and then we can figure it out, okay?"

It was hard to argue with that logic. It would be wise for me to get out of this place, to get back on campus, to rest and regroup and recover, to consider everything that had happened in the sober light of familiar day. Plus, I had taught Constitution 101 one semester. The Fifth Amendment protects you against self-incrimination. Maybe I should use that right now.

Benedict drove. My head spun. The doc had given me a shot that had lifted me up and dropped me in the middle of Loopy Land. I tried to focus, but putting aside the drinking and drugs, the threat to life was hard to shake. I had literally had to fight for survival. What was going on here? What could Natalie have to do with all this?

As we pulled into the staff parking lot, I saw a campus police car near my front door. Benedict looked a question at me. I shrugged and stepped out of the car. The head rush as I stood nearly floored me. I made my way to a standing position and started gingerly up the path. Evelyn Stemmer was the head of campus security. She was a petite woman with a ready smile. The ready smile wasn't there right now.

"We've been trying to reach you, Professor Fisher," she said.

"My cell phone was stolen."

"I see. Do you mind coming with me?"

"Where?"

"President's house. President Tripp needs to speak with you."

Benedict stepped between us. "What's this about, Evelyn?"

She looked at him as though he'd just plopped out of a rhino's rectum. "I'd rather let President Tripp do the talking. Me, I'm just an errand girl."

I was too out of it to protest. What would be the point anyway? Benedict wanted to come with us, but I really didn't think it would behoove my position to have my best friend visit my boss with me. The front seat of the campus police car had some kind of computer in it. I had to sit in the back like a real-life perp.

The president lived in a twenty-two-room, 9,600-square-foot stone residence, done up in a style that the experts called "restrained Gothic Revival." I was not sure what that meant, but it was a pretty impressive structure. I also didn't see the need for the squad car — the villa sat on a hilltop overlooking the athletic fields, maybe four hundred yards from the staff parking lot. Fully renovated two years ago, the home could now play host to not only the president's young family but, more importantly, to a full potpourri of fund-raising events.

I was escorted into an office that looked exactly like a college president's office, just sleeker and more polished. Come to think of it, so did the new president. Jack Tripp was sleek and polished and corporate with floppy hair and capped teeth. He tried to fit in by dressing in tweed, but the tweed was far too tailored and costly to be bona fide professorial. His patches were too evenly cut. The students derisively referred to him as a "poser." Again I wasn't sure exactly what that meant, but it seemed apropos.

I have learned that human beings are all about incentives, so I cut the president some slack. His job, though couched in haughty terms of academia and higher learning, was all about raising money. Period. That was, and perhaps should be, his main concern. The best presidents, I had learned, were often the ones who understood this and thus came in with the least lofty agenda. By that definition, President Tripp was doing a pretty good job.

"Sit, Jacob," Tripp said, looking past me to Officer Stemmer. "Evelyn, close the door on your way out, would you?"

I did as Tripp asked. Evelyn Stemmer did too.

Tripp sat at the ornate desk in front of me. It was a big desk. Too big and corporate and self-important. When I am feeling unkind, I often note that a man's desk, like his car, often seems to involve, uh, compensation. Tripp folded his hands on a desktop large enough to land a helicopter and said, "You look like hell, Jacob."

I bit back the "you should see the other guy" because, in this case, the rejoinder was in serious bad taste. "I had a late night."

"You look injured."

"I'm fine."

"You should get it looked at."

"I have." I shifted in the seat. The meds were making everything hazy, as though my eyes were covered in thin strips of gauze. "What's this about, Jack?"

He spread his hands for a moment and then brought them back to the desk. "Do you want to tell me about last night?"

"What about last night?" I asked.

"You tell me."

So we were playing that game. Fair enough. I'd go first. "I went drinking with a friend at a bar. Had too much. When I came back to my place, two men jumped me. They, uh, kidnapped me."

His eyes widened. "Two men kidnapped you?"

"Yes."

"Who?"

"They said their names were Bob and Otto."

"Bob and Otto?"

"That's what they said."

"And where are these men now?"

"I don't know."

"Are they in custody?"

"No."

"But you've reported the matter to the police?"

"I have," I said. "Do you mind telling me what this is about?"

Tripp lifted his hand, as if he'd suddenly realized the desktop was sticky. He placed the lower parts of his palms together and let the fingertips bounce off one another. "Do you know a student named Barry Watkins?"

My heart skipped a beat. "Is he okay?"

"You know him?"

"Yes. One of the men who grabbed me punched him in the face."

"I see," he said, as though he didn't see at all. "When?"

"We were standing by the van. Barry called out to me and ran over. Before I could so much as turn around, one of the guys punched him. Is Barry okay?"

The fingertips bounced some more. "He is in the hospital with facial fractures. That punch did serious damage."

I sat back. "Damn."

"His parents are rather upset. They are talking about a lawsuit."

Lawsuit — the word that strikes terror in the heart of every bureaucrat. I half expected some lame horror-movie music to start up.

"Barry Watkins also doesn't recall two other men. He remembers calling out to you, running toward you, and that's it. Two other students recall seeing you flee in a van."

"I didn't flee. I got in the back."

"I see," he said in that same tone. "When these other two students arrived, Barry was lying on the ground bleeding. You drove off."

"I wasn't driving. I was in the back."

"I see."

185

Again with the "I see." I leaned closer to him. The desk was completely bare except for one too-neat stack of papers and, of course, the requisite family photograph with the blond wife, two adorable kids, and a dog with floppy hair like Tripp's. Nothing else. Big desk. Nothing on it.

"I wanted to get them as far away from campus as possible," I said, "especially after that display of violence. So I quickly cooperated."

"And by them, you mean the two men who . . . were they abducting you?"

"Yes."

"Who were these men?"

"I don't know."

"They were just, what, kidnapping you for ransom?"

"I doubt it," I said, realizing how crazy it all sounded. "One had broken into my home. The other waited in the van. They insisted I come with them."

"You are a very large man. Powerful. Physically intimidating."

I waited.

"How did they persuade you to go with them?"

I skipped the part about Natalie and dropped the bombshell instead. "They were armed."

186

The eyes widened again. "With guns?"

"Yes."

"For real?"

"They were real guns, yes."

"How do you know?"

I decided not to mention that one had taken shots at me. I wondered whether the police might find bullets near the highway. I'd have to check.

"Did you tell anyone else about this?" Tripp asked when I didn't answer.

"I told the cops, but I'm not sure that they believe me."

He leaned back and started picking at his lip. I knew what he was thinking: How would the students, their parents, and important alumni react if they knew that gunmen had been on campus? Not only had they been on campus, but if I were telling the truth — questionable at best — they had kidnapped a professor and assaulted a student.

"You were quite inebriated at the time, were you not?"

Here we go. "I was."

"We have a campus security camera in the middle of the quad. Your walk was rather more of a weave."

"That's what happens when you have too much to drink."

"We also have reports that you left the Library Bar at one A.M. . . . and yet you weren't seen weaving across campus until three."

Again I waited.

"Where were you for those two hours?"

"Why?"

"Because I'm investigating an assault on a student."

"That we know took place after three A.M. What, you think I planned it for two hours?"

"I see very little need for sarcasm, Jacob. This is a serious matter."

I closed my eyes and felt the room spin. He had a point. "I left with a young lady. It's totally irrelevant. I'd never punch Barry. He visits my office every week."

"Yes, he defended you too. He said that you're his favorite professor. But I have to look at the facts, Jacob. You understand that, don't you?"

"I do."

"Fact: You were drunk."

"I'm a college professor. Drinking is practically a job requirement."

"That's not funny."

"But true. Heck, I've been to parties right here. You're not afraid to hoist a glass or two yourself."

"You're not helping yourself."

"I'm not trying to. I'm trying to get at the truth."

"Then, fact: While you are being vague, it appears as though after drinking you had a one-night stand."

"We shouldn't be vague," I said. "That's exactly what I'm saying. She was over thirty and does not work for the college. So what?"

"So after these episodes, a student got assaulted."

"Not by me."

"Still, there is a connection," he said, leaning back. "I don't see where I have any choice but to ask for you to take a leave of absence."

"For drinking?"

"For all of it," he said.

"I'm in the middle of teaching classes —"

"We will find coverage."

"And I have a responsibility to my students. I can't just abandon them."

"Perhaps," he said, with an edge in his voice, "you should have thought of that before you got drunk."

"Getting drunk isn't a crime."

"No, but your actions afterward . . ." His voice trailed off, and a smile came to his lips. "Funny," he said.

"What?"

"I heard about your run-in with Professor

Trainor years ago. How can you not see the parallel?"

I said nothing.

"There is an old Greek saying," he went on. "The humpback never sees the hump on his own back."

I nodded. "Deep."

"You're making jokes, Jacob, but do you really think you're blameless here?"

I wasn't sure what to think. "I didn't say I was blameless."

"Just a hypocrite?" He sighed a little too deeply. "I don't like doing this to you, Jacob."

"I hear a but."

"You know the but. Are the police investigating your claim?"

I wasn't sure how to answer so I went with the truth. "I don't know."

"Then maybe it's best that you take a leave of absence until this is resolved."

I was about to protest, but then I pulled up. He was right. Forget all the political mumbo jumbo or legal claims here. The truth was, I was indeed putting students in harm's way. My actions *had,* in fact, already gotten one student seriously injured. I could make all the excuses I wanted to, but if I had kept my promise to Natalie, Barry would not be lying in a hospital bed with

190

facial fractures.

Could I take the risk of letting it happen again?

Lest I forgot, Bob was still out there. He might want vengeance for Otto or, at the very least, to finish the job or silence the witness. By staying, wouldn't I be endangering the welfare of my students?

President Tripp started sorting the papers on his desk, a clear sign we were done here. "Pack your things," he said. "I'd like you off campus within the hour."

CHAPTER 16

By noon the next day, I was back in Palmetto Bluff.

I knocked on the door of a home located on a quiet cul-de-sac. Delia Sanderson — Todd Sanderson's, uh, widow, I guess — opened it with a sad smile. She was what some might call a handsome woman in a sinewy, farmhand kind of way. She had strong facial features and big hands.

"Thank you so much for making the trip, Professor."

"Please," I said, feeling a small ping of guilt, "call me Jake."

She stepped aside and invited me inside. The house was nice, done up in that modern faux-Victorian style that seemed to be the rage of these spanking new developments. The property backed onto a golf course. The atmosphere was both green and serene.

"I can't tell you how much I appreciate you coming all this way."

Another ping. "Please," I said, "it's an honor."

"Still. For the college to send a professor all this way . . ."

"It's not a big deal, really." I tried to smile. "It's nice to get away too."

"Well, I'm grateful," Delia Sanderson said. "Our children aren't home right now. I made them go back to school. You need to grieve but you need to do something, you know what I mean?"

"I do," I said.

I hadn't been specific when I made the call yesterday. I just told her that I was a professor at Todd's alma mater and that I hoped to stop by the house to talk about her late husband and offer condolences. Did I hint that I was sort of coming on behalf of the college? Let us say I didn't discourage that thinking.

"Would you like some coffee?" she asked.

I've found that people have a tendency to relax more when they are doing simple tasks and feeling as though they are making their guests feel comfortable. I said yes.

We were standing in the foyer. The formal rooms, where you'd normally take guests, were on the right. The lived-in rooms — den and kitchen — were on the left. I followed her into the kitchen, figuring that the more casual setting might also make her more apt to open up.

There were no signs of the recent break-in, but what exactly did I think I'd find? Blood on the floor? Overturned furniture? Open drawers? Yellow police tape?

The sleek kitchen was expansive with great flow into an even more expansive "media" room. An enormous television hung on the wall. The couch was littered with remotes and Xbox controllers. Yes, I know Xbox. I have one. I love to play Madden. Sue me.

She headed toward one of those coffee-makers that use individual pods. I took a seat on a stool at the kitchen's granite island. She showed me a surprisingly large display of coffee-pod options.

"Which would you like?" she asked.

"You tell me," I said.

"Are you a strong-coffee guy? I bet you are."

"You'd win that bet."

She opened the machine's mouth and put in a pod called Jet Fuel. The machine seemed to eat the pod and piss out the coffee. Appetizing imagery, I know. "Do you take it black?" she asked.

"Not that much a strong-coffee guy," I said, asking for a little milk and sweetener.

She handed me the cup. "You don't look like a college professor."

I get that a lot.

"My tweed jacket is at the cleaner." Then: "I'm sorry for your loss."

"Thank you."

I took a sip of the coffee. Why was I here exactly? I needed to figure out if Delia Sanderson's Todd was Natalie's Todd. If he was the same man, well, how was that possible? What did his death mean? And what secrets was this woman in front of me maybe keeping?

I had no idea, of course, but I was willing to take some chances now. That meant that I might have to push her. I didn't relish that — prodding a woman who was so clearly grieving. Whatever else I thought might be going on here — and really I didn't have a clue — Delia Sanderson was in obvious pain. You could see the pull in her face, the subtle slump in the shoulders, the shatter in the eyes.

"I don't know how to ask this delicately . . . ," I began.

I stopped, hoping she'd take the bait. She did. "But you want to know how he died?"

"If I'm prying . . ."

"It's okay."

"The papers say it happened during a

break-in."

Her face lost color. She spun back toward the coffeemaker. She fiddled with a pod, picked one up, dropped it, chose another.

"I'm sorry," I said. "We don't need to go into this."

"It wasn't a break-in."

I stayed quiet.

"I mean, they didn't steal anything. Isn't that unusual? If it was a break-in, wouldn't you take something? But they just . . ."

She slammed down the mouth of the coffeemaker.

I said, "They?"

"What?"

"You said 'they.' There was more than one burglar?"

She still had her back to me. "I don't know. The police won't speculate. I just don't see how one guy could have done . . ." Her head dropped. I thought that maybe I saw her knees buckle. I started to rise and move toward her, but really, who the hell was I? I stopped and quietly slid back onto the stool.

"We were supposed to be safe here," Delia Sanderson said. "A gated community. It was supposed to keep the bad out."

The development was huge, acres upon acres of cultivated remoteness. There was a

196

gate of sorts, a little hut at the development's entrance, a steel arm that had to be lifted to drive through, a rent-a-cop who nodded and pushed a button. None of that could keep the bad out, not if the bad was determined. The gate was possibly a deterrent for easygoing trouble. It maybe added an extra layer of hassle so that trouble chose to find an easier mark. But true protection? No. The gate was more for show.

"Why do you think there was more than one?" I asked.

"I guess . . . I guess I don't see how one man could cause that much damage."

"What do you mean?"

She shook her head. Using one finger, she wiped one eye, then the other. She turned around and faced me. "Let's talk about something else."

I wanted to push it, but I knew that wouldn't play here. I was a college professor visiting from her late husband's alma mater. Plus, well, I was still a human being. It was time to back up and try another route.

I stood as gently as I knew how and moved toward the refrigerator. There were dozens of family photographs done up in a magnetic collage. The photographs were wonderfully unspectacular, almost too expected: fishing trip, Disney visit, dance recitals, beach-Christmas photograph, school holiday concerts, graduations. The refrigerator missed none of life's little yard markers. I leaned in and studied Todd's face in as many of them as I could.

Was he the same man?

In every image on the refrigerator, he was clean-shaven. The man I had met had that fashionably annoying stubble. You could grow that in a few days, of course, but I found it odd. So again, I wondered: Was this the man I saw marry Natalie?

I could feel Delia's eyes on my back.

"I met your husband once," I said.

"Oh?"

I turned toward her. "Six years ago."

She picked up her coffee — evidently she took it black — and sat at another stool. "Where?"

I kept my eyes on her as I said, "In Vermont."

There was no big jolt or anything like that, but her face did scrunch up a bit. "Vermont?"

"Yes. In a town called Kraftboro."

"You're sure it was Todd?"

"It was in late August," I explained. "I was staying at a retreat."

Now she looked openly confused. "I don't

recall Todd ever going to Vermont."

"Six years ago," I said again. "In August."

"Yes, I heard you say that the first time." There was a hint of impatience in her tone now.

I pointed back toward the refrigerator. "He didn't look exactly like this though."

"I'm not following you."

"His hair was longer," I said, "and he had stubble."

"Todd?"

"Yes."

She considered that and a small smile found her lips. "I get it now."

"Get what?"

"Why you came all this way."

This I was anxious to hear.

"I couldn't figure it out. Todd hadn't been an active member of the alumni or anything like that. It wasn't as though the college would have much more than a passing interest in him. Now all this talk about a man from Vermont . . ." She stopped and shrugged. "You mistook my husband for another man. For this Todd you met in Vermont."

"No, I'm pretty certain it was —"

"Todd has never been to Vermont. I'm sure of that. And every August for the past eight years, he traveled to Africa to perform surgery on the needy. He also shaved every day. I mean, even on a lazy Sunday. Todd never went a day without shaving."

I took another look at the photographs on the refrigerator. Could that be? Could it be that simple? I had the wrong man. I had considered that possibility before but now, finally, I was sort of believing it.

In a sense, that didn't change much anymore. There was still the e-mail from Natalie. There was still Otto and Bob and all that happened. But now, maybe, I could put this connection to rest.

Delia was openly studying me now. "What's going on? Why are you really here?"

I reached into my pocket and plucked out the photograph of Natalie. Strangely enough, I have only one. She didn't like photographs, but I had snapped this one while she was asleep. I don't know why. Or maybe I do. I handed it to Delia Sanderson and waited for a reaction.

"Strange," she said.

"What?"

"Her eyes are closed." She looked up at me. "Did you take this picture?"

"Yes."

"While she was sleeping?"

"Yes. Do you know her?"

"No." She stared down at the photograph.

"She means something to you, doesn't she?"

"Yes."

"So who is she?"

The front door opened. "Mom?"

She put down the photograph and started toward the voice. "Eric? Is everything okay? You're home early."

I followed her down the corridor. I recognized her son from his eulogy at the funeral. He looked past his mother, his gaze boring into me. "Who's this?" he asked. His tone was surprisingly hostile, as though he suspected that I'd come here to hit on his mom or something.

"This is Professor Fisher from Lanford," she said. "He came to ask about your father."

"Ask what?"

"Just paying my respects," I said, shaking the young man's hand. "I'm very sorry for your loss. The entire college is."

He shook my hand and said nothing. We all stood in that front foyer like three awkward strangers who hadn't yet been introduced at a cocktail party. Eric broke the deadlock. "I couldn't find my cleats," he said.

"You left them in the car."

"Oh, right. I'll just grab them and head back."

He rushed back out the door. We both watched him, perhaps with the same thoughts about his fatherless future looming in front of us. There was nothing more to learn here. It was time for me to let this family be.

"I better be going," I said. "Thank you for your time."

"You're welcome."

As I turned toward the door, my line of vision swung past the living room.

My heart stopped.

"Professor Fisher?"

My hand was on the doorknob. Seconds passed. I don't know how many. I didn't turn the knob, didn't move, didn't even breathe. I just stared into the living room, across the Oriental rug, to a spot above the fireplace.

Delia Sanderson again: "Professor?"

Her voice was very far away.

I finally let go of the knob and moved into the living room, across the Oriental carpet, and stared up above the fireplace. Delia Sanderson followed me.

"Are you okay?"

No, I wasn't okay. And I hadn't been wrong. If I had questions before, they all ended now. No coincidence, no mistake, no doubt: Todd Sanderson was the man I saw marry Natalie six years ago.

I felt rather than saw Delia Sanderson standing next to me. "It moves me," she said. "I can stand here for hours and find something new."

I understood. There was the soft morning glow hitting the side, the pinkness that comes with the new day, the dark windows as though the cottage had once been warm but was now abandoned.

It was Natalie's painting.

"Do you like it?" Delia Sanderson asked me.

"Yes," I said. "I like it very much."

Chapter 17

I sat on the couch. Delia Sanderson didn't offer me coffee this time. She poured two fingers' worth of Macallan. It was early and as we've already learned I am not much of a drinker, but I gratefully accepted it with a shaking hand.

"Do you want to tell me what this is about?" Delia Sanderson asked.

I wasn't sure how to explain this without sounding insane, so I started with a question. "How did you get that painting?"

"Todd bought it."

"When?"

"I don't know."

"Think."

"What's the difference?"

"Please," I said, trying to keep my voice steady. "Could you just tell me when and where he bought it?"

She looked up, thinking about it. "The where I don't remember. But the when . . .

it was our anniversary. Five, maybe six years ago."

"It was six," I said.

"Again with six," she said. "I don't understand any of this."

I saw no reason to lie — and worse, I saw no way to say this in a way that would soften the blow. "I showed you a photograph of a sleeping woman, remember?"

"It was only two minutes ago."

"Right. She painted that picture."

Delia frowned. "What are you talking about?"

"Her name is Natalie Avery. That was her in the photograph."

"That . . ." She shook her head. "I don't understand. I thought you taught political science."

"I do."

"So are you some kind of art historian? Is that woman a Lanford alum too?"

"No, it's not like that." I looked back at that cottage on the hill. "I'm looking for her."

"The artist?"

"Yes."

She studied my face. "Is she missing?"

"I don't know."

Our eyes met. She didn't nod, but she

205

didn't have to. "She means a great deal to you."

It wasn't a question, but I answered it anyway. "Yes. I realize that this is making no sense."

"It isn't," Delia Sanderson agreed. "But you believe that my husband knew something about her. That's why you're really here."

"Yes."

"Why?"

Again I saw no reason to lie. "This will sound insane."

She waited.

"Six years ago, I saw your husband marry Natalie Avery in a small chapel in Vermont."

Delia Sanderson blinked twice. She rose from the couch and started to back away from me. "I think you better leave."

"Please just listen to me."

She closed her eyes, but, hey, you can't close your ears. I talked fast. I explained about going to the wedding six years ago, about seeing Todd's obituary, about coming to the funeral, about believing that maybe I was mistaken.

"You were mistaken," she said when I finished. "You have to be."

"So that painting. It's a coincidence?"

She said nothing.

"Mrs. Sanderson?"

"What are you after?" she asked in a soft voice.

"I want to find her."

"Why?"

"You know why."

She nodded. "Because you're in love with her."

"Yes."

"Even though you saw her marry another man six years ago."

I didn't bother responding. The house was maddeningly quiet. We both turned and looked back at that cottage on the hill. I wanted it to change somehow. I wanted the sun to rise a little higher or to see a light on in one of the windows.

Delia Sanderson moved a few yards farther away from me and took out her phone.

"What are you doing?" I asked.

"I googled you yesterday. After you called me."

"Okay."

"I wanted to make sure that you were who you said you were."

"Who else would I be?"

Delia Sanderson ignored my question. "There was a picture of you on the Lanford website. Before I opened the door, I checked through the peephole to make sure."

"I'm not following."

"Better to be safe than sorry, I figured. I worried that maybe whoever murdered my husband . . ."

I understood now. "Would come back for you?"

She shrugged.

"But you saw it was me."

"Yes. So I let you in. But now I'm wondering. I mean, you came here under false pretenses. How do I know that you aren't one of them?"

I wasn't sure what to say.

"So for right now I'm keeping my distance, if that's okay with you. I'm standing pretty close to the front door. If I see you start to rise, I hit this button for nine-one-one and run. Do you understand?"

"I'm not with —"

"Do you understand?"

"Of course," I said. "I won't move from this seat. But can I ask you a question?"

She gestured for me to go ahead.

"How do you know I don't have a gun?"

"I've been watching since you entered. There'd be no place for you to conceal it in that outfit."

I nodded. Then I said, "You don't really believe I'm here to hurt you, do you?"

"I don't. But like the saying goes, better

safe than sorry."

"I know that story about a wedding in Vermont sounds crazy," I said.

"It does," Delia Sanderson said. "And yet, it's too crazy to be a lie."

We gave it another moment. Our eyes wandered back to that cottage up on the hill.

"He was such a good man," Delia Sanderson said. "Todd could have made a fortune in private practice, but he worked almost exclusively for Fresh Start. You know what that is?"

The name was not entirely unfamiliar, but I couldn't place it. "I'm afraid that I don't."

She actually smiled at that. "Wow, you really didn't do your homework before you came. Fresh Start is the charity Todd founded with some other Lanford graduates. It was his passion."

I remembered it now. There had been a mention of it in his obituary, though I didn't know it had any connection to Lanford. "What did Fresh Start do?"

"They operated on cleft palates overseas. They worked on burns and scars and performed various other necessary cosmetic surgeries. The procedures were life-changing. Like the name, they gave people a fresh start. Todd dedicated his life to it.

When you said that you saw him in Vermont, I knew that couldn't be true. He was working in Nigeria."

"Except," I said, "he wasn't."

"So you're telling this widow that her husband lied to her."

"No. I'm telling her that Todd Sanderson was in Vermont on August twenty-eighth, six years ago."

"Marrying your ex-girlfriend, the artist?"

I didn't bother replying.

A tear ran down her cheek. "They hurt Todd. Before they killed him. They hurt him badly. Why would someone do something like that?"

"I don't know."

She shook her head.

"When you say they hurt him," I said slowly, "do you mean that they did more than kill him?"

"Yes."

Again I didn't know how to ask the question with any sort of sensitivity, so I settled on directness: "How did they hurt him?"

But even before she replied, I thought that maybe I knew the answer.

"With tools," Delia Sanderson said, a sob coming to her throat. "They cuffed him to a chair and tortured him with tools."

CHAPTER 18

When my plane landed back in Boston, there was a message on my new phone from Shanta Newlin. "I heard you got kicked off campus. We should talk."

I called her back as I walked through the airport terminal. When Shanta picked up, she asked me where I was.

"Logan Airport," I said.

"Nice trip?"

"Delightful. You said we needed to talk."

"In person. Come straight to my office from the airport."

"I'm not welcome on campus," I said.

"Oh, right, I forgot for a second. Judie's again? Be there in an hour."

Shanta was sitting at the corner table when I arrived. She had a drink in front of her. The drink was bright pink and had a pineapple on top. I pointed at it.

"All you're missing is a little umbrella," I said.

211

"What, you figured me as more a scotch-and-soda girl?"

"Minus the soda."

"Sorry. With me, the fruitier the drink, the better."

I slid into the chair across from her. Shanta picked up the drink and took a sip from the straw.

"I heard you were involved in a student attack," she said.

"Are you working for President Tripp now?"

She frowned over her fruity drink. "What happened?"

I told her the whole story — Bob and Otto, the van, the self-defense killing, the escape from the van, the roll down the hill. Her expression didn't change, but I could see the wheels moving behind her eyes.

"You told the police this?"

"Sort of."

"What do you mean, sort of?"

"I was pretty drunk. They seem to think I fabricated the bit about being kidnapped and killing a guy."

She looked at me as though I were perhaps the biggest fool ever to inhabit this planet. "Did you really tell the police that part?"

"At first. Then Benedict reminded me that maybe it wasn't the best idea to admit to killing a man, even if it was in self-defense."

"You get your legal advice from Benedict?"

I shrugged. Once again I thought about keeping my mouth shut. I had been warned, hadn't I? There was also the promise. Shanta sat back and sipped her drink. The waitress came over and asked what I wanted. I pointed at the fruity drink and indicated that I wanted a "virgin" one of those too. I don't know why. I hate fruity drinks.

"What did you really learn about Natalie?" I asked.

"I told you."

"Right, nothing, zippo, zilch. So why did you want to see me?"

The portobello sandwich came for her, the turkey BLT on rye for me. "I took the liberty of ordering for you," she said.

I didn't touch the sandwich.

"What's going on, Shanta?"

"That's what I want to know. How did you meet Natalie?"

"What difference does that make?"

"Humor me."

Once again she was asking all the questions, and I was giving all the answers. I told her how we met at the retreats in Vermont six years ago.

"What did she tell you about her father?"

"Just that he was dead."

Shanta kept her eyes on mine. "Nothing else?"

"Like what?"

"Like, I don't know" — she took a deep sip and shrugged theatrically — "that he used to be a professor here."

My eyes widened. "Her father?"

"Yep."

"Her father was a professor at Lanford?"

"No, at Judie's Restaurant," Shanta said with an eye roll. "Of course at Lanford."

I was still trying to clear my head. "When?"

"He started about thirty years ago. He taught here for seven years. In the political science department."

"You're kidding?"

"Yes, that's why I called you here. Because I'm such a top-notch kidder."

I did the math. Natalie would have been very young when her father started teaching here — and still a kid when he left. Maybe she didn't remember being here. Maybe that was why she didn't say anything. But wouldn't Natalie have at least known about it? Wouldn't she have said, "Hey, my father taught here too. Same department as you."

I thought about how she came to campus

with those sunglasses and hat on, how she wanted to see so much of it, how she had grown pensive during the walks on the commons.

"Why wouldn't she tell me?" I asked out loud.

"I don't know."

"Was he fired? Where did they go afterward?"

She shrugged. "A better question might be, why did Natalie's mom start using her maiden name?"

"What?"

"Her father's name was Aaron Kleiner. Natalie's mother's maiden name was Avery. She changed it back. And she changed Natalie and Julie's name to her maiden name too."

"Wait, when did her father die?"

"So Natalie never told you?"

"I just got the impression it was a long time ago. Maybe that's it. Maybe he died and that's why they left campus."

Shanta smiled. "I don't think so, Jake."

"Why?"

"Because here's where it gets really interesting. Here's where Daddy is just like his little girl."

I said nothing.

"There is no report he ever died."

I swallowed. "So where is he?"

"Like father, like daughter, Jake."

"What the hell does that mean?" But maybe I already knew.

"I looked into where Professor Aaron Kleiner is now," Shanta said. "Guess what I found?"

I waited.

"That's right — zippo, *nada,* zilch, nothing. Since he left Lanford a quarter century ago, there has been absolutely no sign of Professor Aaron Kleiner."

CHAPTER 19

I found old yearbooks in the school library.

They were in the basement. The books smelled of mold. The glossy pages stuck together as I tried to flip through them. But there he was. Professor Aaron Kleiner. The picture was fairly unremarkable. He was a nice-enough-looking man with the usual posed smile, aiming for happiness but landing somewhere closer to awkward. I stared at his face to see if I could spot any resemblance to Natalie. There might have been. Hard to say. The mind can play tricks, as we all know.

We have a tendency to see what we want to see.

I stared at his face as though it would give me some kind of answer. It didn't. I checked through the other yearbooks. There was nothing more to learn. I scanned through the political science pages and stopped at a group picture taken in front of Clark House.

All of the professors and support staff were there. Professor Kleiner stood right next to department chair Malcolm Hume. The smiles in this photograph were more relaxed, more natural. Mrs. Dinsmore still looked to be about a hundred years old.

Wait. Mrs. Dinsmore . . .

I tucked one of the yearbooks under my arm and hurried toward Clark House. It was after hours, but Mrs. Dinsmore lived at the office. Yes, I had been suspended and was supposed to be off campus, but I doubted that campus police would open fire. So I walked across the quad where the students roamed, with a book I hadn't checked out of the library. Look at me, living on the edge.

I remembered walking here that day six years ago with Natalie. Why hadn't she said anything? Had there been any sign? Did she grow quiet or slow her step? I didn't remember. I just remember yapping happily away about the campus like some freshman tour guide after too many Red Bulls.

Mrs. Dinsmore looked up at me over her half-moon reading glasses. "I thought you were out of here."

"Maybe in body," I said, "but am I ever far from your heart?"

She rolled her eyes. "What do you want?"

I put the yearbook down in front of her. It was open to the group picture. I pointed at Natalie's father. "Do you remember a professor named Aaron Kleiner?"

Mrs. Dinsmore took her time. The reading glasses were mounted to a chain around her neck. She removed them, cleaned them with quaking hands, and put them back on again. Her face was still as stone.

"I remember him," she said softly. "Why do you ask?"

"Do you know why he was fired?"

She looked up at me. "Who said he was fired?"

"Or why he left? Is there anything you can tell me about what happened to him?"

"He hasn't been here in twenty-five years. You were maybe ten when he left."

"I know."

"So why are you asking?"

I didn't even know how to dance around that question. "Do you remember his children?"

"Little girls. Natalie and Julie."

No hesitation. That surprised me. "You remember their names?"

"What about them?"

"Six years ago I met Natalie at a retreat in Vermont. We fell in love."

Mrs. Dinsmore waited for me to say more.

219

"I know this sounds crazy, but I'm trying to find her. I think she may be in danger, and maybe it has something to do with her father, I don't know."

Mrs. Dinsmore kept her eyes on me another second or two. She let her reading glasses drop back to her chest. "He was a good professor. You'd have liked him. His classes were lively. He was terrific at energizing the students."

Her gaze dropped back to the photograph in the yearbook.

"In those days, some of the younger professors doubled as dorm monitors. Aaron Kleiner was one of them. He and his family lived on the bottom floor of the Tingley dormitory. The students loved them. I remember one year, the students chipped in and bought a swing set for the girls. They all built it on a Saturday morning in the courtyard behind Pratt."

She looked off wistfully. "Natalie was an adorable little girl. How does she look now?"

"She's the most beautiful woman in the world," I said.

Mrs. Dinsmore gave me a wry smile. "You're a romantic."

"What happened to them?"

"A few things," she said. "There were rumors about their marriage."

"What kind of rumors?"

"What kind are there always on a college campus? Young kids, distracted wife, attractive man on a campus with impressionable coeds. I tease you about the young girls who stop by your office, but I've seen too many lives ruined by that temptation."

"He had an affair with a student?"

"Maybe. I don't know. Those were the rumors. Have you heard of Vice Chair Roy Horduck?"

"I've seen his name on some plaques."

"Aaron Kleiner accused Horduck of plagiarism. The charges were never brought, but vice chair is a pretty powerful position. Aaron Kleiner got demoted. Then he got involved in a cheating scandal."

"A professor cheated?"

"No, of course not. He made accusations against a student, maybe two. I don't remember the details anymore. That might have been his downfall, I don't know. He started to drink. He behaved more erratically. The rumors started."

She stared down at the photograph again.

"So they asked him to resign?"

"No," Mrs. Dinsmore said.

"Then what happened?"

"One day, his wife walked through that very door." She pointed behind her. I knew what door. I had walked through it a thousand times, but I still looked, as though Natalie's mom might walk through it again. "She was crying. Hysterical, really. I was sitting right where I am now, at this very spot, at this very desk . . ."

Her words faded away.

"She wanted to see Professor Hume. He wasn't here so I called him on the phone. He hurried over. She told him that Professor Kleiner was gone."

"Gone?"

"He'd packed his things and run off with another woman. A former student."

"Who?"

"I don't know. Like I said, she was hysterical. There were no cell phones back in those days. We had no way to reach him. We waited. I remember he had a class that afternoon. He never showed. Professor Hume had to cover that day. The other professors took turns covering until the semester ended. The students were really upset. Parents called, but Professor Hume placated them all by giving everyone an A." She shrugged, pushed the yearbook back toward me, and pretended to get back to work.

"We never heard from him again."

I swallowed. "So what happened to his

wife and daughters?"

"The same, I guess."

"What does that mean?"

"They moved away at the end of the semester. I never heard from them again. I always hoped that they all ended up at another college — that they patched things up. But I guess that wasn't what happened, was it?"

"No."

"So what happened to them?" Mrs. Dinsmore asked.

"I don't know."

CHAPTER 20

Who would know?

Answer: Natalie's sister, Julie. She had blown me off on the phone. I wondered whether I'd have better luck in person.

I was heading back to my car when my cell phone rang. I checked the number on the caller ID. The area code was 802.

Vermont.

I answered the phone and said hello.

"Um, hi. You left your card at the café."

I recognized the voice. "Cookie?"

"We should talk," she said.

My grip on the phone tightened. "I'm listening."

"I don't trust phones," Cookie said. There was a quake in her voice. "Can you get back up here?"

"I can drive up right now if you want."

Cookie gave me directions to her home, not far from the café. I took 91 north and tried unsuccessfully not to speed. My heart pounded in my chest, keeping beat, it seemed, with whatever song was on the radio. By the time I reached the state line, it was near midnight. I had started that morning flying down to see Delia Sanderson. It had been a long day and for just a second, I could feel the exhaustion. I flashed back to the first time I saw Natalie's painting of that cottage on the hill — to Cookie coming up behind me and asking if I liked it.

Why, I asked myself again, had Cookie acted as though she didn't remember me when I stopped in the café?

There was something else that came back to me. Everyone else I met said that there had never been a Creative Recharge retreat, but when Cookie made her denial, she said, "We never worked at the retreat."

I hadn't caught that at the time, but if there had never been a retreat up that hill, wouldn't your response be something like, "Huh? What retreat?"

I slowed as I passed Cookie's bookshop café. There were only two streetlights, both casting long, menacing shadows. No people were present. The small town center was perfectly still, too still, like that scene in a zombie film before the hero gets surrounded by the flesh-eaters. I made a right at the end of the block, drove half a mile, made another right. There were no streetlights now. The only illumination at all came from my headlights. If I was passing houses or buildings, all the lights had been turned off there too. I guess no one out here left their lights on a timer to deter burglars. Smart move. I doubted in this darkness that burglars could find the homes.

I checked my GPS and saw that I was half a mile from my destination. Two more turns. Something akin to dread started seeping into my chest. We have all read about how certain animals and sea creatures can sense danger. They can actually feel threats or even oncoming natural disasters, almost as though they had survival radar or invisible tentacles reaching out and around corners. Somewhere, of course, primitive man must have had this ability too. That sort of survival stuff stays with us. It may lie dormant. It may wither away from lack of use. But that instinctive Neanderthal man is always there, lurking under our khakis and dress shirt.

Right now, to use vernacular from my comic-book youth, my Spidey senses were tingling.

I turned off the headlights and slowed to the curb in pitch darkness practically by sense of touch. There were no stones framing the street. The pavement just gave way to the grass. I didn't know what I was about to do, but the more I thought about this, the more I thought that maybe some measure of care was in order.

I could walk from here.

I slipped out of the car. Once I closed the door, once all the light was gone, I realized just how dark it really was. The night seemed to be a living thing, consuming me, covering my eyes. I waited a minute or two, just standing there, letting my eyes adjust. Eyes adjusting to darkness — another one of those talents we undoubtedly inherited from primitive man. When I could see at least a few feet in front of me, I started on my way. I had my smartphone too. It was loaded up with apps I never used, but the one I did, the one that was probably the most useful and least techie, was the simple flashlight. I debated turning it on but decided against it.

If there was danger here — and I couldn't imagine what that danger might be or what form it might take — I didn't want to give it a heads-up with a shining flashlight. That had been the whole point of parking and sneaking up, right?

I flashed back to being trapped in the back of that van. I had no qualms about what I'd been forced to do to escape — I would do it again, of course, a thousand times over — but there was also no doubt that Otto's final moments would haunt my sleep until the day I died. I would always hear the wet crack of that neck snapping, would always remember the feel of bone and cartilage giving way, ending a life. I had killed someone. I had snuffed out a human being.

Then my thoughts turned to Bob.

I slowed my step. What did Bob do after I escaped down the hill? He must have gotten back in his van, driven away, probably dumped Otto's body someplace, and then . . .

Would he maybe try to find me again?

I thought about the strain in Cookie's voice. What did she want to tell me? And why was it suddenly so urgent? Why call me up here now, late at night, not giving me a chance to think it all through?

I was on Cookie's block now. Small lights were on in a few of the windows, giving the houses a spooky, jack-o'-lantern glow. The house at the end of the cul-de-sac had more lights on than the others.

Cookie's.

I moved to the left to stay out of sight. Her front porch lights were on, so that wouldn't be the way to approach. Not if I wanted to stay unseen. The house was a sprawling one-level, unnaturally long and slightly uneven, as though additions had been stuck on without much forethought. Staying low, I circled toward the side of the house. I tried to stay in the dark. I literally crawled the last ten yards toward the window with the brightest light.

Now what?

I was under the window on all fours. I stayed still and tried to listen. Nothing. There is silence, and then there is rural silence, silence you could feel and reach out and touch, silence with texture and distance. That was what surrounded me now. Real, true, rural silence.

I shifted my weight slightly. My knees cracked, the sound seemingly screaming through the stillness. I got my feet beneath me, my knees deeply bent, my hands on my thighs. I readied to push myself up like a human piston, so that I could take a peek in the window.

Keeping most of my face out of sight, I rose toward the corner of the window so that only one eye and the top right quadrant of my face would be exposed. I blinked in the sudden light and looked into the room.

Cookie was there.

She sat on the couch. Cookie's back was

ramrod straight. Her mouth was set. Denise, her partner, sat next to her. They were holding hands, but their faces were pale and drawn. The tension came off them in waves.

You didn't have to be an expert in body language to see that they were nervous about something. It took me a few more moments to realize what that something was.

A man sat in the chair across from them.

His back was to me so that at first I could only see the top of his head.

My first thought was a panicked one: Could it be Bob?

I raised myself up a few more inches, trying to get a better look at the man. No luck. The chair was big and plush. The man sank deep into it, vanishing from view. I moved to the other side of the window, changing my exposed face quadrant to the upper left. Now I could see the hair was salt-and-pepper curly.

Not Bob. Definitely not Bob.

The man was speaking. The two women listened intently, nodding in unison to whatever he was saying. I turned and pressed my ear against the window. The glass was cold. I tried to make out what the man was saying, but it was still too muffled. I glanced back into the room. The man in the chair leaned a little forward, trying to make a point. Then he tilted his chin just enough so I could see his profile.

I may have gasped out loud.

The man had a beard. That was the key. That was how I was able to recognize him — the beard and the curly hair. I flashed back again to that very first time I saw Natalie, sitting in the chair with her sunglasses on. And next to her, seated to her right, had been a man with a beard and curly hair.

This man.

What the . . . ?

The bearded guy rose out of the plush chair. He started to pace, gesturing wildly. Cookie and Denise tensed up. They held hands so tightly I swore that I could see their knuckles whiten. That was when I noticed something else that sent me reeling — something that made me realize with a stunning thud the importance of running this little reconnaissance mission before walking blindly into the situation.

The bearded man had a gun.

I froze in my half squat. My legs started to shake, from fear or exertion, I wasn't sure which. I lowered myself back down. Now what?

Flee, dopey.

Yep, that seemed the best play. Flee back

to my car. Call the cops. Let them handle it. I tried to picture how that scenario would play out. First off, how long would it take the cops to get here? Wait, would they even believe me? Would they call Cookie and Denise first? Would a SWAT team come out? And now that I really thought about it, what was happening here exactly? Did Beardy kidnap Cookie or Denise and make them call me — or were they all in cahoots together? And if they were in cahoots, what would happen after I called? The cops would show up, and Cookie and Denise would deny everything. Beardy would hide his gun and claim ignorance.

Then again, what was the alternative? I had to bring in the cops, right?

Beardy continued to pace. The tension in the room made it pound out like a heart. Beardy checked his watch. He took out his mobile phone and held it in a walkie-talkie manner. He barked something into it.

Who was he talking to?

Whoa, I thought. What if there were others? It was time to go. Call the cops, don't call the cops, whatever. That guy was armed. I wasn't.

Hasta luego, mofos.

I was taking one last look through the window when I heard the dog bark come from behind me. I froze at the sound. Beardy did not. His head snapped toward the barking — and by extension, me — as though pulled on a string.

Our eyes locked through the window. I saw his widen in surprise. For the briefest of moments — a hundredth of a second, maybe two of them — neither of us moved. We just stared in shock, unsure of what to make of each other, until Beardy raised the gun, pointed it at me, and pulled the trigger.

I fell backward as the bullet crashed through the window.

I dropped to the ground. Shards of glass rained down on me. The dog kept barking. I rolled over, cutting myself on the glass, and got to my feet.

"Stop!"

It was another man's voice coming from my left. I didn't recognize the voice, but the guy was outside. Oh man, I had to get out of there. No time to think or hesitate. I ran full throttle in the other direction. I turned the corner, legs pumping, nearly in the clear.

Or so I thought.

Earlier I had credited my attuned Spidey senses with gifting me the premonition of danger. If that was the case, those same senses had just failed me miserably.

Another man was standing right around the corner. He'd been waiting for me, baseball bat at the ready. I managed to stop my legs, but there was no time for anything else. The meat of the bat came toward me. No chance for me to react. No chance for me to do anything but stand there stupidly. The blow landed flush on my forehead.

I dropped to the ground.

He may have hit me with the bat again. I don't know. My eyes rolled back, and I was gone.

CHAPTER 21

First thing when I woke up: pain.

That was all I could think of: massive, all-consuming pain and how to lessen it. It felt as though my skull had been shattered, that tiny fragments of bone were loose, that their jagged edges were ripping through my most sensitive brain tissue.

I moved my head slightly to the side, but that just made those jagged edges angrier. I stopped, blinked my eyes, blinked them again in an attempt to open them, gave up.

"He's awake."

The voice belonged to Cookie. I tried once more to pry my eyes open. I almost used my fingers against my eyelids. I swam past the hurt. It took a few seconds, but I finally got there. It took a few more seconds to focus and start to take in my new surroundings.

I wasn't outside anymore.

That much was for certain. I looked up at

the exposed wooden beams of a roof. I also wasn't in Cookie's house. She had a one-level ranch. This looked more like a barn or old farmhouse. There was a wooden floor underneath me, not dirt, so I ruled out the barn.

Cookie was there. So was Denise. Beardy came over and looked down at me with pure, unfiltered hatred. I had no idea why. I saw a second man standing by a door to my left. A third man sat in front of a computer screen. I didn't recognize either of them.

Beardy waited, glaring down at me. He probably thought that I would say something obvious like, "Where am I?" I didn't. I used the time to calm myself and try to gather my thoughts.

I had no idea what was going on.

I kept my eyes moving, trying to get a sense of the room. I searched for an escape route. I saw one door and three windows, all closed. The door was guarded too. I remembered that at least one of them was armed with a gun.

I needed to be patient.

"Talk," Beardy said to me.

I didn't. He kicked me in the ribs. I let out a groan, but I didn't move.

"Jed," Cookie said, "don't."

Beardy Jed stared down at me. There was

rage behind his eyes. "How did you find Todd?"

That threw me. I don't know what I'd expected him to ask, but it wasn't that. "What?"

"You heard me," Jed said. "How did you find Todd?"

My head was swimming. I didn't see where a lie here would help me, so I went with the truth. "His obituary."

Jed looked at Cookie. Now I saw confusion on their faces.

"I saw his obituary," I continued. "It was on the college website. That's how I got to his funeral."

Jed wound up to kick me again, but Cookie stopped him with a shake of her head. "I'm not talking about that," Jed spat. "I'm talking about before."

"What before?"

"Don't play dumb. How did you find Todd?"

"I don't know what you're talking about," I said.

The rage behind his eyes exploded. He pulled out the gun and pointed it at me. "You're lying."

I said nothing.

Cookie moved closer to him. "Jed?"

"Back off," he snapped. "You know what

he did? Do you?"

She nodded and did as she was asked. I stayed perfectly still.

"Talk," he said to me again.

"I don't know what you want me to say."

I glanced at the guy sitting by the computer. He looked scared. So did the guy by the door. I thought back to Bob and Otto. They hadn't looked scared. They looked ready and experienced. These guys didn't. I wasn't sure what, if anything, that meant, except that either way, I was in huge trouble.

"One more time," Jed began through gritted teeth. "How did you find Todd?"

"I already told you."

"You killed him!" Jed shouted.

"What? No!"

Jed dropped to his knees and put the muzzle of the gun against my temple. I closed my eyes and waited for the blast. He moved his lips close to my ear.

"If you lie again," he whispered, "I will kill you right here and now."

Cookie: "Jed?"

"Shut up!"

He pressed the muzzle hard enough against my temple to leave an indentation. "Talk."

"I didn't . . ." His eyes told me that another denial would seal my fate. "Why would I kill him?"

"You tell us," Jed said. "But first I want to know how you found him."

Jed's hand was shaking, the muzzle jangling against my temple. His spittle was getting tangled up in his beard. My pain was gone now, replaced by naked fear. Jed wanted to pull that trigger. He wanted to kill me.

"I told you how," I said. "Please. Listen to me."

"You're lying!"

"I'm not —"

"You tortured him, but he wouldn't talk. Todd couldn't help you anyway. He didn't know. He was just helpless and brave, and you, you bastard . . ."

I was seconds from death. I could hear the torment in his voice and knew that he wouldn't listen to reason. I had to do something, had to risk going for the gun, but I was flat on my back. Any move would take too long.

"I never hurt him, I swear."

"And I guess you'll also tell us you didn't visit his widow today."

"No, I did," I said quickly, happy to agree with him.

"But she didn't know anything either, did she?"

"Know about what?"

Again the muzzle dug in a little deeper. "Why did you go down to talk to the widow?"

I met his eye. "You know why," I said.

"What were you looking for?"

"Not what," I said. "Who. I was looking for Natalie."

He nodded now. A chilly smile came to his face. The smile told me that I had given him the right answer — and the wrong one. "Why?" he asked.

"What do you mean, why?"

"Who hired you?"

"No one hired me."

"Jed!"

It wasn't Cookie this time. It was the guy at the computer screen.

Jed turned, annoyed by the interruption. "What?"

"You better take a look at this. We have company."

Jed pulled the gun away from my head. I let out a long breath of relief. The guy by the computer twisted the monitor so Jed could see the screen. It was a surveillance video in black-and-white.

"What are they doing here?" Cookie asked. "If they find him here . . ."

"They're our friends," Jed said. "Let's not

worry until —"

I didn't wait for more. I saw my chance and I took it. Without warning I jumped to my feet and ran toward the guy blocking the door. It seemed as though I were moving in slow motion, as if it were taking much too long to get to that door. I lowered my shoulder, ready to ram into him.

"Stop!"

I was maybe two steps from the guy guarding the door. He was in a crouch, bracing himself for my attack. My brain kept working, calculating and recalculating. In something quicker than seconds — quicker than nanoseconds — I laid out the whole upcoming scenario. How long would it take me to put the guy down? At best, two or three seconds. Then I had to reach for the knob, turn it, fling the door open, run outside.

How long would that all take?

Conclusion: Too long.

Two other men and maybe two women would be on me by then. Or maybe Jed would just shoot. In fact, if he reacted fast enough, he could probably fire a round before I even reached the guy.

In short, calculating the odds, I realized that I had no chance of getting out through the door. Yet here I was, still running toward my adversary with a full head of steam. He was ready for me. He expected me to go for him. So, I assumed, did Jed and the others.

That wouldn't do then, would it?

I needed to surprise them. At the last possible moment, I veered my body right and without so much as a backward glance or even the slightest hesitation, I leapt forward and dived straight through the window.

Still airborne, with yet another window shattering around me, I heard Jed shout, "Get him!"

I tucked my arms and head, landing on the roll, hoping to use my momentum to get smoothly back on my feet. That was a fantasy. I did manage to roll up to my feet, but the momentum didn't suddenly stop. It kept me going, knocking me back to the ground, sending me tumbling. When I finally stopped, I struggled to get back up.

Where the hell was I?

No time to think. I was in the backyard, I guessed. I saw woods. The driveway and front, I assumed, were behind me. I started in that direction, but then I heard the front door open. The three men appeared.

Uh-oh.

I turned and ran into the woods. The darkness swallowed me whole. I couldn't see more than a few feet in front of me, but slowing down wasn't an option. There were men — at least one of whom had a gun — behind me.

"Over there!" I heard someone yell.

"We can't, Jed. You saw what was on the screen."

So I ran. I ran into those woods hard and fast, and eventually I ran face-first into a tree. It was like when Wile E. Coyote runs into a rake — a dull thud followed by vibrations. My brain started shaking. The blow stopped me cold, and I fell to the ground. My already aching head screamed in pain.

I saw the beam of a flashlight coming closer to me.

I tried to roll into some kind of hiding spot. My side hit another tree or, hell, maybe it was the same one. My head screamed in protest. I rolled in the other direction, trying to stay as flat as possible. The flashlight beam sliced through the air right above me.

I could hear footsteps moving closer.

Had to move.

Back toward the house I heard the crunch of tires on gravel. A car was coming up the drive.

"Jed?"

It was a harsh whisper. The flashlight stopped moving. I heard someone call out to Jed again. Now the flashlight went off. I was back in the pure darkness. I heard the footsteps recede.

Get up and run, dumb ass!

My head wouldn't let me. I lay still another moment and then looked back toward the old farmhouse in the distance. Now I could finally see it from the outside for the first time. I stayed still and stared. Once again, the floor beneath me seemed to fall away.

It was the main house of the Creative Recharge retreat.

I was being held in the place where Natalie had stayed.

What the hell was going on?

The car came to a stop. I rose just enough to get a look. When I did, when I saw the car, I felt an entirely new sense of relief.

It was a police squad car.

Now I understood their panic. Jed and his group had a surveillance camera by the entrance. They had seen the cop car coming to my rescue and had panicked. It made sense now.

I started toward my saviors. Jed and his followers wouldn't kill me now. Not in front of cops who had come to rescue me. I was almost to the edge of the woods, maybe thirty yards from the cop car, when another thought entered my head.

How had the cops known where I was?

For that matter, how had the cops known I was in trouble? And why, if they were here to rescue me, had the car driven up at such an unhurried pace? Why had Jed made that comment about their being "our friends"? As I slowed down, the relief now ebbing away, a few more questions entered my head. Why was Jed walking toward the squad car with a big smile and casual wave? Why were the two cops getting out of the car waving back just as casually? Why were they all shaking hands and exchanging backslaps like old buddies?

"Hey, Jed," one called out.

Oh damn. It was Stocky. The other cop was Thin Man Jerry. I decided to stay where I was.

"Hey, fellas," Jed said. "How are you guys?"

"Good, man, when did you get back?"

"A couple of days ago. What's up?"

Stocky said, "You know a guy named Jake Fisher?"

Whoa. So maybe they were here to rescue me?

"No, don't think so," Jed said. The others were all outside now. More handshakes and backslaps. "Guys, you know a . . . what was the name again?"

"Jacob Fisher."

They all shook their heads and muttered their lack of knowledge.

"There's an APB out on him," Stocky said. "College professor. Seems he killed a man."

My blood went cold.

Thin Man Jerry added, "The dope confessed to it even."

"He sounds dangerous," Jed said, "but I don't get what that has to do with us."

"First off, we spotted him trying to get on your land a couple days back."

"My land?"

"Yep. But that's not why we're here now."

I ducked down in the brush, not sure what to do here.

"See, we got a GPS working a trace on a cell phone," Stocky said.

"And," Thin Man Jerry added, "the coordinates are leading us right up here."

"I don't understand."

"Simple, Jed. We can track his iPhone. Not that hard nowadays. Hell, I got a tracker on my kid's phone, for crying out loud. It tells us that our perp is here on your property at this very moment."

"A dangerous killer?"

"Could be, yep. Why don't you all wait

inside now?" He looked back toward his partner. "Jerry?"

Jerry reached back into the car and pulled some sort of handheld device into view. He studied it for a few moments, hit the touch screen, and then declared, "He's within fifty yards — in that direction."

Thin Man Jerry pointed right to where I was hiding.

Several scenarios flew through my brain. One, the most obvious: Surrender. Throw my hands up, walk out of the woods with them held high, and shout, "I give up," as loud as I can. Once I was in police custody I was, if nothing else, safe from Jed and his group.

I was seriously considering doing that — raising my arms, calling out, surrendering — when I saw Jed take out his gun.

Uh-oh.

Stocky said, "Jed, what are you doing?"

"It's my gun. I own it legally. And we're on my property, right?"

"Right, so?"

"So this murderer you're after . . . ," Jed began.

Now I was a murderer.

"He might be armed and dangerous. We aren't letting you guys go after him without backup."

"We don't need backup, Jed. Put that away."

"This is still my property, right?"

"It is."

"So if it's all the same to you, I'm staying right here."

The obvious scenario suddenly didn't seem so obvious. Jed was intent on killing me for two reasons. One, he thought that I had something to do with Todd's murder. That was the reason they had grabbed me in the first place. But now, two, dead men tell no tales. If I surrendered, I could tell the cops what had happened tonight, how they had kidnapped me and fired shots at me. It might be my word against theirs, but there'd be the bullet at Cookie's house matching his gun. There'd be the phone records of Cookie calling me. It might be a tough sell, but I bet Jed didn't want to take the risk.

But if Jed shot me now — even if he fired as I tried to surrender — it could be viewed as either self-defense or, at worst, a jumpy trigger finger. He would shoot and kill me and say that he thought I had a gun or something like that and, really, I already killed one man, according to Stocky and Thin Man Jerry. And all of these Vermont buddies would back Jed's story and the only guy who would contradict them — yours truly — would be worm food.

There was more to consider. If I surrendered, how long would I be jammed up with the police? I was getting closer to the truth. I could feel it. They thought that I killed someone. Heck, I sort of confessed to it. How long could they hold me? A while, I bet.

If they nabbed me now, I'd probably never have a chance to confront Natalie's sister, Julie.

"This way," Thin Man Jerry said.

They started walking to me. Jed lifted his gun, keeping it very much at the ready.

I started to backpedal. My head felt as though it'd been encased in molasses.

"If someone is in those woods," Stocky shouted, "come out now with your hands up."

They moved closer. I slid backward a few more steps and ducked behind a tree. The woods were thick. If I could get deep enough in them, I'd be safe at least for a bit. I picked up a rock and hurled it as far as I could to my left. All eyes turned. Flashlights came on and shone in that direction.

"Over there," someone yelled.

Jed led the way, gun pointed.

Surrender? Oh, I don't think so.

Stocky moved next to Jed. Jed hurried his step, nearly running, but Stocky put up an arm to stop him. "Move slow," Stocky said. "He might be armed."

Jed, of course, knew better, didn't he?

Thin Man Jerry didn't budge. "This thing says he's still over here."

Again he pointed in my direction. They were forty, fifty yards away. Staying low in the thicket, I quickly buried the phone — my second lost in the past three days — under a pile of leaves and hurried away, trying to make as little noise as possible. I started moving backward, deeper into the woods, again trying my best not to make any noise. I kept a few rocks in my hand. I'd throw them if I needed to distract.

The others gathered back around Jerry, all moving slowly toward the phone.

I picked up my pace, getting deeper and deeper into the trees. I couldn't see them anymore, just the flashlights.

"He's close by," Thin Man Jerry said.

"Or," Jed added, seeing the light, I guess, "his cell phone is."

I kept moving, kept low. I really didn't have a plan here. I had no idea what direction to take or how far the woods went. I might be able to escape them, might be able to keep moving, but eventually, unless I found a way out of here, I didn't have a clue how I'd get out of this.

Maybe, I thought, I could double-back to the house.

I heard voices mumbling. They were now too far for me to see them. That was a good thing. I could see the movement stop. The flashlight was lowered.

"He's not here," someone said.

Stocky, annoyed: "I can see that."

"Maybe your tracker is off."

They were, I guessed, right on top of where I'd haphazardly buried the phone. I wondered how long that gave me. Not much time, but probably enough. I rose to keep running and then it happened.

I'm not a doctor or a scientist, so I really can't tell you how adrenaline works. I only know that it does. It had helped me move past the pain from that blow to the head, from my jumping through a window, from my landing hard on the ground. It helped me recover from running face-first into that tree, even as I felt my lip fatten, could taste the bitter blood on my tongue.

What I do know — what I was learning at that very moment — was that adrenaline is not limitless. It was a finite hormone found within our bodies, nothing more. It may be

251

the most potent surge we know, but the effects, as I was quickly experiencing, were only short-term.

That surge eventually peters out.

The pain didn't so much ebb back in as announce itself with the thrash of a reaper's scythe. A bolt of pain ripped through my head, knocking me to my knees. I actually had to cover my mouth with my hand to prevent myself from crying out.

I heard another car coming up the drive. Had Stocky called for backup?

In the distance, I could hear voices:

"It's his phone!"

"What the . . . he buried it!"

"Spread out!"

I could hear rustling behind me. I wondered how much of a lead I had and how well that lead would stand up to flashlights and bullets. Probably not very big or well. I once again considered the idea of surrendering and taking my chances. I once again didn't like it.

I heard Stocky say, "Just back off, Jed. We can handle this."

"It's my land," Jed replied. "Too much land for you two to cover."

"Still —"

"My property, Jerry." There was snap in

Jed's voice. "You're on it without a warrant."

"A warrant?" It was Stocky. "You serious? We're just worried about your safety."

"Me too," Jed answered. "You got no idea where this murderer is hiding, right?"

"Well —"

"For all you know, he could be in the house. Hiding. Waiting for us. No way, bro — we are staying out here with you."

Silence.

Get *up,* I told myself.

"I want everyone to stay in sight," Stocky said. "No heroes. You see something, you scream for help."

I heard murmurs of agreement, then flashlights sliced through the dark. They were spreading out. I couldn't see people in the dark, just the bouncing beams of light. It was enough to know that I was really screwed.

Get up, dumb ass!

My head reeled in agony, but I managed to get to my feet. I stumbled forward like some kind of stiff-legged movie monster. I had made it about three steps, maybe four, when the flashlight sliced across my back.

I quickly jumped behind a tree.

Had I been spotted?

I waited for someone to call out. No one

did. I kept my back against the bark. The only sound now was my own breath. Did that beam of light hit me? I was pretty sure that it had. But I didn't know for sure. I stayed where I was and waited.

Footsteps coming toward me.

I wasn't sure what to do. If someone had spotted me, I was finished. There was no way I could get away. I waited for someone to shout for help.

Nothing, except for the approaching footsteps.

Wait a second. If I had been spotted, why hadn't anyone called out? Maybe I was okay. Maybe I had been mistaken for a tree or something.

Or maybe no one was calling out because they wanted to shoot me?

I tried to coldly consider that for a moment. Suppose, for example, it was Jed. Would he call out? No. If he called out, I might run and then Stocky and Thin Man Jerry would be on me too and it would be harder to kill me. But suppose he had spotted me with his flashlight. What then? If he had indeed seen me, if he knew that I was hiding behind this very tree, well, maybe Jed could sneak up on me alone, gun at the ready, and . . .

Ka-boom.

The footsteps were growing louder.

My brain tried to do that quick-calculating-reptilian thing again — it had already saved me, right? — but after a second or two of neuron burning, I came to a rather startling yet obvious conclusion:

I was finished. There was no way out.

I tried to gather my strength for a big-time sprint, but really, what would that do? I'd expose myself for certain and in the condition I was in I'd never get far. I'd either get shot or captured. Come to think of it, those seemed to be my only two choices now: shot or captured. I preferred captured, thank you very much. The question now was, how could I maximize my chances of captured over shot?

I didn't have a clue.

A beam of light danced in front of me. I pressed my back into the tree and went up on my tippy-toes. Like that was going to help. The footsteps were getting closer. Judging by the sound and the brightness of the light, I would guess that someone was within ten yards of me.

Options flew in and out of my brain. I could stay here and jump the guy. If it was Jed, for example, I could disarm him. But any struggle on my part would not only reveal my location for sure, but if it wasn't

Jed — if it was, for example, Stocky — then it would be open season on using deadly force on me.

So what to do?

Hope that I hadn't been spotted.

Of course, hope wasn't a plan or even an option. It was wishing. It was fanciful thinking. It was leaving my fate in the hands of, well, fate.

The footsteps were only a yard or two away now. I braced myself, unsure what to do, leaving it to that reptilian part of my brain, when I heard a whisper.

"Don't say a word. I know you're behind the tree."

It was Cookie.

"I'm going to walk past you," she said, her voice low. "When I do, get right behind me and walk. Get as close to my back as possible."

"What?"

"Just do it." Her tone left no room for discussion. "Right up close."

Cookie walked past my tree, nearly knocking into it, and kept going. I didn't hesitate. I fell in line right behind her and followed. I could see flashlights in the distance, both on my left and on my right.

"That wasn't an act, was it?" Cookie said.

I didn't know what she meant.

"You loved Natalie, didn't you?"

"Yes," I whispered.

"I'm going to walk you as far as I can. We will hit a path. Take it to the right. Stay low and out of sight. The path will lead to the clearing where the white chapel is. You'll know how to get away from there. I will try to keep them occupied. Get as far away as you can. Don't go home. They'll find you there."

"Who will find me?"

I tried to move in sync with her, matching footstep for footstep like an annoying kid copying another.

"You need to stop, Jake."

"Who will find me?"

"This is bigger than you can imagine. You have no idea what you're up against. None at all."

"Tell me."

"If you don't stop, you'll kill us all." Cookie veered left. I kept with her. "The path is up ahead. I will turn left, you head down to the right. Understand?"

"Where's Natalie? Is she alive?"

"In ten seconds, we will be on the path."

"Tell me."

"You're not listening to me. You've got to leave this alone."

"Then tell me where Natalie is."

In the distance I could hear Stocky yell out something, but I couldn't make out the words. Cookie slowed her step.

"Please," I said.

Her voice was distant, hollow. "I don't know where Natalie is. I don't know if she's dead or alive. Neither does Jed. Neither do any of us."

We hit a path made of crumbled stone. She began to turn to the left. "One last thing, Jake."

"What?"

"If you come back, I won't be the one saving your life." Cookie showed me the gun in her hand. "I'll be the one who ends it."

CHAPTER 22

I recognized the path.

There was a small pond to the right. Natalie and I had gone swimming there late one night. We got out, panting, lying naked in each other's arm, skin against skin. "I never had this," she said slowly. "I mean, I've had this, but . . . never *this*."

I understood. I hadn't either.

I passed the old park bench where Natalie and I used to sit after having coffee and scones at Cookie's. Up ahead, I could see the faint outline of the chapel. I barely glanced at it, didn't need those memories slowing me down right now. I took the path down into town. My car was less than half a mile away. I wondered whether the cops had located it yet. I didn't see how. I wouldn't be able to drive it very long — there was probably an APB on it too — but I didn't see any other way of getting out of town. I'd have to risk it.

The street remained so dark that I was only able to find my car via memory. I practically walked right into it. When I opened the door, the car's interior light burst through the night. I quickly slipped inside and closed the door. Now what? I was, I guessed, a guy on the run. I remembered seeing on some TV show where the fugitive switched license plates with another car. Maybe that would help. Maybe I could find a parked car and do that. Right, sure, except, of course, I didn't have a screwdriver. How could I do it without a screwdriver? I searched my pocket and pulled out a dime. Would that work as a screwdriver?

It would take too long.

I did have a destination in mind. I drove south, careful not to drive too fast or too slowly, constantly hitting the gas and brake, as though the proper speed would somehow make me invisible. The roads were dark. That would probably help. I had to keep in mind that an APB wasn't all-powerful. I probably had some time on my hands if I could keep off main roads.

My iPhone was, of course, gone. I felt naked and impotent without it. Funny how attached we get to those devices. I continued south.

Now what?

I had only sixty dollars on me. That wouldn't get me far. If I used a credit card, the cops would see it and pick me up right away. Well, not right away. They'd have to see the charge come in and then dispatch a squad car or whatever. I don't know how long that took but I doubt it would be instantaneous. Cops are good. They aren't omnipotent.

No choice really. I had to take a calculated risk. Interstate 91, the main highway in this area, was just up ahead. I took it to the first rest area and parked near the back in the least-lit spot I could find. I actually cinched up my collar, as if that would disguise me, and headed inside. When I walked past the small rest-stop convenience store, something snagged my gaze.

They sold pens and markers. Not a lot of them, but maybe . . .

I thought about it for a second, maybe two, and then I headed into the shop. When I checked the small selection of writing utensils, the disappointment hit me harder than I expected.

"Can I help you?"

The girl behind the counter couldn't have been more than twenty. She had blond hair with streaks of pink in it. Yep, pink.

"I like your hair," I said, ever the charmer.

"The pink?" She pointed at the streaks. "It's for breast cancer awareness. Say, are you okay?"

"Sure, why?"

"You got a big bump on your head. I think it's bleeding."

"Oh, that. Right. I'm fine."

"We sell a first aid kit, if you think that'll help."

"Yeah, maybe." I turned back to the pens and markers. "I'm looking for a red marker, but I don't see any here."

"We don't carry any. Just black."

"Oh."

She studied my face. "I got one here though." She reached into a drawer and picked out a red Sharpie marker. "We use it for inventory, to cross out stuff."

I tried not to show how anxious I was. "Is there any way I can purchase it from you?"

"I don't think we're supposed to do that."

"Please," I said. "It is really important."

She thought about it. "Tell you what. You buy the first aid kit and promise to take care of that bump, and I'll throw in the pen."

I made the deal and hurried into the men's room. The clock had to be ticking. A police car would eventually drive by major rest stops and check cars, right? Or wrong? I didn't have a clue. I tried to keep my breathing even and smooth. I checked my face in the mirror. Ugh. There was swelling on my forehead, and an open gash above my eye. I cleaned it out as much as I could, but a big bandage would make me stick out like a sore thumb.

The ATM was next to the vending machines, but that would have to wait a few more minutes.

I rushed out to my car. My car license plate read "704 LI6." The lettering in Massachusetts is red. Using the marker I turned the 0 into an 8, the L into an E, the I into a T, the 6 into an 8. I took a step back. It would never stand up to close inspection, but from any sort of distance, the plate did read "784 ET8."

I would have smiled at my ingenuity, but there was no time. I headed back toward the ATM and debated how to approach the machine. I knew that all ATMs had cameras — who didn't? — but even if I avoided being seen, the authorities would know it was my credit card.

Speed seemed more important here. If they had a picture of me, they had a picture of me.

I have two credit cards. I took out the max on both and hurried back to my car. I got off the highway at the next exit and started taking side roads. When I reached Greenfield, I parked the car on a side street in the center of town. I considered taking the nearest bus, but that would be too obvious. I found a taxi and took it to Springfield. Naturally I paid cash. I took the Peter Pan bus from there to New York City. Throughout all of this travel, my eyes kept shifting all over the place, waiting for — I don't know — a cop or a bad guy to spot and nab me.

Paranoid much?

Once in Manhattan I hired another taxi to take me out to Ramsey, New Jersey, where I knew Julie Pottham, Natalie's sister, lived.

When we reached Ramsey, the driver said, "Okay, bud, where to?"

It was four in the morning — clearly too late (or, depending on your point of view, too early) to visit Natalie's sister. Plus I needed rest. My head hurt. My nerves were shot. I could feel my body quake from exhaustion.

"Let's find a motel."

"There's a Sheraton up this way."

They'd require identification and probably a credit card. "No. Something . . . cheaper."

We found one of those no-tell motels designed for truckers, adulterers, and us fugitives. It was aptly named the Fair Motel. I liked that honesty: We aren't great, we aren't even good, we're "fair." A sign above the awning announced "Hourly Rates" (just like a Ritz-Carlton), "Color TV" (mocking those competitors who still use black-and-white), and my favorite part: "Now Featuring Towels!"

This place wouldn't require ID or credit card or even a pulse.

The woman behind the desk was in her seventies. She looked at me with seen-it-all eyes. Her name tag read MABEL. Her hair had the consistency of hay. I asked for a room in the back.

"Do you have a reservation?" she asked me.

"You're kidding, right?"

"Yeah, I am," Mabel said. "But the rooms in the back are full. Everyone wants a room in the back. Must be the view of the Dumpster. I got a nice room overlooking a Staples store, if you'd like."

Mabel gave me a key to room 12, which ended up not being as nightmarish as I imagined. The place looked *fair*ly clean. I tried not to think what this room had probably witnessed during its lifetime, but then again, if I stopped and thought about it, I wouldn't like to think about that in a Ritz-

Carlton either.

I collapsed into bed with my clothes still on and fell into one of those sleeps where you don't remember falling asleep and have no idea what time it is when you wake up. When morning hit, I reached for my iPhone on the night table but, alas, I remembered that I didn't have it anymore. The police did. Were they going through it? Were they seeing all the places I had searched, all the texts I had sent, all the e-mails I had mailed out? Were they doing the same at my house on campus? If they had gotten a warrant to track me down via my iPhone, wouldn't it stand to reason that they also had enough to search my place? But then again, so what? They wouldn't find anything incriminating. Embarrassing maybe, but who didn't have some Internet searches that were embarrassing?

My head still hurt. A lot. I smelled like a goat. A shower would help but not if I had to change into these same clothes. I stumbled into the bright morning sunlight, shielding my eyes like a vampire or one of those guys who spent too much time in a casino. Mabel was still behind the desk.

"Wow, what time do you get off?" I asked.

"Are you hitting on me?"

"Uh, no."

266

"Because you might want to clean up a little before you make your big move. I got standards."

"Do you have any aspirin or Tylenol?"

Mabel frowned, reached into her purse, and pulled out a small arsenal of painkillers. Tylenol, Advil, Aleve, Bayer. I chose the Tylenol, downed two, and thanked her.

"The Target down the road has a big-n-tall section," Mabel said. "Maybe you want to buy some new clothes."

Great suggestion. I headed over and bought a pair of jeans and a flannel shirt, not to mention a few undergarments. I also bought a travel-size toothbrush, toothpaste, and deodorant. My plan was not to stay on the run for very long, but there was still one thing I wanted to do before I surrendered to the authorities.

Talk to Natalie's sister in person.

Last purchase: A disposable cell phone. I called Benedict's cell, home, and office. No answer at any of them. It was probably too early for him. I wondered who else I should try and decided to call Shanta. She answered on the first ring.

"Hello?"

"It's Jake."

"What's this phone number you're calling from?"

267

"It's a disposable phone," I said.

There was a pause. "Do you want to tell me what's going on?"

"Two Vermont cops were looking for me."

"Why?"

I quickly explained.

"Wait," Shanta said, "you ran away from cops?"

"I didn't trust the situation. I thought those people would kill me."

"So surrender now."

"Not quite yet."

"Jake, listen to me. If you're a fugitive, if law enforcement officials are looking for you—"

"I just need to do something first."

"You need to surrender."

"I will, but . . ."

"But what? Are you out of your mind?"

Maybe. "Uh, no."

"Where the hell are you?"

I said nothing.

"Jake? This isn't a game. Where are you?"

"I'll call you back."

I quickly hung up, mad at myself. Calling Shanta had been a mistake. She was a friend, but she also had other responsibilities and agendas here.

Okay, deep breath. Now what?

I called Natalie's sister.

"Hello?"

It was Julie. I hung up. She was home. That was all I needed to know. The phone number for a taxi service had been prominently displayed in my motel room. I guess a lot of people don't like to come to or leave the Fair Motel with their real cars. I called that number and asked for a cab to pick me up at Target. I ducked into the men's room, did as much washing as a sink would allow, and changed into my new duds.

Fifteen minutes later, I rang Julie Pottham's doorbell.

She had one of those screen-glass doors in front of the wooden one, so she could open one, see who it was, but still be locked behind the glass. When Julie saw who was standing on her front stoop, her eyes grew big and her hand fluttered toward her mouth.

"Do you still want to pretend you don't know who I am?" I asked.

"If you don't leave right now, I am going to call the cops."

"Why did you lie to me, Julie?"

"Get off my property."

"No. You can call the cops, and they can drag me away, but I will come back. Or I'll follow you to work. Or I'll come back at night. I'm not going away until you answer my questions."

Julie's eyes darted left and then right. Her hair was still mousy brown. She hadn't changed much in the past six years. "Leave my sister alone. She's happily married."

"To whom?"

"What?"

"Todd is dead."

That slowed her down. "What are you talking about?"

"He was murdered."

Her eyes widened. "What? Oh my God, what did you do?"

"What? Me? No. You think . . . ?" This conversation was quickly spinning out of control. "It has nothing to do with me. Todd was found in the home he shared with his wife and two kids."

"Kids? They don't have kids."

I looked at her.

"I mean, she would have told me . . ." Julie's voice drifted off. She looked shell-shocked. I hadn't expected that. I figured that she knew what was going on, was part of it, whatever the hell "it" was.

"Julie," I said slowly, trying to get her refocused, "why did you pretend you didn't know me when I called?"

Her voice was still far away. "Where?" she asked.

"What?"

"Where was Todd murdered?"

"He lived in Palmetto Bluff, South Carolina."

She shook her head. "That makes no sense. You've made a mistake. Or you're lying."

"No," I said.

"If Todd was dead — murdered, according to you — Natalie would have told me."

I licked my lips, tried to keep the desperation out of my voice. "So you're in touch with her?"

No answer.

"Julie?"

"Natalie worried this might happen."

"What might happen?"

Her eyes finally found focus. They hit mine like a laser. "Natalie thought you'd come to me someday. She even told me what to say if you did."

I swallowed. "What did she say?"

" 'Remind him of his promise.' "

Silence.

I took a step closer to her. "I kept that promise," I said. "I kept it for six years. Let me in, Julie."

"No."

"Todd is dead. If there was a promise, I kept it. It's over now."

"I don't believe you."

"Check the Lanford website. You'll see an obituary."

"What?"

"On the computer. Todd Sanderson. Check his obituary. I'll wait."

Without another word, she stepped back and closed the door. I didn't know what that meant. I didn't know if that meant she was going to check the website or if she had had enough. I had nowhere else to go. I stayed there, facing the door, waiting. Ten minutes later Julie was back. She unlocked the screen door and gestured for me to come inside.

I sat on the couch. Julie sat across from me, stunned. Her eyes looked like shattered marbles.

"I don't understand," she said. "It says he's married with kids. I thought . . ."

"You thought what?"

She shook her head sharply. "Why are you so interested in this anyway? Natalie dumped you. I saw you at the wedding. I thought you'd never show up, but Natalie knew you would. Why? Are you some kind of masochist?"

"Natalie knew I'd show?"

"Yes."

I nodded.

"What?" she asked.

"She knew I'd have to see for myself."

"Why?"

"Because I didn't believe it."

"That she could fall in love with another man?"

"Yes."

"But she did," Julie said. "And she made you promise to stay away."

"I knew that promise was wrong. Even as I made it, even as I watched her exchange vows with another man, I never believed that Natalie stopped loving me. I know that sounds delusional. I know that sounds like I'm wearing the thickest pair of rose-tinted glasses in the history of mankind or I'm some sort of egomaniac who can't accept the truth. But I know. I know how I felt when I was with her — and I know how she felt. All that stuff we scoff at about two hearts beating as one, about sun shining on a cloudy day, about a connection that went beyond physical, beyond spiritual — now suddenly I got it. Natalie and I had it all. You can't lie about that. If there is a false note in that kind of love, you hear it. There were too many moments that stole my breath. I lived for her laugh. When I looked into her eyes, I could see forever. When I held her, I knew — once in a lifetime, if you're lucky. We'd found a place rare and special, a place with color and texture, and if you're this lucky, you regret any moment of your life that you're not in this place because it feels like a sad waste. You pity others because they will never know these continuous bursts of passion. Natalie made me feel alive. She made everything around us crackle and surprise. That's how I felt — and I *know* that Natalie felt the same. We weren't blinded by love. Just the opposite. It made us both clear-eyed and that was why it will never let me go. I should never have made that promise. There was confusion in my head but never my heart. I should have kept listening to my heart."

There were tears running down my face when I finished.

"You really believe that, don't you?"

I nodded. "No matter what you tell me."

"And yet —" Julie said.

I finished the thought for her. "And yet Natalie broke it off with me and married her old boyfriend."

Julie made a face. "Old boyfriend?"

"Yes."

"Todd wasn't an old boyfriend."

"What?"

"They'd just met. It was all ridiculously sudden."

I tried to clear my head. "But she said that they'd dated before, that they even lived together and were in love and they'd broken it off and then realized that they belonged together . . ."

But Julie was shaking her head. The floor underneath me gave way.

"It was a whirlwind romance," she said. "That was what Natalie told me. I couldn't understand the sudden rush to get married. But Natalie, well, she was an artist. She was unpredictable. She had, as you put it, these bursts of passion."

It made no sense. None of this made any sense. Or maybe, for the first time, the confusion was leading to some kind of clarity.

"Where is Natalie?" I asked.

Julie tucked her hair behind her ear and looked off.

"Please tell me."

"I don't get any of this," Julie said.

"I know. I want to help."

"She warned me. She warned me not to tell you anything."

I didn't know how to reply to that.

"I think it's best if you go now," Julie said.

No chance, but maybe it was time to circle in from another direction, keep her off balance. "Where is your father?" I asked her.

275

When I'd first confronted her at the door, a slow stun had come to her face. Now it looked as though I'd slapped her. "What?"

"He taught at Lanford — in my department even. Where is he now?"

"What does he have to do with anything?"

Good question, I thought. Great question even. "Natalie never told me about him."

"She didn't?" Julie gave a halfhearted shrug. "Maybe you two weren't as close as you thought."

"She came with me to campus and she never said one word about him. Why?"

Julie considered that for a moment. "He left us twenty-five years ago, you know. I was five years old. Natalie was nine. I barely remember him."

"Where did he go?"

"What difference does it make?"

"Please. Where did he go?"

"He ran off with a student, but that didn't last. My mother . . . She never forgave him. He got remarried and started a new family."

"Where are they?"

"I don't know and I don't care. My mother said he moved out west someplace. That's all I know. I had no interest."

"And Natalie?"

"What about her?"

"Did she have an interest in her father?"

"An interest? It wasn't up to her. He ran off."

"Did Natalie know where he was?"

"No. But . . . I think he's the reason Natalie was always so screwed up when it came to men. When we were little, she was convinced that one day Dad would come back and we'd be a family. Even after he remarried. Even after he had other kids. He was no good, Mom said. He was dead to her — and me."

"But not to Natalie."

Julie didn't reply. She seemed lost in a thought.

"What?" I asked.

"My mother is in a home now. Complications due to diabetes. I tried to care for her but . . ." Her voice faded away. "See, Mom never remarried. She never had a life. My father took all that away from her. And yet Natalie still longed for some kind of reconciliation. She still thought, I don't know, that it wasn't too late. Natalie was such a dreamer. It's like finding Dad would prove a point — like then she could meet a man that would never leave and that would prove that Dad didn't mean to leave us either."

"Julie?"

"What?"

I made sure that she was looking directly into my eyes. "She met that man."

Julie looked out her back window, blinked hard. A tear ran down her cheek.

"Where is Natalie?" I asked.

Julie shook her head.

"I won't leave until you tell me. Please. If she still has no interest in seeing me —"

"Of course she has no interest," Julie snapped, suddenly angry. "If she had an interest, wouldn't she have contacted you on her own? You were right before."

"About what?"

"About being delusional. About wearing those rose-tinted glasses."

"Then help me take them off," I said, unfazed. "Once and for all. Help me see the truth."

I don't know if my words reached her. I would not be dissuaded. I looked at her and maybe she saw that. Maybe that was why she finally caved.

"After the wedding, Natalie and Todd moved to Denmark," Julie said. "That was their home, but they traveled a lot. Todd worked as a doctor for a charity. I forget the name of it. Something about beginnings maybe."

"Fresh Start."

"Yes, that's it. So they traveled to poorer

278

countries. Todd would do medical procedures on the needy. Natalie would do her artwork and teach. She loved it. They were happy. Or so I thought."

"When was the last time you saw her?"

"At the wedding."

"Wait. You haven't seen your sister in six years?"

"That's right. After the wedding, Natalie explained to me that her life with Todd was going to be a glorious journey. She warned me that it might be a long time before I saw her again."

I couldn't believe what I was hearing. "And you've never gone over and visited? She's never come back?"

"No. Like I said, she warned me. I get postcards from Denmark. That's it."

"How about e-mail or talking on the phone?"

"She doesn't have either. She thought that modern technology was clouding her thinking and harming her work."

I made a face. "She told you that?"

"Yes."

"And you bought it? What if there was an emergency?"

Julie shrugged. "This was the life she wanted."

"Didn't you find this arrangement odd?"

"Yes. In fact, I made a lot of the arguments you're making now. But what could I do? She made it clear — this was what she wanted. This was the start of a whole new journey. Who was I to stand in the way?"

I shook my head in disbelief and to clear it. "When was the last time you got a postcard from her?"

"It's been a while. Months, maybe half a year."

I sat back. "So in reality, you don't know where she is, do you?"

"I would say Denmark, but in truth, no, I guess I don't. I also don't understand how her husband could have been living with another woman in South Carolina or any of this. I mean, nothing makes sense anymore. I don't know where she is."

A sharp knock on the door startled us both. Julie actually reached for my hand as though she needed comfort. There was a second knock and then a voice called out.

"Jacob Fisher? This is the police. The house is surrounded. Come out with your hands in the air."

CHAPTER 23

I refused to say a word until my attorney —
Benedict — was present.

That took some time. The lead officer
identified himself as Jim Mulholland of the
New York Police Department. I couldn't
figure out that jurisdiction. Lanford College
is in Massachusetts. I had killed Otto along
Route 91 still within that state. I had
ventured into Vermont and when they
picked me up I was in New Jersey. Other
than taking public transportation through
Manhattan, I could not figure out how the
NYPD could possibly be involved in this
mess.

Mulholland was a burly man with a thick
mustache that brought on visions of Mag-
num PI. He stressed that I was not under
arrest and that I could leave anytime, but
boy, they would really, *really* appreciate my
cooperation. He chatted politely, if not
inanely, as he drove me to a Midtown

precinct. He offered me soda, coffee, sandwiches, whatever I wanted. I was suddenly hungry and accepted. I was about to dig in when I remembered that it was guilty men who ate in custody. I had read that somewhere. The guilty man knows what is going on, so he can sleep and eat. It is the innocent man who is too confused and nervous to do either.

Then again, which was I?

I ate the sandwich and even enjoyed every bite. Every once in a while, Mulholland or his partner, Susan Telesco, a tall blonde with jeans and a turtleneck, would try to engage me in conversation. I would shake them off and remind them that I had invoked my right to counsel. Three hours later, Benedict showed up. The four of us — Mulholland, Telesco, Benedict, and yours truly — sat around a table in an interrogation room that had been done up to not be overly intimidating. Of course it wasn't as though I had a lot of experience in interrogation rooms, but I always expected them to be somewhat stark. This one was more a soft beige.

"Do you know why you're here?" Mulholland asked.

Benedict frowned. "Really?"

"What?"

"How did you expect us to answer that exactly? With a confession perhaps? 'Oh yes, Detective Mulholland, I assume you've arrested me because I shot up two liquor stores'? Can we skip amateur hour and just get to the heart of this?"

"Listen," Mulholland said, adjusting himself in the chair, "we're on your side."

"Oh boy."

"No, I mean it. We just need to clean up some details, and then we all go home better people for what happened."

"What are you talking about?" Benedict asked.

Mulholland nodded at Telesco. She opened a folder and slid a sheet of paper across the table. When I saw the mug shots — front view, side view — my blood hummed in my veins.

It was Otto.

"Do you know this man?" Telesco asked me.

"Don't answer." I wasn't about to, but Benedict put a hand on my arm just in case. "Who is he?"

"His name is Otto Devereaux."

The name sent a chill through me. They had shown me their faces. They had used at least Otto's real name. That could only mean one thing — they never intended for me to leave that van alive.

"Recently, your client stated that he had an altercation with a man matching Otto Devereaux's description on a highway in Massachusetts. In that statement, your client said that he had been forced to kill Mr. Devereaux in self-defense."

"My client retracted that statement. He was disoriented and under the influence of alcohol."

"You don't understand," Mulholland said. "We aren't here to bust his chops. If we could, we'd give him a medal." He spread his hands. "We are all on the same side here."

"Oh?"

"Otto Devereaux was a career scumbag of almost biblical proportions. We could show his full oeuvre, but it would take too long. Let's just lead with some of the highlights. Murder, assault, extortion. His nickname was Home Depot because he liked using tools on his victims. He enforced for the legendary Ache brothers until someone decided that he was too violent for them. Then he worked on his own or for whatever desperate bad guy needed a true sicko." He smiled at me. "Look, Jake, I don't know how you got the drop on this guy, but what you did was a blessing for society."

"So," Benedict said, "theoretically speaking, you're here to thank us?"

"Nothing theoretical about it. You're a hero. We want to shake your hand."

No one shook hands.

"Tell me," Benedict said, "where did you find his body?"

"That's not important."

"What was the cause of death?"

"That's not important either."

Benedict said, smiling broadly, "Is this really the way to treat your hero?" He nodded toward me. "If there is nothing else, I think we will be leaving now."

Mulholland glanced over at Telesco. I thought that I saw a small smile on her face. I didn't like it. "Okay," he said, "if that's how you want to play it."

"Meaning?"

"Meaning nothing. You're free to go."

"Sorry we couldn't help," Benedict said.

"Don't worry about it. Like I said, we just wanted to thank the man who took this guy out."

"Uh-huh." We were both standing now. "We can find our way out."

We were nearly out the door when Susan Telesco said, "Oh, Professor Fisher?"

I turned.

"Do you mind if we show you one more

photograph?"

They both looked up at me as though they couldn't be bothered, as though they had all the time in the world and my answer was meaningless. I could look at the picture or I could walk out the door. No biggie. I didn't move. They didn't move.

"Professor Fisher?" Telesco said.

She slid the photograph out of the folder facedown, as if we were playing blackjack in a casino. I could see the glint in her eye now. The room dropped ten degrees.

"Show me," I said.

She flipped over the photograph. I froze.

"Do you know this woman?" she asked.

I didn't reply. I stared at the photograph. Yes, of course, I knew the woman.

It was Natalie.

"Professor Fisher?"

"I know her."

The photograph was black-and-white. It looked like a still frame from some kind of surveillance video. Natalie was hurrying down a corridor.

"What can you tell me about her?"

Benedict put a hand on my shoulder. "Why are you asking my client?"

Telesco pinned me down with her eyes. "You were visiting her sister when we found you. Would you mind telling us what you were doing there?"

"And again," Benedict said, "why are you asking my client?"

"The woman's name is Natalie Avery. We've previously spoken at length to her sister, Julie Pottham. She claims that her sister lives in Denmark."

I spoke this time. "What do you want with her?"

"I'm not at liberty to discuss that."

"Then neither am I," I said.

Telesco looked at Mulholland. He shrugged. "Okay, then. You're free to go."

We all stood there, playing this game of chicken. To mix metaphors, I had no cards here so I was the first to blink. "We used to date," I said.

They waited for more.

Benedict said, "Jake . . . ," but I waved him off.

"I'm looking for her."

"Why?"

I glanced at Benedict. He seemed to be as curious as the cops. "I loved her," I said. "I never really got over her. So I was hoping . . . I don't know. I was hoping for some kind of reconciliation."

Telesco wrote something down. "Why now?"

That anonymous e-mail came back to me:

You made a promise.

I sat back down and pulled the photograph closer. I swallowed hard. Natalie's shoulders were hunched. Her beautiful face . . . I could feel myself well up . . . she looked terrified. My finger found her face, as if somehow she could feel my touch and would find comfort. I hated this. I hated seeing her so scared.

"Where was this taken?" I asked.

"It's not important."

"The hell it isn't. You're looking for her, aren't you? Why?"

They looked at each other again. Telesco nodded. "Let's just say," Mulholland began slowly, "that Natalie is a person of interest."

"Is she in trouble?"

"Not from us."

"What's that supposed to mean?"

"What do you think it means?" For the first time, I saw the facade drop and could see a flash of anger on Mulholland's face. "We've been looking for her" — he grabbed the photograph of Otto — "but so were he and his friends. Who would you rather found her first?"

I stared at the photograph, my vision blurring and clearing, when I noticed something else. I tried not to move, tried not to change the expression on my face. In the bottom right-hand corner, there was a time-date stamp. It read: 11:47 P.M., May 24 . . . six years ago.

This picture had been taken a few weeks before Natalie and I met.

"Professor Fisher?"

"I don't know where she is."

"But you're looking?"

"Yes."

"Why now?"

I shrugged. "I missed her."

"But why now?"

"It could have been a year ago. It could have been a year later. It was just the time."

They didn't believe me. Too bad.

"Have you had any luck?"

"No."

"We can help her," Mulholland said.

I said nothing.

"If Otto's friends find her first . . ."

"Why are they looking for her? Hell, why are you looking for her?"

They changed subjects. "You were in Vermont. Two police officers identified you and we found your iPhone up there. Why?"

"It is where we dated."

"She stayed at that farm?"

I was talking too much. "We met in Vermont. She got married in the chapel up there."

"And how did your phone end up there?"

"He must have dropped it," Benedict said. "By the way, can we get it back?"

"Sure. That can be arranged, no problem." Silence.

I looked at Telesco. "Have you been searching for her for the last six years?"

"In the beginning. But not so much in recent years, no."

"Why not?" I asked. "I mean, well, the same question you asked me: Why now?"

Again they exchanged a glance. Mulholland said to Telesco, "Tell him."

Telesco looked at me. "We stopped looking for her because we were sure that she was dead."

I had somehow expected that answer. "Why did you think that?"

"It doesn't involve you. You need to help us here."

"I don't know anything."

"If you tell us what you know," Telesco said, her voice suddenly hard, "we forget all about Otto."

Benedict: "What the hell is that supposed to mean?"

"What do you think it means? Your client claims self-defense."

"So?"

"You asked about the cause of death. Here's your answer: He snapped a man's neck. I have news for you. A broken neck is rarely the result of self-defense."

"First off, we deny that he had anything to do with the death of this felon —"

She put her hand up. "Save it."

"It doesn't matter," I said. "You can make all the threats you want. I don't know anything."

"Otto didn't believe that, did he?"

Bob's voice: *"Where is she?"*

Mulholland leaned close to me. "Are you dumb enough to think this is the end of it? You think they'll just forget about you now? They underestimated you the first time. They won't do that again."

"Who are 'they'?" I asked.

"Some seriously bad men," he said. "That's all you need to know."

"That makes no sense," Benedict said.

"Listen to me closely. They can find Natalie first," Mulholland said, "or we can. It's your choice."

Again I said, "I really don't know anything."

Which was true enough. But more than that, Mulholland had left off one last option, much as it might seem like a long shot. I could find her.

CHAPTER 24

Benedict drove. "You want to fill me in?"

"It's a long story," I said.

"It's a long drive. Speaking of which, where am I going to drop you off?"

Good question. I couldn't go back to campus, not only because I was unwelcome, but as Detectives Mulholland and Telesco reminded me, some very bad people might be interested in finding me. I wondered whether Jed and Cookie were part of the same bad people as Bob and Otto or if I had two different groups of bad people after me. Doubtful. Bob and Otto were cool professionals. Grabbing me had been another day at the office. Jed and Cookie were bumbling amateurs — unsure, angry, scared. I wasn't sure what that meant, but I suspected that it was important.

"I'm not sure."

"I'll start back toward campus, okay? You fill me in on what's going on."

So I did. Benedict kept his eyes on the road, nodding every once in a while. His face remained set, his hands always at ten and two. When I finished he said nothing for several seconds. Then: "Jake?"

"Yes?"

"You need to stop this," Benedict said.

"I'm not sure I can."

"A lot of people want to kill you."

"I was never popular to begin with," I said.

"True enough, but you've stumbled into some serious doo-doo."

"You humanities professors and your big words."

"I'm not joking," he said.

I knew that.

"These people in Vermont," Benedict said. "Who were they?"

"Old friends, in a way. I mean, that's the weirdest part. Jed and Cookie were both there the first time I met Natalie."

"And now they want to kill you?"

"Jed thinks that I had something to do with Todd Sanderson's murder. But I can't figure out why he'd care or how he knew Todd. There has to be some connection between them."

"A connection between this Jed guy and Todd Sanderson?"

"Yes."

"The answer is obvious, isn't it?"

I nodded. "Natalie," I said.

"Yep."

I thought about that. "The first time I saw Natalie, she was sitting next to Jed. I even had a passing thought that maybe they were dating."

"Well then," Benedict said, "now it sounds like all three of you have something of a connection."

"Meaning?"

"Carnal knowledge of Natalie."

I didn't like that. "You don't know that for sure," I protested weakly.

"May I state the obvious?"

"If you must."

"I've known my share of women," Benedict said. "At the risk of bragging, some might even call me an expert on the subject."

I made a face. "Risk?"

"Some women are just trouble. You understand what I'm saying?"

"Trouble."

"Right."

"And I guess you're going to tell me Natalie is one of these women."

"You, Jed, Todd," Benedict said. "No offense, but there is only one explanation for all this."

"And that is?"

"Your Natalie is a big ol' can of crazy."

I frowned. We drove a little more.

"I have that guest cottage I use as an office," Benedict said. "You can stay there until this all cools down."

"Thank you."

We drove a little more.

"Jake?"

"Yeah?"

"We always fall harder for the crazy ones," Benedict said. "That's our problem as men. We all claim we hate the drama, but we don't."

"That's deep, Benedict."

"Can I ask you one more thing?"

"Sure."

I thought I saw his grip tighten on the wheel. "How did you happen to see Todd's obituary?"

I turned to face him. "What?"

"His obituary. How did you see it?"

I wondered if the confusion was showing on my face. "It was on the front page of the college website. What exactly are you trying to ask?"

"Nothing. I was just wondering, that's all."

"I told you about it in my office — and you encouraged me to go down to the funeral, remember?"

"I do," Benedict said. "And now I'm encouraging you to let this go."

I didn't reply. We drove for a while in silence. Benedict interrupted it.

"One other thing that's bothering me," he said.

"What's that?"

"How do you think the police found you at Natalie's sister's house?"

I had wondered the same thing, but now I realized the answer was obvious. "Shanta."

"She knew where you were?"

I explained about my calling her and my stupidity in keeping the disposable phone. If the police can track you by your phone, it stood to reason that if they knew the number (which would have popped up on Shanta's caller ID), they could track you by a disposable phone too. I still had it in my pocket and debated chucking it out the window. No need. The cops weren't the ones I was worried about anymore.

After President Tripp requested my departure, I had packed a suitcase and my laptop and stored them in my office at Clark House. I wondered whether someone might be, I don't know, staking out my campus house or that office. It seemed like overkill, but what the heck. Benedict had the idea of having us park far away. We looked to see if there was anything suspicious. There wasn't.

"We can send a student in to pick up your stuff," he said.

I shook my head. "I already got one student hurt in this."

"There's no risk here."

"Still."

Clark House was closed. I carefully entered via the back entrance. I grabbed my stuff and hurried back toward Benedict's car. No one shot me. Score one for the good guys. Benedict drove to the back of his property and dropped me off at the guest cottage.

"Thank you," I said.

"I got a bunch of papers to grade. You'll be all right?"

"Sure."

"You should see a doctor about your head."

I did have a residual headache. If it was from some kind of concussion, exhaustion, stress, or some combination of those, I had no idea. Either way I didn't think a doctor could help. I thanked Benedict again and settled into the room. I took out my laptop and set it up on the desk.

It was time, I thought, to do some cyber-sleuthing.

You may wonder what qualifies me to be

a top-notch investigator or how I would know how to cyber-sleuth. I'm not and I don't. But I know how to type stuff in a Google search field. That was what I started to do now.

First, I searched for a date: May 24, six years ago.

That had been the date on the surveillance photograph the NYPD had shown me. It stood to reason that whatever had happened that day, well, it was probably a crime. It might have been reported in the news. Was that a long shot? I guess. But it could be a start.

When I hit the return button, a bunch of hits about a tornado in Kansas popped up first. I would need to narrow this down. I added "NYC" into the search field and hit the return button again. The first story told me that the New York Rangers had lost to the Buffalo Sabres 2 to 1. Second link: the New York Mets beat the Arizona Diamondbacks 5 to 3. Man, we are a sports-obsessed society.

I finally located a site that ran daily New York newspapers and their archives. Over the past two weeks, the front pages of many newspapers were discussing the brazen string of bank robberies in New York City. They hit at night and left no clue and had earned the nickname "the Invisibles." Catchy. Then I hit the link for the archives for May 24 six years ago and started cyber-paging through the metro sections.

Top stories for that day: An armed man attacked the French consulate. Police took down a heroin ring operated by a Ukrainian gang. A cop named Jordan Smith accused of rape was having his day in court. A house fire in Staten Island had been deemed suspicious. A hedge fund manager from Solem Hamilton had been indicted in some kind of Ponzi scheme. A state comptroller was accused of ethics violations.

This didn't help. Or maybe it did. Maybe Natalie had been part of the Ukrainian gang. Maybe she knew the hedge fund manager — the surveillance photo looked like the lobby of an office building — or the state comptroller. Where was I on that day six years ago? May 24. School would have been coming to a close. In fact, classes would probably be over right around then.

Six years ago.

My life had been in turmoil, as Benedict had recently reminded me at the Library Bar. My father had died of a heart attack a month earlier. My thesis wasn't going well. May 24. That would have been right around the time Professor Trainor had thrown his graduation party with the underage drinking. I had wanted him seriously censured, putting a bit of tension between Professor Hume and myself.

But my life wasn't the point here. Natalie's was.

The surveillance photograph had been taken May 24. I thought about that for a moment. Suppose there had been some kind of crime or incident on May 24. Okay, right, that was certainly the possibility I had been going on, but now I was following through on the thought. If the incident took place on May 24, when would the papers report it?

May 25, not May 24.

This was not a brilliant insight, but it did make some sense. I found the papers for May 25 and again searched the metro sections. Top stories: Local philanthropist Archer Minor was gunned down. A fire in Chelsea kills two. An unarmed teen was shot by police. Man kills his ex-wife. High school principal arrested for embezzling school funds.

This was a waste of time.

I closed my eyes and rubbed them. Giving up sounded really good right now. I could lie down and close my eyes. I could keep my promise and honor the wishes, it seemed, of the woman I thought was my true love. Of course, as Benedict had pointed out, maybe Todd and Jed thought that Natalie was their true love. A flush of something primordial — let's call it jealousy — whooshed through me.

Sorry, I didn't buy it.

Jed wasn't attacking me as a jealous lover. Todd . . . I didn't know what the hell was going on there, but it didn't matter. I couldn't back away. I wasn't built that way — who is, really? How could any reasonable person live with so many questions left unanswered?

A small voice in my head replied: Well, at least you'd *live*.

Didn't matter. Couldn't be done. I had been attacked, threatened, assaulted, arrested, and I had even killed a man . . .

Whoa, hold the phone. I had killed a man — and now I knew his name.

I leaned forward and googled a name: Otto Devereaux.

I expected to find an obituary on top. I didn't. The first hit was a forum for "gangster enthusiasts." Yes, for real. I clicked into the discussion boards, but you had to create a profile. I quickly did.

There was a topic called "RIP, OTTO." I hit the link:

Holy crap! Otto Devereaux, one of the toughest mob hit men and extortionists, got his neck snapped! His body was dumped on the side of Saw Mill Parkway like some piece of garbage. Respekt, Otto. You knew how to kill, bro.

I shook my head. What next — a fan site for convicted pedophiles?

There were about a dozen comments from people remembering some of Otto's most horrible deeds and, yes, praising his work. They say that you can find any sort of depravity on the Internet. I had stumbled across a site devoted to admirers of violent gangsters. Some world.

On the fourteenth comment, I hit pay dirt:

Otto is being laid to rest at the Franklin Funeral Home in Queens this Saturday. The funeral is private, so you can't go to pay your respects, but admirers can still send flowers. Here's the address.

The post listed an address in Flushing, Queens.

There was a sketchpad on the desk. I grabbed a pencil and leaned back with it. I wrote down Natalie's name on the left. I wrote down Todd's beneath it. I jotted down other names — mine, Jed, Cookie, Bob, Otto — any name I could come up with at all. Delia Sanderson; Eban Trainor; Natalie's father, Aaron Kleiner, and mother, Sylvia Avery; Julie Pottham; Malcolm Hume even. All of them. Then on the right side of the page, I drew a timeline from top to bottom.

Go back as far as I could. Where did this first start?

I didn't know.

So back to the beginning.

Twenty-five years ago, Natalie's father, who taught here at Lanford, had run off with a student. According to Julie Pottham, dear old Dad had relocated and remarried. The only problem was, there was no sign of him anywhere. How had Shanta put it? Like father, like daughter. Both Natalie and her father had seemingly vanished into thin air. Both were completely off the grid.

I drew a line connecting Natalie and her father.

How could I learn more about this connection? I thought about what Julie had said. Her information about her father's remarriage came from her mother. Maybe Mom knew more than she was saying. Maybe she had an address for Dad. Either way, I needed to talk to her. But how? She was in a home. That was what Julie had said. I didn't know which home and somehow I doubted that Julie would be forthcoming. Still, it couldn't be too difficult to track Mrs. Avery down.

I circled Sylvia Avery, Natalie's mother.

Back to the timeline. I moved up through the years until I reached twenty years ago when Todd Sanderson was a student. He had nearly been expelled after his father's suicide. I thought back to his student file and his obituary. Both had mentioned that Todd had made amends by launching a charity.

I wrote down *Fresh Start* on my pad.

One, Fresh Start had been birthed on this very campus in the wake of Todd's personal turmoil. Two, six years ago, Natalie told her sister that she and Todd were going to travel around the world doing good works for Fresh Start. Three, Delia Sanderson, Todd's real wife, told me that Fresh Start had been her husband's passion. Four, Professor Hume, my very own beloved mentor, had been the faculty adviser during Fresh Start's creation.

I started tapping the paper with my pencil. Fresh Start was all over this. Whatever "this" was.

I needed to look into that charity. If Natalie had indeed traveled for Fresh Start, someone there might at the very least have a lead on where she was. Again I started doing web searches. Fresh Start helped people get new starts, though the work seemed a bit unfocused. They worked with kids who needed cleft palates repaired, for example. They helped with political dissidents who needed asylum. They helped people with bankruptcy issues. They helped you find new employment, no matter what issues you've had in the past.

In short, as the mantra on the bottom of the home page said, "We help anyone who truly, desperately needs a fresh start."

I frowned. Could that be more vague?

There was a link to donate. Fresh Start was a 501(c)(3) charity, so all contributions were tax deductible. No officers were listed — no mention of Todd Sanderson or Malcolm Hume or anyone. There was no office address. The phone number had an 843 area code — South Carolina. I dialed the number. An answering machine picked up. I didn't leave a message.

I found a company online that investigates various charities "so that you may give with confidence." For a small fee, they would send you a complete report on any charity, including an IRS Form 990 (whatever that was) and a "comprehensive analysis with full financial data, mission-driven decisions, officers' biographies, charity holdings, money spent on fund-raising and all other activities." I paid the small fee. An e-mail came to me saying that the report would be in my e-mail the following day.

I could wait that long. My head throbbed like a stubbed toe. My craving for sleep was overwhelming, emanating from the marrow of my bones. Tomorrow morning I would head to Otto Devereaux's funeral, but for now, the body needed rest and nourishment. I took a shower, grabbed a bite to eat, and slept the sleep of the dead, which, based on what was going on around me, seemed apropos.

CHAPTER 25

Benedict leaned into the car window of his own car. "I don't like this."

I didn't bother responding. We had been through this a dozen times already. "Thanks for letting me borrow your car."

I had left my car with its altered license plate on the street in Greenfield. At some point I would have to figure out a way to retrieve it, but it could wait.

"I can go with you," Benedict said.

"You have a class."

Benedict didn't argue. We never miss class. I had hurt enough students, in ways small and big, by taking up this bizarre quest. I wouldn't allow more to pay even a minor price.

"So your plan is to show up at this gangster's funeral?"

"More or less."

"Sounds like less to me."

Hard to argue. I planned on staking out

Otto Devereaux's funeral. My hope was that I could somehow learn why he attacked me, who he worked for, why they were searching for Natalie. I wasn't big on the details — like how I'd accomplish this — but I had no job right now and sitting around idly waiting to be found by Bob or Jed didn't seem like a terrific alternative either.

Better to be proactive. That was what I would tell my students.

Route 95 in Connecticut and New York is basically a series of construction areas masquerading as an interstate highway. Still I made decent time. The Franklin Funeral Home was located on Northern Boulevard in the Flushing section of Queens. For some odd reason, the picture on their website was of Central Park's beloved Bow Bridge, a place you've seen lovers get married in pretty much every romantic comedy that takes place in Manhattan. I had no idea why they had that, as opposed to the photographs of their actual funeral home, until I pulled up to it.

Some final resting spot.

The Franklin Funeral Home looked as though it'd been built to house two dentists' offices with maybe room for a proctologist, circa 1978. The facade was the yellowing stucco of a smoker's teeth. Weddings, parties, celebrations often reflect the celebrants. Funerals rarely do. Death is truly the great equalizer, so much so that all funeral services, except the ones in movies, end up being the same. They are always colorless and rote and offer not so much solace and comfort as formula and ritual.

So now what? I couldn't just go in. Suppose Bob was there? I could try to stay in the back, but guys my size do not blend well. There was a man in a black suit directing people where to park. I pulled up and tried to smile as though I was heading for a funeral, whatever that meant. The man in the black suit asked, "Are you here for the Devereaux or Johnson funeral?"

Because I was quick on my feet, I said, "Johnson."

"You can park on the left."

I pulled into the spacious lot. The Johnson funeral, it seemed, was taking place by the front entrance. There was a tent set up out back for Devereaux's. I found a parking spot in the right corner. I backed into it, giving me a perfect view of the Devereaux tent. If by some chance someone in the Johnson party or the Franklin Funeral staff noticed me, I could pull off being bereaved and needing a moment.

I thought back to the last time I was at a

funeral, just six days ago in that small white chapel in Palmetto Bluff. If I still had my timeline on me, there would be a six-year gap between a wedding in one white chapel and a funeral in another. Six years. I wondered how many of those days passed without Natalie in some way crossing my mind, and I realized that the answer was none.

But right now, the bigger question was, what had those six years been like for her?

A stretch limousine pulled up to the front of the tent. Another strange death ritual: The one time we all get to ride in cars we equate with luxury and excess is when we are mourning the death of a beloved. Then again, when better? Two dark-suited men came over and opened the limo doors, red-carpet style. A slender woman in her mid-thirties was helped out. She was holding hands with a long-haired little boy who looked to be six or seven. The little boy wore a black suit, which struck me as borderline obscene. Little boys should never wear black suits.

The obvious had not dawned on me until this very moment: Otto might have had a family. Otto might have had a slender wife who shared his bed and dreams. He might have had a long-haired son who loved him and played ball with him in the yard. Other people poured out of the car. An elderly woman wept hard in a handkerchief kept crumpled up in her fist. She had to be half carried toward the tent by a couple in their thirties. Otto's mother and maybe siblings, I didn't know. The family made a receiving line by the front of the tent. They greeted mourners, the devastation obvious in their bearings and on their faces. The little boy looked lost, confused, scared, like someone had sneaked up on him and punched him in the stomach.

That someone being me.

I sat perfectly still. I had thought about Otto as some contained entity. I thought killing him was merely a personal tragedy, the end of one isolated human life. But none of us are truly contained. Death ripples, echoes.

In the end though, hard as it might have been to watch the result of my actions, it didn't change the fact that my actions were justified. I sat a little straighter and kept a closer eye on the mourners. I expected that the line would look like a casting call for *Sopranos* extras. There were some of those, no question about it, but the crowd was a pretty varied bunch. They shook hands with the family, embraced them, offered kisses.

Some held the hugs a long time. Some did the quick back-pat and release. At one point, the woman I pegged as Otto's mother nearly fainted, but two men caught her.

I had killed her son. The thought was both obvious and surreal.

Another stretch limousine pulled up and stopped directly in front of the receiving line. Everyone seemed to freeze for a moment. Two men who looked like New York Jets offensive linemen opened the back door. A tall, skinny man with slicked-down hair stepped out. I saw the crowd start whispering. The man was in his seventies, I'd guess, and looked vaguely familiar, but I couldn't place him. The man didn't wait at the end of the line — the line parted for him like the Red Sea for Moses. The man had one of those thin mustaches that looked as though it'd been sketched on with a pencil. He nodded as he approached the family, accepting handshakes and greetings.

Whoever this guy was, he was important.

The thin man with the thin mustache stopped and greeted each family member. One — a guy I pegged as Otto's brother-in-law — took a knee. The thin man shook his head, and the man apologetically stood back up. One of the offensive linemen stayed a step in front of the thin man. The other stayed a step behind him. No one followed them down the receiving line.

When the thin man shook hands with Otto's mother, the final person on the line, he turned and headed back toward his limo. One of the offensive linemen opened the back door. The thin man slid inside. The door closed. One offensive lineman drove. The other sat in the passenger seat. The stretch limousine was put in reverse. Everyone stayed still as the thin man made his exit.

For a full minute after he was gone, no one moved. I saw one woman cross herself. Then the line started up again. The family accepted condolences. I waited, wondering who the thin man was and if it mattered. Otto's mother started sobbing again.

As I watched, her knees buckled. She fell into the arms of a man, sobbing into his chest. I froze. The man helped her back up and let her cry. I could see him stroke her back and offer her words of condolence. She held on for a long time. The man stood and waited with extreme patience.

It was Bob.

I ducked down in my seat, even though I was probably a solid hundred yards away. My heart started pounding. I took a deep breath and risked another look. Bob was gently pulling Otto's mom off him. He smiled at her and moved toward a group of men standing maybe ten yards away.

There were five of them. One produced a pack of cigarettes. All the men took a cigarette, except Bob. Good to know my gangster was somewhat health conscious. I took out my phone, found the camera app, and zoomed onto Bob's face. I snapped four photos.

So now what?

Wait here, I guessed. Wait for the funeral and then follow Bob home.

And then?

I didn't know. I really didn't. The key was to find out his real name and identity and hope that led to his motive for asking about Natalie. He had clearly been the boss. He'd have to know the reasons, right? I could also just watch him get in his car and then I could write down his license plate number. Maybe Shanta would help track down his real name from that, except that I no longer fully trusted her and for all I knew, Bob had driven to the funeral with his smoker pals.

Four of the men peeled off the group and headed inside, leaving Bob alone with one guy. The guy was younger and wore a suit so shiny it looked like a disco ball. Bob seemed to be giving Shiny Suit instructions.

Shiny Suit nodded a lot. When Bob was done, he headed into the funeral. Shiny Suit did not. Instead he swaggered with almost cartoon exaggeration in the other direction, toward a bright white Cadillac Escalade.

I bit my lower lip, trying to decide what to do. The funeral would take some time — half an hour, hour, something like that. There was no reason to just sit here. I might as well follow Shiny Suit and see where it led.

I started up the car and pulled onto Northern Boulevard behind him. This felt weird — "tailing a perp" — but it seemed a day for the weird. I didn't know how far to stay behind the Escalade. Would he spot me following him? I doubted it, even though I had a Massachusetts license plate in the state of New York. He made a right onto Francis Lewis Boulevard. I stayed two cars behind him. Crafty. I felt like Starsky and Hutch. One of them anyway.

When I'm nervous, I tell myself a lot of dumb jokes.

Shiny Suit pulled off at a mega-nursery called Global Garden. Great, I thought. He's picking up flower arrangements for Otto's funeral. Another weird thing about funerals: Wear black but kill something as colorful as flowers to decorate. The store, however, was closed. I wasn't sure what to make of that, so I didn't make anything of it yet. Shiny Suit pulled in to the back. I did likewise, though I stayed to the side, at a pretty good distance. Shiny Suit stepped down from the driver's seat of the Escalade and swaggered over toward the store's back door. Shiny Suit was big on the swagger. I didn't want to prejudge but based on the company he kept, the glistening of his suit, and the poser-like swagger, I somehow suspected that Shiny Suit was what the students today technically refer to as a douchebag. He rapped on the back door with his pinkie ring and waited, bouncing on his feet like a boxer listening to the ring introduction. I thought the bouncing around was for show. It wasn't.

A kid — he could have been one of my students — wearing a bright green store apron and a backward-facing Brooklyn Nets baseball cap opened the door, stepped out, and Shiny Suit sucker-punched him in the face.

Oh man. What had I stumbled across?

The cap flew to the ground. The kid followed, holding his nose. Shiny Suit grabbed him by the hair. He lowered his face so that I feared he might bite the kid's probably-broken nose and started yelling at him.

Then he stood back up and threw a kick in the kid's ribs. The kid rocked back and forth in pain.

Okay, enough.

Working on a rather heady albeit dangerous blend of fear and instinct, I opened my car door. The fear could be controlled. I had learned how to do that during my years as a bouncer. Anyone with an iota of humanity experiences fear during physical altercations. That is how we are built. The key is harnessing it, not letting it paralyze or weaken you. Experience helps.

"Stop!" I shouted, and then — here was where the instinct part came in — I added, "Police!"

Shiny Suit's head spun toward me.

I reached into my pocket and took out my wallet. I flipped it open. No, I don't have a badge, but he would be too far away to see. My attitude would sell it. I stayed firm, calm.

The kid scrambled back toward the door. He stopped to scoop up his Brooklyn Nets baseball cap, jammed it onto his head with the bill facing back, and disappeared into the building. I didn't care. I closed my wallet and started walking toward Shiny Suit. He, too, must have had some experience in this. He didn't run. He didn't look guilty.

He didn't try to explain. He just waited patiently for me to approach.

"I have one question for you," I said. "If you answer it, we forget all about this."

"All about what?" Shiny Suit replied. He smiled. His tiny teeth looked like Tic Tacs. "I don't see anything to forget, do you?"

The iPhone was in my hand, displaying the clearest photo I had of Bob. "Who is this man?"

Shiny Suit looked at it. He smiled at me again. "Let me see your badge."

Uh-oh. So much for attitude selling it.

"Just tell me —"

"You ain't no cop." Shiny Suit found this funny. "You know how I know?"

I didn't respond. The door to the shop opened a crack. I could see the kid peeking out. He met my eye and nodded his gratitude.

"If you were a cop, you'd know who that is."

"So just tell me his name and . . ."

Shiny Suit started to reach into his pocket. He could have been reaching for a gun. He could have been reaching for a knife. He could have been reaching for a tissue. I didn't know which. I didn't ask. I probably didn't care.

I had had enough.

Without saying a word or issuing a warning of any sort, I snapped my fist into his nose. I could hear the cracking sound, like I'd stepped on a big beetle. Blood ran down his face. Even through the small crack in the door, I could see the kid smiling.

"What the — ?"

I snapped another punch, aiming again for the definitely-broken nose. "Who is he?" I asked. "What's his name?"

Shiny Suit cupped his nose as though it were a dying bird he wanted to save. I swept his leg. He went down in almost the exact spot the kid had been in less than a minute earlier. Behind him, the crack in the door disappeared. The kid wanted no part of this, I guessed. I didn't blame him. The blood was messing up my man's shiny suit. I bet it would wipe right off like vinyl. I bent down with my fist cocked.

"Who is he?"

"Oh man." Shiny Suit's voice had a tinge of awe in the nasal. "You're such a dead man."

That almost slowed me down. "Who is he?"

I showed him the fist again. He held up his hand in a pitiful defensive move. I could punch right through it.

"Okay, okay," he said. "Danny Zuker.

That's who you're messing with, pal. Danny Zuker."

Unlike Otto, Bob hadn't used his real name.

"You're a dead man, bro."

"I heard you the first time," I snapped, but even I could hear the fear in my voice.

"Danny ain't a forgiving guy either. Oh man, you are so dead. You hear what I'm saying? You know what you are?"

"A dead man, yeah, I got it. Lie on your stomach. Put your right cheek on the pavement."

"Why?"

I cocked the fist again. He lay on his stomach and put the wrong cheek down. I told him that. He turned his head the other way. I grabbed his wallet out of his back pocket.

"You robbing me now?"

"Shut up."

I checked his ID and read his name out loud: "Edward Locke from right here in Flushing, New York."

"Yeah, so?"

"So now I know your name. And where you live. See, two can play at that game."

He chuckled at that.

"What?"

"No one plays that game like Danny Zuker."

I dropped his wallet onto the pavement. "So you plan to tell him about our little altercation?" I asked.

"Our little what?"

"Are you going to tell him about this?"

I could see him smile through the blood. "The minute you're gone, bro. Why, you wanna threaten me some more?"

"No, not at all, I think you should tell him," I said, using my calmest voice. "But, well, how will it look?"

With his face still on the pavement, he frowned. "How will what look?"

"You, Edward Locke, just got taken down by some chump you don't know. He broke your nose, ruined your nice suit — and how did you save yourself from a bigger beating? Well, you sung like a bird."

"What?"

"You sold out Danny Zuker after two punches."

"I did not! No way I'd ever —"

"You gave me his name after only two punches. Do you think that will impress Danny? You seem to know him pretty well. How do you think he'll react to your story of selling him out like that?"

"I didn't sell him out!"

"Think he'll see it that way?"

Silence.

"Up to you," I said, "but here's what I might suggest. If you say nothing, Danny will never know about this. He won't know you messed up. He won't know someone got the jump on you. He won't know that you sold him out after only two punches."

More silence.

"We understand each other, Edward?"

He didn't reply and I didn't bother pushing for one. It was time to leave now. I doubted that Edward would be able to see the license plate from here — Benedict's license plate — but I didn't want to take any chances.

"I'm going to leave now. Keep your face down until I'm gone and then all this goes away."

"Except for my broken nose," he pouted.

"That'll heal too. Just stay down."

Keeping an eye on him, I walked backward to the car. Edward Locke never so much as budged. I got in my car and drove away. I felt pretty good about myself, which, ironically, was not something I was proud of. I got back on Northern Boulevard and drove past the funeral home. No reason to stop there. I had stirred up enough trouble for now. When I stopped at the next traffic light,

I quickly checked my e-mail. Bingo. There was one from the website who investigated charities. The subject read:

Here is your complete analysis on Fresh Start

It could wait till I was back, couldn't it? Or maybe . . . I kept my eyes peeled. It didn't take long. Two blocks up I spotted a place called the Cybercraft Internet Café. It was far enough away from the funeral home, not that I thought that they'd go searching nearby parking lots for me.

The place looked like an overcrowded tech department. There were dozens of computers lined up in narrow cubbies along the wall. They were all taken. No customer, other than yours truly, looked older than twenty.

"It's going to be a wait," a pure slacker yah-dude with more piercings than teeth told me.

"That's okay," I said.

It could indeed wait. I wanted to get home. I was just about to leave when a group of what had to be gamers let out a shout, slapped one another on the back, offered up complicated handshakes of congratulations, and rose from the terminals.

"Who won?" Slacker Yah-Dude asked.

"Randy Corwick, man."

Slacker Yah-Dude liked that. "Pay up." Then to me he said, "How long you need a terminal for, Pops?"

"Ten minutes," I said.

"You got five. Use terminal six. It's hot, man. Don't cool it down with something lame."

Terrific. I quickly signed on and opened up my e-mail. I downloaded the financial report on Fresh Start. It was eighteen pages. There was an income statement, expense graphs, revenue graphs, profitability graphs, liquidity graphs, a graph on useful versus depreciated life of building and equipment, something about liability composition, a balance sheet, something called a comparables analysis . . .

I teach political science. I do not understand business or numbers.

Toward the back I found a history of the organization. It had indeed been founded twenty years ago by three people. Professor Malcolm Hume was listed as the academic adviser. Two students were listed as copresidents. One was Todd Sanderson. The other was Jedediah Drachman.

My blood chilled. What's a common nickname for someone named Jedediah?

Jed.

I still had no idea what was going on, but it was all about Fresh Start.

"Time's up, Pops." It was Slacker Yah-Dude. "Another terminal will be open in fifteen."

I shook my head. I paid the rental fee and stumbled back to my car. Was my mentor somehow involved in this? What kind of good works did Fresh Start do that involved trying to kill me? I didn't know. It was time to head home and maybe discuss this all with Benedict. Maybe he'd have a clue.

I started up Benedict's car and, still dazed, headed west on Northern Boulevard. I had programmed the address for the Franklin Funeral Home into the GPS, but for the ride back, I figured that I could just hit "Previous Destinations" and Benedict would have his home in there. So when I hit the next red light, I turned the knob and clicked on "Previous Destinations." I was about to scan down for Benedict's address in Lanford, Massachusetts, but my gaze stopped cold at the first address, the place Benedict had most recently visited. The address didn't read Lanford, Massachusetts.

It read Kraftboro, Vermont.

CHAPTER 26

My world tilted, teetered, rocked, and flipped itself upside down.

I just stared at the GPS. The full address was listed as 260 VT-14, Kraftboro, Vermont. I knew the address. I had put it in my own GPS not long ago.

It was the address of the Creative Recharge Colony.

My best friend had visited the retreat where Natalie had stayed six years ago. He had visited the place where she married Todd. He had visited the place where, most recently, Jed and his gang had tried to kill me.

For several seconds, maybe longer, I could not move. I sat in the car. The car radio was on, but I couldn't tell you what was playing. It felt as though the world had shut down. It took reality a while to get through my haze, but when it did, it hit me like a surprise left hook.

I was alone.

Even my best friend had lied — check that: was *still* lying — to me.

Wait, I said to myself. There had to be a reasonable answer.

Like what? What possible explanation could there be for having that address in Benedict's GPS? What the hell was going on? Who could I trust?

I only knew the answer to that last question: No one.

I'm a big guy. I consider myself pretty independent. But right here, right now, I didn't think that I had ever felt so small or such gut-wrenching loneliness.

I shook my head. Okay, Jake, snap out of it. Enough with the self-pity. Time to act.

First I checked through the rest of the addresses in Benedict's GPS. There was nothing of interest. I did find his home address, so I set it up to lead me home. I started on my way. I flipped stations on the radio, searching for that ever-elusive perfect song. Never found it. I whistled along with what crappy song came on. It didn't help. The construction sites on Route 95 pounded the hell out of what was left of my psyche.

I spent most of the ride having imaginary conversations with Benedict. I actually rehearsed how I'd approach him, what I'd say, what he might answer, how I'd counter.

My grip on the wheel tightened when I pulled onto Benedict's street. I checked the time. He had a seminar for another hour, so he wouldn't be home. Good. I parked by the guest cottage and started toward his house. Again I debated what to do. The truth was, I needed more information. I wasn't ready to interrogate him yet. I didn't know enough. The simple Francis Bacon axiom, one we constantly stressed to our students, applied here: Knowledge is power.

Benedict hid a spare house key in a fake rock by his garbage can. One may wonder how I know this, so I will tell you: We are best friends. We have no secrets from each other.

Another voice in my head: Was it all a lie? Was our friendship never real?

I thought what Cookie had whispered to me in those dark woods: *If you don't stop, you'll kill us all.*

It was not meant to be hyperbole and yet here I was, not stopping, risking in a way I could still not fathom "all" these lives. Who was "all"? Was I always, in a sense, risking them? Was Benedict supposed to, I don't know, keep an eye on me or something?

Let's not get completely paranoid here.

Right, okay, a step at a time. There was

still the possibility of an innocent explanation for the Vermont address being on his GPS. I was not the most creative fellow. I have a habit of seeing things linearly. Maybe someone else borrowed his car, for example. Maybe someone even stole it. Maybe one of his late-night conquests wanted to visit an organic farm. Maybe I was once again practicing self-delusion.

I put the key in the lock. Was I really about to cross this line? Was I really going to snoop on my closest friend?

Bet your ass.

I entered through the back door. My apartment would kindly be described as functional. Benedict's resembled a third-world prince's harem. The den featured dozens of upscale, brightly hued beanbag chairs. There were vibrant tapestries on the walls. Slim African sculptures stood tall in all four corners. The room was over the top in a thousand ways, but I had always felt comfortable here. The big yellow beanbag was my favorite. I had watched a lot of football on that. I had played a lot of Xbox there.

The Xbox controllers were lying on it now. I stared down at them, though I didn't really think the controllers would offer up much information. I wondered what I was

330

looking for. A clue, I guess. Something that would tell me why Benedict would have driven up to that farm/retreat/kidnapper-hideout in Kraftboro, Vermont. What that might be, I didn't have the slightest.

I started going through the drawers. I searched the ones in the kitchen first. Nothing. I took the spare bedroom next. Nothing. I tried the closet and bureau in the den. More nothing. I headed into the bedroom and tried there. Nothing. Benedict had a desk in there with a computer on it. I checked the drawers underneath it. Nothing.

I found a file drawer. I checked the file cabinet. There were routine bills. There were student papers. There were class schedules. As far as anything truly personal, there was — drum roll, please — nothing.

Absolutely nothing.

I thought about that. Who doesn't have anything personal in their house? Then again what would you find in my house? More than this, certainly. There would be some old photographs, a few personal letters, something that indicated my past.

Benedict had none of that. So what?

I kept looking. I was hoping to find something that would link Benedict to the Creative Recharge Colony or Vermont or anything really. I tried to sit at his desk. Benedict is a lot smaller than I am, so my knees couldn't fit under the desk. I leaned forward and hit a key on the computer. The screen lit up. Like most people, Benedict had not shut down his computer. I suddenly realized how old-fashioned my house search had been thus far. No one keeps secrets in their drawers anymore.

We keep them on the computer.

I opened up his Microsoft Office and looked for the most recent documents. The first listed was a Word document called VBM-WXY.doc. Strange name. I clicked on it.

The file wouldn't open. It was password protected.

Whoa.

There was no point in trying to guess the password. I didn't have a clue. I tried to think of another way around that. Nothing came to mind. The rest of the files under "Recent" were student recommendations. Two were for medical schools, two for law schools, one for business school.

So what was in the password-protected one?

No idea. I clicked on the Mail icon on the bottom. The mail, too, required a password to enter. I looked around the desk for a slip of paper with a password — lots of people did that — but I found nothing. Another dead end.

Now what?

I clicked on his web browser. His Yahoo! news page popped up. Not much to learn here. I clicked the history page and finally hit something approaching pay dirt. Benedict had been on Facebook recently. I clicked the link. A profile for a man named, believe it or not, John Smith, came up. John Smith had no photograph of himself. He had no friends. He had no status reports. His address was listed as New York, NY.

This computer was signed in to this Facebook under the name John Smith.

Hmm. I thought about that. It was a fake account. I know a lot of people have them. A friend of mine uses a music service that goes through Facebook, showing all his friends every song he listens to. He didn't like that, so he created a dummy account like this one. Now no one can see what songs he likes.

The fact that Benedict had a dummy account meant nothing. What was more interesting though, as I typed his name into the search engine, was that Benedict Edwards didn't have a real Facebook account. There were two Benedict Edwardses listed in the

Facebook directory. One was a musician from Oklahoma City, the other was a dancer from Tampa, Florida. Neither was my Benedict Edwards.

Again, so what? A lot of people don't have Facebook accounts. I had one set up, but I've almost never used it. My profile picture was the yearbook photograph. I accepted friends maybe once a week. I probably had about fifty of them. I had originally signed up because people were sending me links to photographs and the like and the only way I could view them was to sign in to a Facebook account. Other than that, social media in general held very little appeal to me.

So maybe that was what Benedict had done. We were on many of the same e-mail lists. He had probably set up the dummy account so he could view Facebook links.

When I looked down the history page, that theory immediately imploded. The first listing was for a man on Facebook named Kevin Backus. I clicked the link. For a second, I thought that maybe it was another dummy account for Benedict, that Kevin Backus was merely an online pseudonym. But that wasn't the case. Kevin Backus was just some nondescript guy. He wore sunglasses in his profile picture and posed with his thumb up. I frowned at that.

I racked my brain. Kevin Backus. Neither his name nor his face was familiar.

I hit the "about" page. It was blank. It didn't list a home, a school, an occupation, any of that. The only thing that had been filled out was "in a relationship." He was, according to this, in a relationship with a woman named Marie-Anne Cantin.

I rubbed my chin. Marie-Anne Cantin. That name didn't ring a bell either. So, why had Benedict been on this Kevin Backus's page? I didn't know, but I suspected it was hugely important. I could start googling him. I looked again at the name Marie-Anne Cantin. It was typed in blue, meaning that she also had a profile. I only had to click on her name.

That was what I did.

When her page came up — when I saw Marie-Anne Cantin's profile photograph — I recognized the face almost immediately.

Benedict carried her picture in his wallet.

Oh man. I swallowed, sat back, caught my breath. Now I got it. I could almost feel Benedict's pain. I had lost the great love of my life. Benedict, it seemed, had done the same. Marie-Anne Cantin was indeed a stunning woman. I would describe her as high-cheekboned, regal, African American except, as I looked closer at her profile, that last part would be inaccurate.

She wasn't African American. She was, well, African. Marie-Anne Cantin, according to her Facebook page, lived in Ghana.

This fact was, I guess, interesting, albeit in a not-my-business way. Somewhere along the way, Benedict had met this woman. He had fallen in love with her. He carried a torch for her. What that could possibly have to do with his visiting Kraftboro, Vermont . . .

Hold the phone.

Hadn't I, too, fallen in love with a woman? I, too, still carried a torch for her. And I, too, had been up in Kraftboro, Vermont.

Was Kevin Backus Benedict's very own Todd Sanderson?

I frowned. That felt like a stretch. And wrong. Still, wrong as it felt, I needed to investigate this. Marie-Anne Cantin was the only lead I had right now. I clicked her "about" link. It was impressive. She had studied economics at Oxford University and had received a law degree at Harvard. She was legal counsel for the United Nations. She both lived in and was from Accra, the capital of Ghana. She was, as I already knew, "in a relationship" with Kevin Backus.

Now what?

I clicked on her pictures, but they were

set on private. No way to view them. An idea came to me. I hit the back arrow until I was on Kevin Backus's page again. His photographs were not set on private. I could see them all. Okay, good. I started clicking through them. I don't know why. I don't know what I expected to find.

Kevin Backus had his photographs in various albums. I started with the one simply titled "Happy Times." There were twenty, twenty-five pictures of either my boy Kevin with his main squeeze, Marie-Anne, or just Marie-Anne alone, obviously snapped by Kevin. They looked happy. Check that. She looked happy. He looked deliriously happy. I pictured Benedict sitting here, clicking through these photographs of the woman he loved with this Kevin guy. I could see the glass of scotch in his hand. I could see the room growing dark. I could see the blue light of the screen bouncing off Benedict's oversize Ant-Man glasses. I could see a lone tear running down his cheek.

Too much?

Facebook loved to torture ex-loves by keeping them front and center. You couldn't escape your exes anymore. Their lives were right here for you to see. Man, that sucked. So this was what Benedict did at night — tormented himself. I didn't know any of this for certain, of course, but I was pretty sure that was how it played out. I remembered that drunken night in the bar, the way he carefully took out the well-creased photograph of Marie-Anne. I could still hear the agony in his slurred words:

"The only girl I'll ever love."

Benedict, you poor bastard.

Poor bastard perhaps, but I still didn't have a clue what this meant or how it related to Benedict's recent visit to Vermont. I clicked through some more albums. There was one titled "Family." Kevin had two brothers and a sister. His mother appeared in a number of photographs. I didn't see any sign of a father. There was an album called "Kintampo Falls" and another for "Mole National Park." Most of the photographs there were shots of wildlife and natural wonders.

The last album was called "Oxford Graduation." Curious. That was where Marie-Anne Cantin had studied economics. Could Kevin and Marie-Anne have attended together? Could they be college sweethearts? I doubted it. It seemed like a long time to be "in a relationship," but, hey, who knew?

The photographs in this album were considerably older. Judging by the hairstyles, clothing, and Kevin's face, I would say at least fifteen, maybe twenty years earlier. I would bet that these photographs predated digital cameras. Kevin had probably scanned them into his computer. I skimmed through the thumbs, not expecting to see anything of interest, when a photograph in the second row made me pull up.

My hand was shaking. I grabbed the mouse, managed to move the cursor so that it hovered over the image, and clicked. The photograph grew bigger. It was a group photograph. Eight people, all in black graduation gowns, stood with big smiles on their faces. I recognized Kevin Backus. He stood on the far right next to a woman I didn't know. Their body language suggested that they were a couple. In fact, as I looked closer, it appeared that I was looking at four couples on their graduation day. I couldn't be sure, of course. It could have been that they were just lined up boy-girl, but I didn't think that was all.

My eye was immediately drawn to the woman on the left. It was Marie-Anne Cantin. She wore a killer smile, absolutely devastating. It was a smile that could twist a man's heart. A man could fall in love just being on the receiving end of that smile. A man would want to see the smile every day and be the one who could make it appear. He would want it all to himself.

Man, I got it, Benedict. I really, truly got it.

Marie-Anne was gazing lovingly at a man I didn't recognize.

At least, not at first.

He, too, was African or African American. His head was shaved. He had no facial hair. He did not wear glasses. That was why I didn't recognize him at first. That was why, even when I looked hard, I couldn't be sure. Except it was the only thing that made sense.

Benedict.

There were only two problems. One, Benedict hadn't graduated from Oxford University. Two, the name underneath the picture didn't read Benedict Edwards. It read Jamal W. Langston.

Huh?

Maybe it wasn't Benedict. Maybe Jamal W. Langston just looked like Benedict.

I frowned. Yeah, right, sure, that made sense. And maybe Benedict just happened to be carrying a torch for a woman who had long ago dated a man who looked just like him!

Dopey theory.

So what other theory did I have? The obvious: Benedict Edwards was really Jamal W. Langston.

I didn't get it. Or maybe I did. Maybe the pieces were finally, if not coming together, all on the same table. I googled Jamal W. Langston. The first link came from a newspaper called the *Statesman*. It was, according to the link, "Ghana's oldest mainstream newspaper — Founded in 1949."

I clicked the article. When I saw what it was — when I read the headline — I nearly screamed out loud, and yet, at the same time, some of those puzzle pieces were starting to come together.

It was Jamal W. Langston's obituary.

How could that be . . . ? I started reading, my eyes growing wide as a few of the puzzle pieces finally started to click into place.

From behind me, a tired voice sent a chill straight down my spine: "Man, I wish you hadn't seen that."

I slowly turned toward Benedict. He had a gun in his hand.

CHAPTER 27

If I'd been ranking the many surreal moments I'd been experiencing in recent days, having my best friend point a gun at me would have just elbowed its way into the top spot. I shook my head. How had I not seen it or sensed anything? His eyeglasses and their frames were beyond ridiculous. The haircut almost dared me to question his sanity or personal space-time continuum.

Benedict stood there wearing a green turtleneck, beige corduroys, and a tweed jacket — with a gun in his hand. Part of me wanted to laugh out loud. I had a million questions for him, but I started with the one I had been asking repeatedly from the beginning.

"Where's Natalie?"

If he was surprised by what I'd asked, his face didn't show it. "I don't know."

I pointed at the gun in his hand. "Are you

going to shoot me?"

"I took an oath," he said. "I made a promise."

"To shoot me?"

"To kill anyone who learned my secret."

"Even your maybe best friend?"

"Even him."

I nodded. "I get it, you know."

"Get what?"

"Jamal W. Langston," I said, gesturing toward the screen. "He was a crusading prosecutor. He took on the deadly drug cartels of Ghana without worry about his own safety. He brought them down when no one else could. The man died a hero."

I waited for him to say something. He didn't.

"Brave guy," I said.

"Foolish guy," Benedict corrected.

"The cartels swore vengeance on him — and if the article is to be believed, they got it. Jamal W. Langston was burned alive. But he wasn't, was he?"

"Depends."

"Depends on what?"

"No, Jamal wasn't burned alive," Benedict said. "But the cartels still got their vengeance."

The proverbial veil was being lifted from my eyes. Well, no, it felt more like a camera coming into focus. The indistinguishable blob in the distance was gaining shape and form. Turn by turn — or in this case, moment by moment — the focus was growing sharper. Natalie, the retreat, our sudden breakup, the wedding, the NYPD, that surveillance photo, her mysterious e-mail to me, the promise she forced me to make six years ago . . . it was all coming together now.

"You faked your own death to save this woman, didn't you?"

"Her," he said. "And me too, I guess."

"But mostly her."

He didn't respond. Instead Benedict — or should I call him Jamal? — moved toward the computer screen. His eyes were moist as he reached his finger out and gently touched Marie-Anne's face.

"Who is she?" I asked.

"My wife."

"Does she know what you've done?"

"No."

"Wait," I said, my head spinning with the realization. "Even she thinks you're dead?"

He nodded. "Those are the rules. That's part of the oath we take. It is the only way to make sure everyone stays safe."

I thought again about him sitting here, looking up that Facebook page, staring at those photographs, her status, her life updates — like the one about her being "in a relationship" with another man.

"Who is Kevin Backus?" I asked.

Benedict managed something like a smile. "Kevin is an old friend. He waited a long time for his chance. It's okay. I don't want her to be alone. He's a good man."

Even the silence pierced the heart.

"Are you going to tell me what's going on?" I asked.

"Nothing to tell."

"I think there is."

He shook his head. "I already told you. I don't know where Natalie is. I've never met her. I've never even heard her name except through you."

"I'm having trouble believing that."

"Too bad." He still had the gun in his hand. "What made you suspect me?"

"The GPS in your car. It showed you'd gone to the retreat in Kraftboro, Vermont."

He made a face. "Dumb of me."

"Why did you drive up there?"

"Why do you think?"

"I don't know."

"I was trying to save your life. I pulled into Jed's farm right after the cops. Seems you didn't need my help."

I remembered now — that car coming up

the driveway as the cops found my buried phone.

"Are you going to shoot me?" I asked.

"You should have listened to Cookie."

"I couldn't. You of all people should understand that."

"Me?" There was something akin to fury in his voice now. "Are you out of your mind? You said it before. I did all this to keep the woman I loved safe. But you? You're trying to get her killed."

"Are you going to shoot me, yes or no?"

"I need you to understand."

"I think I do," I said. "Like we said before, you worked as a prosecutor. You put some really bad people in jail. They tried to seek vengeance on you."

"They did more than try," he said softly, gazing again at Marie-Anne's photograph. "They took her. They even . . . they even hurt her."

"Oh no," I said.

His eyes filled with tears. "It was a warning. I managed to get her back. But that was when I knew for certain that the two of us had to leave."

"So why didn't you?"

"They'd find us. The Ghana cartel smuggles for the Latin Americans. Their tentacles can reach anyplace. Wherever we'd go, they'd track us down. I thought about faking both of our deaths, but . . ."

"But what?"

"But Malcolm said they'd never buy it."

I swallowed. "Malcolm Hume?"

He nodded. "See, Fresh Start had people in the area. They heard about my situation. Professor Hume was put in charge of me. He went off protocol though. Sent me here because I thought I could be of value as both a teacher and, if they needed me, someone to help others."

"You mean, someone like Natalie?"

"I don't know about that."

"Yeah, you do."

"It is very compartmentalized. Different people deal with different aspects and different members. I only worked with Malcolm. I spent some time in that training facility in Vermont, but until a few days ago I never knew about Todd Sanderson, for example."

"So our friendship," I said. "Was that part of your work? Were you supposed to keep an eye on me?"

"No. Why would we need to keep an eye on you?"

"Because of Natalie."

"I told you. I never met her. I don't know anything about her case."

347

"But she does have a case, doesn't she?"

"You don't get it. I don't know." He shook his head. "No one has ever said anything to me about your Natalie."

"But it makes sense, right? You'll grant me that?"

He didn't respond.

"You didn't call it a retreat," I said. "You called it a training center. How brilliant, really. Disguising it as some kind of artist retreat in such a remote area. Who'd suspect, right?"

"I've said too much already," Benedict said. "It isn't important."

"Like hell it isn't. Fresh Start. I should have guessed by the name. That's what they do. They give people who need it a fresh start. A drug cartel wanted you dead. So they saved you. Gave you a fresh start. I don't know what that entails — fake IDs, I guess. A plausible reason for a person to vanish. A dead body in your case. Or maybe you paid off a coroner or a cop, I don't know. Maybe some kind of training on how to behave, learn a language or a new accent, maybe wear a disguise like yours. By the way, can you take those stupid glasses off now?"

He almost smiled. "Can't. I used to wear contact lenses."

I shook my head. "So six years ago, Natalie is up at this training center. I don't know why yet. I assume that it has something to do with that surveillance photograph the NYPD showed us. Maybe she committed a crime, but my guess is, she witnessed something. Something big."

I stopped. Something here wasn't adding up, but I pushed on.

"We met," I said. "We fell in love. That was probably frowned upon or maybe, I don't know, she was up there for another reason when we started our relationship. I don't really get what happened exactly, but all of a sudden Natalie had to vanish. She had to vanish fast. If she wanted to take me too, how would your organization have reacted?"

"Not positively."

"Right. Like with you and Marie-Anne." I barely stopped to think about it now, the pieces just falling into place. "But Natalie also knew me. She knew how I felt about her. She knew that if she just broke up with me, I'd never buy it. She knew if she suddenly disappeared, vanished, I'd follow her to the ends of the earth. That I'd never give up on her."

Benedict just stared at me, not saying a word.

"So what happened next?" I went on. "I guess that your organization could have faked her death, like with you, but nobody would buy it in her case. If guys like Danny Zuker and the NYPD were looking for her, they'd need some pretty solid proof that she was dead. They'd need to see her body and with DNA, well, I don't know. It wouldn't work. So she staged that fake wedding. In many ways it was perfect. It would convince me and, at the same time, it would convince her sister and close friends. Several birds, one stone. She told me that Todd was an old boyfriend that she had recently decided was her true love. That was a lot more plausible than a guy she'd just met. But when I asked Julie about him, she said she had never met Todd. She just thought it was a whirlwind romance. Either way, even if we all felt it was odd, what could we do about it? Natalie was married and gone."

I looked up at him.

"Am I right, Benedict? Or Jamal? Or whatever the hell your name is? Am I at least close?"

"I don't know. I'm not lying. I know nothing about Natalie."

"Are you going to shoot me?"

He still had the gun in hand. "No, Jake, I don't think so."

"Why not? What about your precious oath?"

"The oath is for real. You have no idea how real." He reached into his pocket and pulled out a small box. My grandmother used to keep her pills in one just like it. "We all carry one of these."

"What's in it?" I asked.

He opened it. There was only one black-and-yellow capsule inside. "Cyanide," he said simply, the word chilling the room. "Whoever grabbed Todd Sanderson, well, he must have caught Todd off guard, before he had a chance to jam it in his mouth." He took a step toward me. "You see now, don't you? You see why Natalie made you promise?"

I just stood there, unable to move.

"If you find her, you kill her. It is as simple as that. If the organization is compromised, a lot of people will die. Good people. People like your Natalie and my Marie-Anne. People like you and me. Do you understand now? Do you understand why you have to let it go?"

I did. But I still raged against the machine. "There has to be another way."

"There isn't."

"You just haven't thought of it yet."

"I have," he said in the gentlest voice I

have ever heard. "More times than you can imagine. For years and years. You have no idea."

He put the pillbox back in his pocket.

"You know what I'm saying is the truth, Jake. You are my best friend. With the exception of a woman I will never get to see or touch again, you are the most important person in my life. Please, Jake. Please don't make me kill you."

CHAPTER 28

I almost bought it.

Check that: I did buy it for a long while. At first blush, Benedict — he wanted to make sure that I always called him that, that there would never be any slipup — seemed to be absolutely right. I had to back off.

I didn't know all the details, of course. I didn't know what the full deal was with Fresh Start. I didn't know for certain why Natalie had vanished or where she had gone. Truth was, I didn't even know if she was alive. The NYPD had suspected that she was dead. I didn't know why, but they probably surmised that if guys like Danny Zuker and Otto Devereaux want you dead, someone like Natalie doesn't survive and stay out of sight for six years.

There was more I didn't know. I didn't know how Fresh Start worked or about the training center doubling as a retreat or about Jed or Cookie or what role everyone played in this organization. I didn't know how many people they'd helped vanish or when they had started, though according to that charity report, it all began twenty years ago, when Todd Sanderson was a student. I could probably build a comfortable house with what I didn't know. That no longer mattered. What did matter, of course, was that lives were at stake. I understood the oath. I understood that those who had made such sacrifices and taken such risks would kill to protect themselves and their loved ones.

There was also tremendous comfort in knowing that my relationship with Natalie had not been a lie, that she had, it seemed, sacrificed the truest love I'd ever known in order to save our lives. But that knowledge and its accompanying utter helplessness tore a hole straight through my heart. The pain was back — different maybe, but even more potent.

How to lessen that pain? Yep, you guessed it. Benedict and I hit the Library Bar. We didn't pretend the arms of a stranger would help this time. We knew that only friends like Jack Daniel's and Ketel One could blot out or at least blur images this searing.

We were pretty deep into our Jack-Ketel friendship when I asked one simple question. "Why can't I be with her?"

Benedict didn't reply. He was suddenly fascinated by something at the bottom of his drink. He hoped that I'd let it go. I didn't.

"Why can't I vanish too and live alone with her?"

"Because," he said.

"Because?" I repeated. "What are you, five years old?"

"You'd be willing to do that, Jake? Give up teaching, your life here, all of it?"

"Yes." There was no hesitation. "Of course I would."

Benedict stared back down at his drink. "Yeah, I get that," he said in the saddest voice.

"So?" I said.

Benedict closed his eyes. "Sorry. You can't."

"Why not?"

"Two reasons," he said. "One, it isn't done. That's just part of our protocol, part of how we compartmentalize. It's too dangerous."

"But I could do it," I said, hearing the pleading in my voice coming right through the slur. "It's been six years. I say I'm moving overseas or —"

"You're talking too loudly."

"Sorry."

"Jake?"

"Yes?"

He met my eye and held it. "This is the last time we talk about this. Any of this. I know how hard it is, but you have to promise me you won't raise it again. Do you understand?"

I didn't reply directly. "You said there were two reasons I couldn't be with her."

"Right."

"What's the second?"

He dropped his eyes and finished his drink in one enormous gulp. He held the liquor in his mouth and signaled to the bartender for another. The bartender frowned. We had been keeping him busy.

"Benedict?"

He lifted his glass, tried to drain out the last drops. Then he said, "No one knows where Natalie is."

I made a face. "I get that there's secrecy —"

"Not just secrecy." He kept an impatient eye toward the bartender now. "No one knows where she is."

"Come on. Someone must."

He shook his head. "That's part of it. That's our saving grace. That's what's keeping our people alive right now. Or so I hope.

Todd was tortured. You know that, right? He could give up certain things — the retreat in Vermont, some members — but not even he knows where they go after they get their" — he made quote marks in the air — " 'fresh start.' "

"But they know who you are."

"Only Malcolm does. I was the exception because I came from overseas. The rest? Fresh Start set them up. They are given all the tools. Then, for everyone's safety, they go out on their own and tell no one where they end up. That's what I mean by compartmentalizing. We all know just enough — and not any more than that."

Nobody knew where Natalie was. I tried to let that sink in. It wouldn't. Natalie was in danger, and I could do nothing about it. Natalie was out there alone, and I couldn't be with her.

Benedict shut down then. He had explained as much as he ever would. I knew that now. As we left the bar and staggered back to the house, I made my own promise of sorts. I would back off. I would let it go. I could deal with this pain — I had dealt with it in other forms for six years — in exchange for the safety of the woman I loved.

I could live without Natalie, but I couldn't

live if I did something that would put her in danger. I had been warned repeatedly. Now it was time to listen.

I was out of it.

That was what I told myself as I stumbled into the guest cottage. That was what I planned to do as my head hit the pillow and I closed my eyes. That was what I believed when I flipped onto my back and watched the ceiling spin from too much drink. That was what I was sure was the truth up until — according the bedside digital alarm clock — 6:18 A.M., when I remembered something that had almost escaped my mind:

Natalie's father.

I sat up in bed, my entire body suddenly rigid.

I still didn't know what happened to Professor Aaron Kleiner.

There was, I supposed, the off chance that Julie Pottham was right, that her father ran off with a student and then remarried, but if that was the case, Shanta would have found him with no problem. No, he had vanished.

Just like his daughter Natalie would some twenty years later.

Perhaps there was a simple explanation. Perhaps Fresh Start had helped him too. But, no, Fresh Start had been created twenty years ago. Could Professor Kleiner's disappearance have been the organization's precursor? Malcolm Hume knew Natalie's father. In fact, Natalie's mother had come to him when Aaron Kleiner first abandoned the family. So maybe my mentor helped him vanish and then, what, years later, formed a group under the guise of a charity to help others like him?

Maybe.

Except twenty years later, his daughter suddenly had to vanish too? Does that make sense?

It didn't.

And why would the NYPD have shown me a surveillance photograph from six years ago? How could that relate to Natalie's father? What about Danny Zuker and Otto Devereaux? How could whatever was going on now, with Natalie, be related to her father who vanished twenty-five years ago?

Good questions.

I got out of bed and debated my next move. But what next move? I had promised Benedict that I would stay out of this. Moreover, I now understood in a very real, very concrete way the dangers of continuing this quest, not only for me but for the woman I loved. Natalie had chosen to vanish. Whether it was to protect herself or me or both, I had to not only respect her wishes but her judgment. She had scrutinized her predicament with more knowledge than I had, weighed the pros and cons, and decided that she had to disappear.

Who was I to mess that up?

So once again, I was about to let it go, was about to surrender to living with this horrible albeit necessary frustration, when another thought struck me so hard I almost stumbled. I stayed perfectly still, mulling it over in my mind, looking at it from every conceivable angle. Yes, it was there — something we had all overlooked. Something that changed the very nature of what Benedict had convinced me to do.

Benedict was heading to class when I sprinted outside. When he saw the look on my face, he froze too. "What's wrong?"

"I can't let it go."

He sighed. "We went over this."

"I know," I said, "but we were missing something."

His eyes moved from side to side as though he were afraid someone nearby might be eavesdropping. "Jake, you promised —"

"It didn't start with me."

"What?"

"This new danger. The NYPD asking

questions. Otto Devereaux and Danny Zuker. Fresh Start under siege. It didn't start with me. I didn't kick that all up by trying to find Natalie. That's not how it started."

"I don't understand what you're talking about."

"Todd's murder," I said. "That's what got me involved. You guys keep thinking that I'm the one who breached your group. I'm not. Someone already knew. Someone found out about Todd and tortured and killed him. That's how I got involved — when I saw Todd's obituary."

"That doesn't change anything," Benedict said.

"Of course it does. If Natalie was tucked away safely someplace, okay, I get it. I should leave it alone. But don't you see? She's in danger. Someone knows that she didn't really get married and disappear overseas. Someone went so far as to kill Todd. Someone is after her — and Natalie doesn't even know it."

Benedict started rubbing his chin.

"They're looking for her," I said. "I can't just back away. Don't you see?"

He shook his head. "I don't see." His voice was so weary, so broken and exhausted. "I don't see how you can do anything but get her killed. Listen to me, Jake. I get your point, but we've circled the wagons. We've protected the group. Everyone has gone underground until this blows over."

"But Natalie is —"

"Is safe, as long as you leave it alone. If you don't — if we are all discovered — it could mean death not only to her but to Marie-Anne and me and many, many others. I get what you're saying, but you're not seeing straight. You don't want to accept the truth. You want her so badly that you're twisting the facts into a call for action. Don't you see that?"

I shook my head. "I don't. I really don't."

He glanced at his watch. "Look, I have to go to class. Let's talk about this later. Don't do anything until then, okay?"

I said nothing.

"Promise me, Jake."

I promised. This time, however, I kept the promise for closer to six minutes than six years.

CHAPTER 29

I hit the bank and took out four thousand dollars in cash. The window teller had to get permission from the head teller, who had to find the bank manager. I tried to remember the last time I had used a bank teller rather than the ATM, but I couldn't dredge up the memory.

I stopped at CVS and bought two disposable phones. Knowing that the cops could trace your phone anytime it was on, I powered down my iPhone and stuck it back in my pocket. If I needed to make calls, I'd use the disposables and keep them off as much as possible. If the cops could trace these phones, so, I figured, might a guy like Danny Zuker. I didn't know this for a fact, but my paranoia level was justifiably at an all-time high.

I might not be able to stay off the grid long, but if I could for a few days, that would be all I'd need.

First things first. Benedict said that no one involved with Fresh Start knew where Natalie was. I wasn't so sure. The organization had started at Lanford at the behest, in part anyway, of one Professor Malcolm Hume.

It was time to call my old mentor.

The last time I saw the man whose office I now inhabit was two years ago at a poly-sci seminar on Constitutional abuses. He flew up from Florida looking robust and tan. His teeth were shockingly white. Like many retired Floridians, he appeared rested and happy and very old. We had a nice time, but there was a distance between us now. Malcolm Hume could be like that. I loved the man. Aside from my own father, he was the closest thing I had to a role model. But he had made it clear that retirement was an ending. He had always detested the academic hangers-on, those elderly professors and administrators who stayed on well past their expiration date, like aging ballplayers who won't face the inevitable. Once he left our hallowed halls, Professor Hume didn't enjoy returning. He didn't buy into nostalgia or living off past laurels. Even at the age of eighty, Malcolm Hume was a forward-looking guy. The past was just that to him. The past.

So despite what I considered our rich history, we didn't speak regularly. This part of his life was over. Malcolm Hume now enjoyed golf and his mystery book club and his bridge group down in Florida. Fresh Start, too, might have been something he put behind him. I didn't know how he'd respond to my call — if it would agitate him or not. I didn't much care either.

I needed answers.

I dialed his phone number down in Vero Beach. After five rings his machine picked up. Malcolm's booming recorded voice, graveled a bit with age, invited me to leave a message. I was about to, but then I realized that I didn't really have a callback number, what with my phone off most of the time. I would try him again later.

Now what?

My brain started buzzing again, settling for the umpteenth time on Natalie's father. He was the key here. Who, I wondered, could possibly shine some light on what happened to him? The answer was fairly obvious: Natalie's mom.

I considered calling Julie Pottham and asking her if I could speak to her mother, but again that felt like a complete waste of time. I headed to the local library and signed in to use the Internet. I searched for

Sylvia Avery. The address listed was Julie Pottham's in Ramsey, New Jersey. I leaned back for a second and considered that. I brought up the Yellow Pages website and asked for all assisted-living facilities in the Ramsey area. Three came up. I called them and asked to speak to Sylvia Avery. All three said that they had no "resident" (they all used that term) with that name. I headed back to the computer and spread out the search to Bergen County, New Jersey. Too many came up. I brought up the map and started calling the ones closest to Ramsey. On the sixth call, the operator at Hyde Park Assisted Living said, "Sylvia? I believe she's doing crafts with Louise. Would you like to leave a message?"

Crafts with Louise. Like she was a child at summer camp. "No, I'll call back, thanks. Do you have visiting hours?"

"We prefer that guests come between eight A.M. and eight P.M."

"Thank you."

I hung up. I checked the Hyde Park Assisted Living website. They had a daily schedule online. Crafts with Louise was listed. According to the itinerary, Scrabble Club was next, followed by Armchair Travel Social — I had no idea what that meant — and then Baking Memories. Tomorrow, there would be a three-hour outing to the Paramus Park Mall, but today, nope, everything was in house. Good.

I headed over to the rent-a-car dealership and asked for a mid-size. I got a Ford Fusion. I had to use a credit card, but that couldn't be helped. Time for another road trip — this time to visit Natalie's mother. I wasn't too worried about her not being there when I arrived. Residents in assisted living rarely take unscheduled trips. If by some chance she did, it would be brief. I could wait. I had nowhere else to go anyway. Who knows? Maybe another delightful evening with Mabel at the Fair Motel was in the cards.

When I had just hit Route 95, my mind immediately went to my ride on this very road just . . . wow, it'd been yesterday. I thought about that. I pulled over and took out my iPhone. I turned it on. There were e-mails and phone calls. I noticed three from Shanta. I ignored them. I brought up the web and did a quick Google search for Danny Zuker. There was a famous one working in Hollywood who dominated the hits. I tried putting in the name and the word *mobster*. Nothing. I brought up the forum for gangster enthusiasts. There was nothing on Danny Zuker.

Now what?

I could be spelling the name wrong. I tried Zucker and Zooker and Zoocker. Nothing significant. The exit toward Flushing was nearby. It would be a detour but not a horrible one. I decided to take a chance. I pulled off and found Francis Lewis Boulevard. The Global Garden mega-nursery and garden shop, the place where I had smacked Edward around, was open. I thought about those punches. I had always prided myself on being a rule follower, and I had self-justified my violence of yesterday by claiming that I was rescuing that kid, but the truth was, I didn't have to punch Edward in the nose. I needed information. I broke laws to get it. One could easily rationalize what I had done. The case for obtaining that information while giving Edward a touch of comeuppance was certainly compelling.

But more to the point — and this was something I would need to explore when I had the time — I wondered whether part of me enjoyed it. Did I really need to punch Edward to get the information? Not really. There were other ways. And awful as it was to even let the thought enter my head, hadn't a small part of me taken some pleasure in Otto's death? In my classes, I often talk about the importance of primitive instincts in philosophy and political theory. Did I think I was immune? Maybe the rules that I cherish aren't there to protect others so much as they're there to protect us from ourselves.

In his class on Early Political Thought, Malcolm Hume loved to explore the fine lines. I had balked at such talk. There is right. There is wrong.

So which side of the line was I on now?

I parked near the front, passed a big sale on "Perennials and Pottery," and headed inside. The store was huge. The pungent odor of mulch filled the air. I started toward the left, circled through fresh flowers, shrubbery, home accessories, patio furniture, soil, peat moss — whatever that was. My eyes checked out everyone with the bright green worker's apron. It took about five minutes, but I found the kid, interestingly enough, working in the fertilizer section.

There was a bandage on his nose. His eyes were black. He still wore the Brooklyn Nets baseball cap with the brim facing back. He was helping a customer, loading bags of fertilizer into a cart. The customer was telling him something. The kid nodded with enthusiasm. He had an earring. The hair that peeked out from under the cap looked streaky blond, probably something out of a bottle. The kid worked hard, smiling the entire time, making sure all the customer's needs were being met. I was impressed.

I moved so that I was standing behind him and waited. I tried to figure out an angle of approach so that the kid couldn't make a run for it. When he finished with this current customer, he immediately started looking for someone else to help. I moved up behind him and tapped him on the shoulder.

He turned, the smile at the ready. "Can I . . . ?"

He stopped when he saw my face. I was ready for him to break into a sprint. I wasn't sure what I'd do about it. I was close enough to grab him if he tried, but that would draw the wrong kind of attention. I braced myself and waited for his reaction.

"Dude!" He threw his arms around me, pulling me in tight for a hug. I had not expected that, but I went with it. "Thank you, man. Thank you so much."

"Um, you're welcome."

"Oh man, you're my hero, you know that? Edward is such a dickweed. Picks on me because he knows I ain't that tough. Thanks, man. Thanks a lot."

I said he was welcome again.

"So what's your deal?" he asked. "You

ain't a cop. I know that. So are you, like, I don't know, a superhero or something?"

"Superhero?"

"I mean, you hang out and rescue people and stuff. And then you ask about his MM contact?" His face suddenly darkened. "Man, I hope you got a whole Avengers group behind you or something if you're gonna take him on."

"That's what I wanted to ask you," I said.

"Oh?"

"Edward works for a guy named Danny Zuker, right?"

"You know it."

"Who is Danny Zuker?"

"Sickest dude ever. He'd kill a puppy because it got in his way. You can't believe the psycho-crazy in that guy. He makes Edward pee in his pants. For real."

Terrific. "Who does Danny work for?"

The kid took half a step back. "You don't know?"

"No. That's why I'm here."

"For real?"

"Yes?"

"I was joking, dude — about you being a superhero. I figured, hey, you saw me getting the crap beaten out of me and, I don't know, you're a big dude and you hate bullies and stuff. That wasn't it?"

"No. I need some information."

"I hope one of your superpowers is that you're bulletproof. If you mess with those guys . . ."

"I'll be careful," I said.

"I don't want you to get hurt or nothing, just because you did me a solid, you know?"

"I know," I said, trying my best competent professorial tone. "Just tell me what you know."

The kid shrugged. "Eddie is my bookie. That's all. I'm behind, and he enjoys hurting people. But he's small-time. Like I said, he works for Danny Z. Danny's way high up in MM."

"What's MM?"

"I'd bend my nose with my finger to show you what I mean, but my nose is friggin' killing me."

I nodded. "So Danny Z is with the Mafia? Is that what you're trying to say?"

"I don't know if they call it that. I mean, I only heard that word in really old movies and whatever. I can only tell you Danny Z works directly for the head of MM. That guy is a legend."

"What's his name?"

"You for real? You don't know? How do you live here and not know?"

"I don't live here."

"Oh."

"Are you going to tell me?"

"I owe you. So sure. Like I said, Danny Z is like the right-hand man for MM."

"And MM is?"

An elderly woman stepped between us. "Hello, Harold."

He gave her a big smile. "Hello, Mrs. H. How did those petunias work out for you?"

"You were so right about the placement in the window box. You're a genius with arrangements."

"Thank you."

"If you have time . . ."

"Let me just finish with this gentleman and I'll be right with you."

Mrs. H shuffled away. Harold watched her, smiling all the way.

"Harold," I said, trying to get him back on topic, "who is MM?"

"Come on, man, don't you read the papers? MM. Danny Z reports directly to the biggest, baddest boy of them all — Maxwell Minor."

Something clicked. My face must have shown it because Harold said, "Whoa, dude, you okay?"

My pulse raced. My blood started humming in my ears. I could have looked it up on my iPhone, but I really needed a full screen. "I need to use a computer."

"Owner doesn't let anyone use the Internet here. It's all blocked off."

I thanked him and hurried out. Minor. I had heard that name before in connection to all this. I drove like a madman to Northern Boulevard. I found the same Cybercraft Internet Café. The same yah-dude was behind the desk. If he recognized me, he didn't show it. There were four terminals open. I grabbed one and quickly typed in the address for the New York local newspapers. Clicking on archives, I asked for May 25 again — the day after the surveillance photograph of Natalie had been taken. The computer seemed to be taking forever to grant my search request.

Come on, come on . . .

And then the headline popped up:

PHILANTHROPIST GUNNED DOWN

Archer Minor Executed in His Office

I wanted to shout "Eureka!" out loud, but I controlled myself. Minor. Oh, that couldn't be a coincidence. I clicked the article and read:

Archer Minor, son of reputed mob leader

Maxwell Minor and victim's rights advocate, was executed in his high-rise law office on Park Avenue last night, apparently the victim of a hit authorized by his own father. Known as the Minor son who's gone straight, Archer Minor worked with crime victims, even going so far as to publicly denounce his father in recent weeks and promising the DA's office to provide proof of his familial wrongdoings.

The article didn't have too many other details. I went back to the search engine and looked up Archer Minor. There was at least an article a day for the next week. I started sifting through them, looking for some kind of clue, some kind of connection between Archer Minor and Natalie. An article that came out two days after the shooting snagged my attention:

NYPD SEARCHING FOR WITNESS IN MINOR SLAY

A source inside the NYPD claims that the department is currently looking for a woman who may have witnessed the murder of local gangster's-kid-turned-hero Archer Minor. The NYPD would not comment directly. "We are actively seeking out many leads," Anda Olsen, department spokesperson, said. "We expect to have a suspect in custody soon."

It fit. Or it sort of fit.

I conjured up that surveillance photo of Natalie in what looked like the lobby of an office building. Okay, so now what? Put it together. Somehow, Natalie had been there that night, in Minor's law office. She saw the murder. That would explain the fear on her face. She ran off, hoping it would go away, but then the NYPD must have gone through the surveillance video and found her walking through the lobby.

There was still something big here, something I was missing. I kept reading:

When asked for a motive for the crime, Olsen said, "We believe that Archer Minor was killed because he wanted to do the right thing." Today, Mayor Bloomberg called Archer Minor a hero. "He overcame his family name and history to be one of the great New Yorkers. His tireless work on behalf of victims and in bringing those who commit violent crimes to justice will never be forgotten."

Many are wondering why Archer Minor, who had recently denounced his father,

Maxwell Minor, and his reputed organized-crime syndicate known as MM, was not placed in protective custody. "It was at his request," Olsen said. A source close to Minor's widow said that her husband had worked his whole life to make up for his father's crimes. "Archer started out just wanting to get a good education and go straight," the source said, "but no matter how fast he ran, Archer could never do enough to escape that horrible shadow."

It was not for a lack of trying. Archer Minor was a vocal advocate for crime-victims' rights. After attending Columbia Law School, he worked closely with law enforcement officials. He represented victims of violent crimes, trying to get lengthier sentences for those convicted and restitution for his clients' suffering.

The NYPD would not speculate, but one popular albeit shocking theory of the crime is that Maxwell Minor put out a hit on his own son. Maxwell Minor has not directly denied the charge, but he did release the following brief statement: "My family and I are devastated by the death of my son Archer. I ask the media to allow my family to mourn in private."

I licked my lips and hit the "next page"

link. When I saw the photograph of Maxwell Minor, I wasn't the least bit surprised. It was the man with the thin mustache from Otto Devereaux's funeral.

It was coming together now.

I realized that I'd been holding my breath. I sat back and tried to relax for a moment. I put my hands behind my head and closed my eyes. My mental timeline/connection sheet had all kinds of new little lines on it. Natalie had been there the night of Archer Minor's high-profile murder. She had, I theorized, witnessed the crime. At some point, the NYPD realized it was Natalie in that surveillance video. Natalie, fearing for her life, decided to hide.

I would continue to check, but it was a pretty safe bet that no one had ever been convicted of Archer Minor's murder. That was why the NYPD, all these years later, was still looking for Natalie.

So what happened next?

Natalie hooked up with Fresh Start. How did that happen? I had no idea. But, really, how did anyone hook up with Fresh Start? The organization kept an eye out, I supposed. Like with Benedict né Jamal. They approached those they felt needed and deserved their help.

Anyway, Natalie was sent up to the Creative Recharge Colony, which was, at least in part, a front for the organization. A brilliant one, I might add. Perhaps some of the attendees were really there for artistic reasons. Certainly Natalie was able to do both. Talk about hiding in plain sight. Natalie was probably told to hide there until they saw how the Archer Minor case played out. Maybe the cops would be able to make an arrest without her, and then she could return to her normal life. Maybe the NYPD wouldn't, or at least hadn't yet been able to, identify the woman in the photograph. Whatever. I was guessing here, but I was probably close.

At some point, reality reared its ugly head, crashing in and killing any hope of staying put with her new boyfriend. The choice became clear: Vanish or die.

So she vanished.

I read a few more articles on the case, but there wasn't much new. Archer Minor was portrayed as something of a heroic enigma. He'd been raised to be the baddest of bad guys. His older brother had been executed "gangland style" as the papers called it, while Archer was still in college. Archer was then supposed to take over the family business. It almost reminded me of *The Godfather* movie, except this particular good son never caved. Archer Minor not only flat-out refused to join MM, he worked tire-lessly to take it down.

Again I wondered what would have led my sweet Natalie to be in that law office late at night. She could have been a client, I supposed, but that wouldn't explain being there so late. She may have known Archer Minor, but I had no clue how. I was just about to give up on that, chalk up her visit to random chance, when I read a small, colorless obituary.

What the . . . ?

I actually had to close my eyes, rub them, and then read the obituary from the top again. Because this couldn't be. Just when things had been starting to make sense — just when I thought I was making some progress — I once again got smacked down from my blind side:

Archer Minor, age 41, of Manhattan, for-merly of Flushing, Queens, New York. Mr. Minor was a senior partner at the law firm of Pashaian, Dressner and Rosenburgh, located in the Lock-Horne Building at 245 Park Avenue in New York City. Archer received many awards and citations for his charitable work. He attended Saint

Francis Prep and was graduated summa cum laude from Lanford College . . .

CHAPTER 30

Through the phone line, I heard Mrs. Dinsmore sigh. "Aren't you supposed to be on suspension?"

"You miss me. Admit it."

Even in the midst of this ever-growing combination of horror and confusion, Mrs. Dinsmore made me feel grounded. There were few constants. Messing around with Mrs. Dinsmore was one of them. It was comforting to hold on to my own version of ritual while the rest of the world spun madly on.

"Suspension probably includes calling college support staff," Mrs. Dinsmore said.

"Even if it's just for phone sex?"

I could feel her disapproving glare from 160 miles away. "What do you want, funny man?"

"I need a huge favor," I said.

"And in return?"

"Didn't you hear what I said about phone sex?"

"Jake?"

I don't think she had ever called me by my first name.

"Yes?"

Her voice was suddenly tender. "What's wrong? Getting suspended is not like you. You're a role model here."

"It's a really long story."

"You were asking me about Professor Kleiner's daughter. The one you're in love with."

"Yes."

"Are you still looking for her?"

"Yes."

"Does your suspension have something to do with that?"

"It does."

Silence. Then Mrs. Dinsmore cleared her throat.

"What do you need, Professor Fisher?"

"A student file."

"Again?"

"Yes."

"You need the student's permission," Mrs. Dinsmore said. "I told you that last time."

"And like last time, the student is dead."

"Oh," she said. "What's his name?"

"Archer Minor."

There was a pause.

"Did you know him?" I asked.

"As a student, no."

"But?"

"But I remember reading in the *Lanford News* that he was murdered a few years ago."

"Six years ago," I said.

I started up the car, keeping the phone to my ear.

"Let me see if I understand this," Mrs. Dinsmore said. "You're looking for Natalie Avery, correct?"

"Correct."

"And in searching for her, you've needed to look at the personal files of not one but two murdered students."

Strangely enough, I hadn't thought of it that way. "I guess that's true," I said.

"If I may be bold, this isn't sounding like much of a love story."

I said nothing. A few seconds passed.

"I'll call you back," Mrs. Dinsmore said before hanging up.

The Hyde Park Assisted Living facility resembled a Marriott Courtyard.

A nice one, grant you, upscale with one of those Victorian gazebos in front, but everything screamed chain, impersonal, prefab.

The main building was three stories with faux turrets on the corners. An oversize sign read ASSISTED LIVING ENTRANCE. I followed the path, walked up a wheelchair ramp, and opened the door.

The woman at the desk had a helmety beehive hairdo last seen on a senator's wife circa 1964. She hit me with a smile so wooden I could have knocked on it for luck.

"May I help you?"

I smiled and spread my arms. I had read somewhere that spreading your arms makes you appear more open and trusting while folded arms make you seem the opposite. I didn't know if that was true. It felt as though I might swoop someone up and carry him away. "I'm here to see Sylvia Avery," I said.

"Would she be expecting you?" Beehive asked.

"No, I don't think so. I just happened to be in the neighborhood."

She looked doubtful. I couldn't blame her. I doubt too many people just happen to drop in on assisted-living facilities. "Do you mind signing in?"

"Not at all."

She spun an oversize guestbook, the kind I usually associate with weddings, funerals, and hotels in old movies, toward me and handed me a large quill pen. I signed my name. The woman spun the guestbook back toward her.

"Mr. Fisher," she said, reading the name very slowly. She looked up at me and blinked. "May I ask how you know Miss Avery?"

"Through her daughter Natalie. I thought it'd be nice to visit."

"I'm sure Sylvia will appreciate that." Beehive gestured to her left. "Our living room is available and inviting. Would it be okay if you met there?"

Inviting? "Sure," I said.

Beehive stood. "I'll be right back. Make yourself comfortable."

I moved into the available, inviting living room. I realized what was up. Beehive wanted the meeting in a public place just in case I wasn't on the up-and-up. Made sense. Better safe than sorry and all that. The couches looked nice enough, what with their floral prints, and yet they didn't look like something that could make one comfortable. Nothing here did. The décor resembled that of a model home perfectly laid out to accentuate the positives, but the smell of antiseptic, industrial-strength cleaner, and — yes, dare I say it — the elderly was unmistakable. I stayed standing.

There was an old woman with a walker and tattered bathrobe standing in the corner. She was talking to a wall, gesturing wildly.

My new disposable number started buzzing. I looked at the caller ID, but I had only given this number to one person: Mrs. Dinsmore. There was a sign about no cell phone use, but as I've now learned, I sometimes live on the edge. I moved into a corner, turned my face to the wall, à la the old woman with the walker, and whispered, "Hello?"

"I have Archer Minor's file," Mrs. Dinsmore said. "Do you want me to e-mail it to you?"

"That would be great. Do you have it right there?"

"Yes."

"Is there anything strange about it?"

"I didn't look at it yet. Strange how?"

"Would you mind taking a quick peek?"

"What am I looking for?"

I thought about that. "How about a connection between the two murder victims. Were they in the same dorm? Did they take any of the same classes?"

"That one is easy. No. Archer Minor was graduated before Todd Sanderson even matriculated here. Anything else?"

As I did the math in my head, a cold hand

387

reached into my chest.

Mrs. Dinsmore said, "Are you still there?"

I swallowed. "Was Archer Minor on campus when Professor Kleiner ran off?"

There was a brief pause. Then Mrs. Dinsmore said in a faraway voice: "I think he would have been a freshman or sophomore."

"Could you check to see if — ?"

"One step ahead of you." I could hear file pages being flipped. I glanced behind me. From across the room the old woman with the walker and tattered bathrobe winked at me suggestively. I winked back with equal suggestion. Why not?

Then Mrs. Dinsmore said, "Jake?"

Again she used my first name.

"Yes?"

"Archer Minor was enrolled in Professor Kleiner's class called Citizenship and Pluralism. According to this, he received an A."

Beehive returned, pushing Natalie's mother in a wheelchair. I recognized Sylvia Avery from the wedding six years ago. The years hadn't been so kind to her up until then and judging by what I was seeing now, that hadn't gotten any better.

With the phone still to my ear, I asked Mrs. Dinsmore, "When?"

"When what?"

"When did Archer Minor take that class?"

"Let me see." Then I heard Mrs. Dinsmore's small gasp, but I already knew the answer. "It was the semester Professor Kleiner resigned."

I nodded to myself. Ergo the A. Everyone got them that semester.

My mind was whirling a thousand ways to Sunday. Still reeling, I thanked Mrs. Dinsmore and hung up as Beehive rolled Sylvia Avery right to me. I had hoped that we would be alone, but Beehive waited. I cleared my throat.

"Miss Avery, you may not remember me —"

"Natalie's wedding," she said without hesitation. "You were the mopey guy she dumped."

I looked toward Beehive. Beehive put her hand on Sylvia Avery's shoulder. "Are you okay, Sylvia?"

"Of course I'm okay," she snapped. "Go away and leave us alone."

The wooden smile did not so much as flicker, but then again wood never does. Beehive moved back to the desk. She gave us one more look as though to say, *I may not be sitting right with you but I'll be watching.*

"You're too tall," Sylvia Avery said to me.

"Sorry."

"Don't be sorry. Just sit the hell down so I don't strain my neck."

"Oh," I said. "Sorry."

"Again with the sorry. Sit, sit."

I sat on the couch. She studied me for a bit. "What do you want?"

Sylvia Avery looked small and wizened in that wheelchair, but then again who looks big and hardy in them? I answered her with a question of my own.

"Have you heard from Natalie at all?"

She gave me the suspicious stink eye. "Who wants to know?"

"Uh, me."

"I get cards now and then. Why?"

"But you haven't seen her?"

"Nope. That's okay though. She's a free spirit, you know. When you set a free spirit free, it flies off. That's what it's supposed to do."

"Do you know where this free spirit landed?"

"Not that it's any of your business, but she lives overseas. Happy as can be with Todd. I'm looking forward to those two having kids one day." Her eyes narrowed a bit. "What's your name again?"

"Jake Fisher."

"You married, Jake?"

"No."

"Ever been married?"

"No."

"You got a serious girlfriend?"

I didn't bother answering.

"Shame." Sylvia Avery shook her head. "Big, strong man like you. You should be married. You should be making a girl feel safe. You shouldn't be alone."

I didn't like where this conversational route was taking us. It was time to change it up.

"Miss Avery?"

"Yes?"

"Do you know what I do for a living?"

She looked me up and down. "You look like a linebacker."

"I'm a college professor," I said.

"Oh."

I turned my body so that I could get a clearer look at her reaction to what I was about to say. "I teach political science at Lanford College."

Whatever color had remained in her cheeks drained away.

"Mrs. Kleiner?"

"That's not my name."

"It was though, wasn't it? You changed it back after your husband left Lanford."

She closed her eyes. "Who told you about that?"

"It's a long story."

"Did Natalie say something?"

"No," I said. "Never. Not even when I brought her to campus."

"Good." Her quivering hand came up to her mouth. "My God, how can you know about this?"

"I need to speak to your ex-husband."

"What?" Her eyes widened in fright. "Oh no, this can't be . . ."

"What can't be?"

She sat there, hand on mouth, saying nothing.

"Please, Miss Avery. It is very important I talk to him."

Sylvia Avery squeezed her eyes shut tight like a little kid wishing away a monster. I glanced over her shoulder. Beehive was watching us with open curiosity. I forced up a smile as fake as hers to show that all was okay.

Sylvia Avery's voice was a whisper. "Why are you bringing this up now?"

"I need to speak to him."

"It was such a long, long time ago. Do you know what I had to do to move past that? Do you know how painful this is?"

"I don't want to hurt anyone."

"No? Then stop. Why on earth would you need to find that man? Do you know what

392

his running off did to Natalie?"

I waited, hoping that she'd say more. She did.

"You need to understand. Julie, well, she was young. She barely remembered her father. But Natalie? She never got over it. She never let him go."

Her hand fluttered back toward her face. She looked off. I waited some more, but it was clear that Sylvia Avery had stopped talking for the moment.

I tried to stay firm. "Where is Professor Kleiner now?"

"California," she said.

"Where in California?"

"I don't know."

"Los Angeles area? San Francisco? San Diego? It's a big state."

"I said, I don't know. We don't speak."

"So how do you know he's in California?"

That made her pause. I saw something skitter across her face. "I don't," she said. "He may have moved."

A lie.

"You told your daughters he remarried."

"That's right."

"How did you know?"

"Aaron called and told me."

"I thought you didn't speak."

"Not in a very long time."

"What's his wife's name?"

She shook her head. "I don't know. And I would not tell you if I did."

"Why not? Your daughters, okay, I get that. You were protecting them. But why wouldn't you tell me?"

Her eyes shifted from left to right. I decided to bluff.

"I checked the marital records," I said. "You two were never divorced."

Sylvia Avery let out a small groan. There was no way Beehive could have heard it, but her ears still perked up like a dog's hearing a sound no one else could. I gave Beehive the same "all's fine" smile.

"How did your husband remarry if you two were never divorced?"

"You'll have to ask him."

"What happened, Miss Avery?"

She shook her head. "Let it be."

"He didn't run away with a coed, did he?"

"Yes, he did," she said. Now it was her turn to try to sound firm. But it wasn't there. It was too defensive, too practiced. "Yes, Aaron ran off and left me."

"Lanford College is a small campus, you know that, right?"

"Of course I know it. I lived there for seven years. So what?"

"A female student quitting to run off with

a professor would have made news. Her parents would have called. There would have been staff meetings. Something. I checked the records. No one dropped out when your husband vanished. No female student dropped her classes. No female student was unaccounted for."

This again was a bluff but a good one. Campuses as small as Lanford do not keep secrets well. If a student ran off with a professor, everyone, especially Mrs. Dinsmore, would know her name.

"Maybe she was at Strickland. That state college down the street. I think she went there."

"That's not what happened," I said.

"Please," Miss Avery said. "What are you trying to do?"

"Your husband vanished. And now, twenty-five years later, so has your daughter."

That got her attention. "What?" She shook her head too firmly, reminding me of a stubborn child. "I told you. Natalie lives overseas."

"No, Miss Avery. She doesn't. She never married Todd. That was a ruse. Todd was already married. Someone murdered him a little more than a week ago."

It was one bombshell too many. Sylvia

Avery's head lolled first to the side and then down as though her neck had turned to rubber. Behind her, I saw Beehive pick up the phone. She kept her eye on me and started talking to someone. The wooden smile was gone.

"Natalie was such a happy girl." Her head was still down, her chin on her chest. "You can't imagine. Or maybe you can. You loved her. You got to see the real her, but that was much later. After so much changed back."

"Changed back from what?"

"See, when Natalie was little, my God, that girl lived for her father. He'd come through the door after class, and she'd run to him screaming with joy." Sylvia Avery finally lifted her head. There was a distant smile on her face, her eyes seeing the long-ago memory. "Aaron would pick her up and twirl her and she'd laugh so hard . . ."

She shook her head. "We were all so damn happy."

"What happened, Miss Avery?"

"He ran off."

"Why?"

She shook her head. "It doesn't matter."

"Of course it does."

"Poor Natalie. She couldn't let it go and now . . ."

"Now what?"

396

"You don't understand. You can never understand."

"Then make me understand."

"Why? Who the hell are you?"

"I'm the man who loves her," I said. "I'm the man she loves."

She didn't know how to react to that. Her eyes were still on the floor, almost as though she didn't have the strength to lift even her gaze. "When her father ran off, Natalie changed. She grew so sullen. I lost that little girl. It was like Aaron took her happiness with him. She couldn't accept it. Why would her father abandon her? What did she do wrong? Why didn't he love her anymore?"

I pictured this, my Natalie as a child, feeling lost and abandoned by her own father. I could feel the pain in my chest.

"She had trust issues for so long. You have no idea. She pushed everyone away and yet she never gave up hope." She looked up at me. "Do you know anything about hope, Jake?"

"I think I do," I said.

"It's the cruelest thing in the world. Death is better. When you're dead, the pain stops. But hope keeps raising you way up high, only to drop you to the hard ground. Hope cradles your heart in its hand and then it crushes it with a fist. Over and over. It never stops. That's what hope does."

She put her hands on her lap and looked at me hard. "So, you see, I tried to take that hope away."

I nodded. "You tried to make Natalie forget about her father," I said.

"Yes."

"By saying he ran off and abandoned all of you?"

Her eyes began to well up. "I thought that was best. Do you see? I thought that would make Natalie forget him."

"You told Natalie that her father got remarried," I said. "You told her that he had other children. But all that was a lie, wasn't it?"

Sylvia Avery wouldn't answer. The expression on her face hardened.

"Miss Avery?"

She looked up at me. "Leave me alone."

"I need to know —"

"I don't care what you need to know. I want you to leave me alone."

She started to wheel back. I grabbed hold of her chair. The chair came to a sudden halt. The blanket on her lap fell toward the floor. When I looked down, my hand released the chair without any command from her. Half of her right leg had been amputated. She pulled the blanket up, slower than she had to. She wanted me to see.

"Diabetes," she said to me. "I lost it three years ago."

"I'm sorry."

"Believe me, it was nothing." I reached out again, but she knocked my hand away. "Good-bye, Jake. Leave my family alone." She started to wheel back. No choice now. I had to go nuclear.

"Do you remember a student named Archer Minor?"

Her chair stopped. Her mouth went slack.

"Archer Minor was enrolled in your husband's class at Lanford," I said. "Do you remember him?"

"How . . . ?" Her lips moved but no words came out for a few moments. Then: "Please." If her voice had sounded merely frightened before, she was downright terrified now. "Please leave this alone."

"Archer Minor is dead, you know. He was murdered."

"Good riddance," she said, and then she shut her mouth tightly, as though she regretted the words the moment they came out.

"Please tell me what happened."

"Let it go."

"I can't."

"I don't understand what this has to do with you. It isn't your business." She shook her head. "It makes sense."

"What does?"

"That Natalie would fall for you."

"How's that?"

"You're a dreamer, like her father. He couldn't let things go either. Some people can't. I'm an old woman. Listen to me. The world is messy, Jake. Some people want it to be black-and-white. Those people always pay a price. My husband was one of them. He couldn't let it go. And you, Jake, are heading down that same path."

I heard distant echoes in her past, from Malcolm Hume and Eban Trainor, from Benedict too. I thought about my own recent thoughts, about what it had felt like to punch and even kill a man.

"What happened with Archer Minor?" I asked.

"You won't quit. You'll keep digging until everyone dies."

"It will stay between you and me," I said. "It won't leave this room. Just tell me."

"And if I say no?"

"I'll keep digging. What happened with Archer Minor?"

She looked off again, fingers plucking at her lip as though in deep thought. I sat up a little straighter, trying to meet her eye.

"You know how they say the apple doesn't

fall far from the tree?"

"Yes," I said.

"That kid tried. Archer Minor wanted to be the apple that fell and rolled away. He wanted to be good. He wanted to escape what he was. Aaron understood that. He tried to help him."

She took her time adjusting the blanket in her lap.

"So what happened?" I asked.

"Archer was in over his head at Lanford. In high school his father could pressure the teachers. They gave him A's. I don't know if he really earned that high SAT score on his résumé. I don't know how he got past admissions, but academically, that boy was in over his head."

She stopped again.

"Please go on."

"There's no reason," she said.

Then I remembered something Mrs. Dinsmore had said when I first asked her about Professor Aaron Kleiner.

"There was a cheating scandal, wasn't there?"

Her body language told me that I'd hit pay dirt.

"Did it involve Archer Minor?" I asked.

She didn't reply. She didn't have to.

"Miss Avery?"

"He bought a term paper from a student who'd graduated the year before. The other student had gotten an A on it. Archer just retyped it and handed it in as his own. Didn't change one single word. He figured there'd be no way Aaron would remember. But Aaron remembers everything."

I knew the school rules. That sort of cheating was an automatic expulsion at Lanford.

"Did your husband report him?"

"I told him not to. I told him to give Archer a second chance. I didn't care about the second chance, of course. I just knew."

"You knew his family would be upset."

"Aaron reported it anyway."

"To whom?"

"The chairman of the department."

My heart sank. "Malcolm Hume?"

"Yes."

I sat back. "What did Malcolm say?"

"He wanted Aaron to drop it. He said to go home and think about it."

I thought back to my case with Eban Trainor. He had said something similar to me, hadn't he? Malcolm Hume. You do not get to be secretary of state without compromise, without cutting deals and negotiating terms and understanding that the world was loaded up with gray.

"I'm very tired, Jake."

"I don't understand something."

"Let it go."

"Archer Minor was never reported. He graduated summa cum laude."

"We started getting threatening phone calls. A man visited me. He came into the house when I was in the shower. When I came out, he was just sitting on my bed. He was holding pictures of Natalie and Julie. He didn't say anything. He just sat on my bed and held the pictures. Then he got up and left. Can you imagine what that was like?"

I thought about Danny Zuker breaking in and sitting on my own bed. "You told your husband?"

"Of course."

"And?"

She took her time on this one. "I think he finally understood the danger. But it was too late."

"What did he do?"

"Aaron left. For our sake."

I nodded, seeing it now. "But you couldn't tell Natalie that. You couldn't tell anyone. They'd be in danger. So you told them he ran off. Then you moved away and changed your name."

"Yes," she said.

But I was missing something. I was missing a lot, I suspected. There was something that wasn't adding up here, something niggling at the back of my brain, but I couldn't see it yet. How, for example, did Natalie come across Archer Minor twenty years later?

"Natalie thought her father abandoned her," I said.

She just closed her eyes.

"But you said that she wouldn't let it go."

"She wouldn't stop pressing me. She was so sad. I should have never told her that. But what choice did I have? Everything I did, I did to protect my girls. You don't understand. You don't understand what a mother has to do sometimes. I needed to protect my girls, you see?"

"I do," I said.

"And look what happened. Look what I did." She put her hands to her face and started to sob. The old woman with the walker and tattered bathrobe stopped talking to the wall. Beehive looked like she was readying herself to intervene. "I should have made up some other story. Natalie just kept pressing me, demanding to know what happened to her father. She never stopped."

I saw it now. "So you eventually told her the truth."

"It ruined her life, don't you see? Growing up thinking your father did that to you. She needed closure. I never gave her that. So, yes, I finally told her the truth. I told her that her father loved her. I told her that she didn't do anything wrong. I told her that he would never, ever, abandon her."

I nodded along with her words. "So you told her about Archer Minor. That was why she was there that day."

She didn't say anything. She just sobbed. Beehive was having no more of this. She was on her way over.

"Where is your husband now, Miss Avery?"

"I don't know."

"And Natalie? Where is she?"

"I don't know that either. But, Jake?"

Beehive was by her side. "I think that's enough."

I ignored her. "What, Miss Avery?"

"Let it go. For all our sakes. Don't be like my husband."

CHAPTER 31

When I reached the highway, I flipped on my iPhone. I didn't think anyone was tracking me but if they were, they'd find me on Route 287 near the Palisades Mall. I didn't think that would help them very much. I pulled over to the right. There were two more e-mails and three calls from Shanta, each more urgent than the last. That added up to five. In the first two e-mails, she politely asked me to contact her. In the next two, her request was more urgent. In the final, she threw out the big net:

To: Jacob Fisher
From: Shanta Newlin

Jake,
Stop ignoring me. I found an important connection between Natalie Avery and Todd Sanderson.

Shanta

Whoa. I took the Tappan Zee Bridge and pulled over at the first exit. I turned off the iPhone and picked up one of the disposables. I dialed Shanta's number and waited. She answered on the second ring.

"I get it," she said. "You're mad at me."

"You gave the NYPD that disposable number. You helped them track me down."

"Guilty, but it was for your own good. You could have gotten shot or picked up for resisting arrest."

"Except I didn't resist arrest. I ran away from some nut jobs who were trying to kill me."

"I know Mulholland. He's a good guy. I didn't want some hot-head taking a shot at you."

"For what? I was barely a suspect."

"It doesn't matter, Jake. You don't have to trust me. That's fine. But we need to talk."

I put the car in park and turned off the engine. "You said you found a connection between Natalie Avery and Todd Sanderson."

"Yep."

"What is it?"

"I'll tell you when we talk. In person."

I thought about that.

"Look, Jake, the FBI wanted to bring you in for a full-fledged interrogation. I told

407

them I could better handle it for them."

"The FBI?"

"Yep."

"What do they want with me?"

"Just come in, Jake. It's fine, trust me."

"Right."

"You can talk to me or the FBI." Shanta sighed. "Look, if I tell you what it's about, do you promise you'll come in and talk to me?"

I thought about it. "Yes."

"Promise?"

"Cross my heart. Now what's this about?"

"It's about bank robberies, Jake."

The new rule-breaking, live-on-the-edge me broke plenty of speed laws on the way back to Lanford, Massachusetts. I tried sorting out some of what I learned, putting it in order, testing out various theories and suppositions, rejecting them, trying again. In some ways, it was all coming together; in others, there were pieces that felt too forced for a natural fit.

I was still missing a lot, including the biggie: Where was Natalie?

Twenty-five years ago, Professor Aaron Kleiner had gone to his department chairman, Professor Malcolm Hume, because he caught a student plagiarizing (really, just outright buying) a term paper. My old mentor asked him, in so many words, to let it go — just as he had asked me to do with Professor Eban Trainor.

I wondered whether it was Archer Minor himself who threatened Aaron Kleiner's family or had it been hired hands of MM? It didn't matter. They intimidated Kleiner to the point where he knew that he had to make himself disappear. I tried to put myself in his place. Kleiner probably felt scared, cornered, trapped.

Who would he go to for help?

First thought again: Malcolm Hume.

And years later, when Kleiner's daughter was in the same situation, scared, cornered, trapped . . .

My old mentor's fingerprints were all over this. I really had to talk to him. I dialed Malcolm's number in Florida and again got no answer.

Shanta Newlin lived in a brick town house that my mother would have described as "cutesy." There were overflowing flower boxes and arched windows. Everything was perfectly symmetrical. I walked up the stone walk and rang the doorbell. I was surprised to see a little girl come to the door.

"Who are you?" the little girl said.

"I'm Jake. Who are you?"

The kid was five, maybe six years old. She was about to answer when Shanta came rushing over with a harried look on her face. Shanta had her hair tied back, but strands were falling in her eyes. Sweat dotted her brow.

"I have it, Mackenzie," Shanta told the little girl. "What did I tell you about answering the door without an adult around?"

"Nothing."

"Well, yes, I guess that's true." She cleared her throat. "You should never open a door unless an adult is around."

She pointed at me. "He's around. He's an adult."

Shanta gave me an exasperated look. I shrugged. The kid had a point. Shanta invited me in and told Mackenzie to play in the den.

"Can I go outside?" Mackenzie asked. "I want to go on the swing."

Shanta glanced at me. I shrugged again. I was getting good with the shrugs. "Sure, we can all go out back," Shanta said with a smile so forced I worried it required staples.

I still had no idea who Mackenzie was or what she was doing there, but I had bigger concerns. We headed into the yard. There was a brand-new cedar-wood swing set complete with rocking horse, sliding board, covered fort, and sandbox. As far as I knew, Shanta lived by herself, making this something of a curiosity. Mackenzie jumped on the rocking horse.

"My fiancé's daughter," Shanta said in a way of explanation.

"Oh."

"We're getting married in the fall. He's moving in here."

"Sounds nice."

We watched Mackenzie rock the horse with gusto. She gave Shanta the stink eye.

"That kid hates me," Shanta said.

"Didn't you read fairy tales when you were a kid? You're the evil stepmother."

"Thanks, that helps." Shanta turned her eyes up toward me. "Wow, you look awful."

"Is this the part where I say, 'You should see the other guy'?"

"What are you doing to yourself, Jake?"

"I'm looking for someone I love."

"Does she even want to be found?"

"The heart doesn't ask questions."

"The penis doesn't ask questions," she said. "The heart usually has a little more intelligence."

True enough, I thought. "What is this about a bank robbery?"

She shaded her eyes from the sun. "Impatient, are we?"

"Not in the mood for games, that's for sure."

"Fair enough. Do you remember when you first asked me to check on Natalie Avery?"

"Yes."

"When I put her name through the systems it got two hits. One involved the NYPD. That was the big one. She was a person of great importance to them. I was sworn to secrecy about it. You are my friend. I want you to trust me. But I'm also a law enforcement officer. I'm not allowed to tell friends about ongoing investigations. You get that, right?"

I gave the smallest nod I could muster, more so she'd move on than to signal agreement.

"At the time, I barely noticed the other one," Shanta said. "They weren't interested in finding her or even talking to her. It was the most casual of mentions."

"What was it?"

"I'll get to that in a second. Just let me play it out, okay?"

I gave another small nod. First the shrugs, now the nods.

"I'm going to offer up a show of good faith here," she said. "I don't have to, but I spoke to the NYPD, and they gave me permission. You have to understand. I'm not breaking any legal confidences here."

"Just friends' confidences," I said.

"Low blow."

"Yeah, I know."

"And unfair. I was trying to help you."

"Okay, I'm sorry. What's up with the NYPD?"

She gave me a second or two to stew. "The NYPD believe that Natalie Avery witnessed a murder — that she, in fact, saw the killer and can positively identify him. The NYPD further believe that the perp is a major figure in organized crime. In short, your Natalie has the ability to put away one of the leading mob figures in New York City."

I waited for her to say more. She didn't.

"What else?" I asked.

"That's all I can tell you."

I shook my head. "You must think I'm an idiot."

"What?"

"The NYPD questioned me. They showed me a surveillance video and said that they needed to talk to her. I knew all that already. More to the point, *you* knew that I knew that already. A show of good faith. Come off it. You're hoping to gain my confidence by telling me what I already knew."

"That's not true."

413

"Who's the murder victim?"

"I'm not at liberty —"

"Archer Minor, son of Maxwell Minor. The police believe that Maxwell put out the hit on his own kid."

She looked stunned. "How did you know that?"

"It wasn't hard to figure out. Tell me one thing."

Shanta shook her head. "I can't."

"You still owe me the show of good faith, right? Does the NYPD know why Natalie was there that night? Just tell me that."

Her eyes moved back to the swing set. Mackenzie was off the rocking horse and heading up toward the slide. "They don't know."

"No idea?"

"The NYPD went through the Lock-Horne Building's security footage. It is pretty state-of-the-art. The first video they got was of your girlfriend running down the corridor on the twenty-second floor. There was also footage of her on the elevator, but the clearest shot — the one they showed you — was when she was exiting out the lobby on the ground floor."

"Any video of the killer?"

"I can't tell you more."

"I would say, 'can't or won't,' but that's

such a hoary cliché."

She frowned. I thought that she was frowning at what I said, but I could see that wasn't it. Mackenzie was standing on top of the sliding board. "Mackenzie, that's dangerous."

"I do it all the time," the girl retorted.

"I don't care what you do all the time. Please sit down and slide."

She sat down. She didn't slide.

"The bank robbery?" I asked.

Shanta shook her head — again this action was not directed at what I had said, but at the stubborn girl at the top of the sliding board. "Have you heard anything about the rash of bank robberies in the New York area?"

I recalled a few articles I'd read. "The banks get hit at night when they're closed. The media calls the robbers the Invisibles or something."

"Right."

"What does Natalie have to do with them?"

"Her name came up in connection with one of the robberies — specifically the one on Canal Street in downtown Manhattan two weeks ago. It had been considered to be safer than Fort Knox. The thieves got twelve thousand in cash and busted open four hundred safety-deposit boxes."

"Twelve thousand doesn't sound like a ton."

"It's not. Despite what you see in the movies, banks don't store millions of dollars in vaults. But those safety-deposit boxes could be worth a fortune. That's where these guys are cleaning up. When my grandmother died, my mother put her four-carat diamond ring in a safety-deposit box to give me one day. That ring is probably worth forty grand alone. Who knows how much stuff is there? The insurance claim for one of their earlier robberies was three-point-seven million. Of course people lie. All of a sudden some expensive family heirloom happened to be in the box. But you see my point."

I saw her point. I didn't much care about it. "And Natalie's name came up with respect to this Canal Street robbery."

"Yes."

"How?"

"In a very, very small way." Shanta put her index finger and thumb half an inch apart to indicate how small. "Almost meaningless, really. It wouldn't be anything to care about on its own."

"But you do care."

"Now I do, yes."

"Why?"

"Because so much of what's surrounding your true love makes no sense anymore."

I couldn't argue with that.

"So what do you make of that?" she asked.

"Make of what? I don't know what to say here. I don't even know where Natalie is, much less how she might be connected in a very, very small way to a bank robbery."

"That's my point. I didn't think it mattered either, until I started looking up the other name you mentioned. Todd Sanderson."

"I didn't ask you to look him up."

"Yeah, but I did anyway. Got two hits on him too. Naturally the big hit surrounded the fact that he was murdered a week ago."

"Wait, Todd is also linked to this same bank robbery?"

"Yes. Did you ever read Oscar Wilde?"

I made a face. "Yes."

"He has a wonderful quote: 'To lose one parent may be regarded as a misfortune; to lose both looks like carelessness.' "

"From *The Importance of Being Earnest*," I said because I am an academic and can't help myself.

"Right. One of the people you asked about comes up in a bank robbery? That's nothing to get excited about. But two? That's not a coincidence."

And, I thought, a week or so after the bank robbery, Todd Sanderson was murdered.

"So was Todd's connection to the bank robbery also very, very small?" I asked.

"No. It was just small, I'd say."

"What was it?"

"Mackenzie!"

I turned toward the scream and saw a woman who looked a bit too much like Shanta Newlin for my taste. Same height, same relative weight, same hairstyle. The woman had her eyes wide open as though a plane had suddenly crashed in the backyard. I followed her gaze. Mackenzie was back standing on the slide.

Shanta was mortified. "I'm so sorry, Candace. I told her to sit down."

"You *told* her?" Candace repeated incredulously.

"I'm sorry. I was watching her. I was just talking to a friend."

"And that's an excuse?"

Mackenzie, with a smile that said, *My work is done here,* sat, slid down the slide, and ran toward Candace. "Hi, Mommy."

Mommy. No surprise there.

"Let me show you out," Shanta tried.

"We're already out," Candace said. "We can just go around the front."

"Wait, Mackenzie drew the nicest picture. It's inside. I bet she'll want to take it home."

Candace and Mackenzie were already heading toward the front of the house. "I have hundreds of my daughter's drawings," Candace called back. "Keep it."

Shanta watched them both disappear into the front yard. Her normal military posture was gone. "What the hell am I doing, Jake?"

"Trying," I said. "Living."

She shook her head. "This will never work."

"Do you love him?"

"Yes."

"It'll work. It'll just be messy."

"How did you get to be so wise?"

"I was educated at Lanford College," I said, "and I watch a lot of daytime talk shows."

Shanta turned and looked back toward the swing set. "Todd Sanderson had a safety-deposit box at the Canal Street bank," she said. "He was one of the victims of the robbery. That's all. On the surface of it, he's pretty meaningless too."

"But a week later, he gets murdered," I said.

"Yes."

"Wait, does the FBI think he has something to do with the robberies?"

"I'm not privy to the full investigation."

"But?"

"I didn't see how it could be connected — the bank robbery in Manhattan and his murder down in Palmetto Bluff."

"But now?"

"Well, your Natalie's name came up too."

"In a very, very small way."

"Yes."

"How small?"

"After a robbery like this, the FBI does an inventory of everything. I mean, everything. So when the safety-deposit boxes are blown up, most people have all kinds of important papers in them. Stocks and bonds, powers of attorney, deeds to homes, all that. A lot of that ended up on the floor, of course. Why would a thief want any paperwork? So the FBI goes through all that and catalogs it. So, for example, one guy was holding his brother's car deed. The brother's name goes on the list."

I was trying to keep up with what she was saying. "So let me see if I follow. Natalie's name was on one of those documents from the safety-deposit box?"

"Yes."

"But she didn't have a box of her own there?"

"No. It was found in a box belonging to

Todd Sanderson."

"So what was it? What's the document?"

Shanta turned and met my eye. "Her last will and testament."

CHAPTER 32

The FBI, Shanta said, wanted to know what I knew about all of this. I told her the truth: I knew nothing. I asked Shanta what the will and testament said. It was pretty simple: All of her assets should be split equally between her mother and sister. She had also left a request to be cremated, and interestingly enough, she wanted her ashes to be spread in the woods overlooking the quad at Lanford College.

I thought about the will and testament. I thought about where it had been found. The answer wasn't yet in my grasp, but it felt as though I were circling right above it.

As I started to leave, Shanta asked, "Are you sure you don't have any thoughts about this?"

"I'm sure," I said.

But I thought now that maybe I did. I just didn't want to share them with Shanta or the FBI. I trusted her as far as I could trust anyone who had openly told me that her first allegiance was to law enforcement. To tell her about Fresh Start, for example, would be catastrophic. But more to the point — and this was key — Natalie had not trusted law enforcement.

Why?

It was something I had never really considered before. Natalie could have trusted the cops and testified and gone into witness protection or something like that. But she didn't. Why? What did she know that prevented her from doing that? And if she didn't trust the cops, why on earth should I?

Once again I took out my cell phone and tried Malcolm Hume's number in Florida. Once again there was no answer. Enough. I hurried over to Clark House. Mrs. Dinsmore was just settling into her desk. She looked up at me over the half-moon reading glasses. "You're not supposed to be here."

I didn't bother defending or cracking wise. I told her about trying to reach Malcolm Hume.

"He's not in Vero Beach," she said.

"Do you know where he is?"

"I do."

"Could you tell me?"

She took her time shuffling papers and

sliding a paperclip into place. "He's staying at his cabin off Lake Canet."

I had been invited once many years ago for a fishing trip, but I didn't go. I hate fishing. I didn't get it, but then again I was never one for ease-back, Zen-type activities. I have trouble turning myself off. I'd rather read than relax. I'd rather keep the mind engaged. But I remembered that the property had been in Mrs. Hume's family for generations. He joked that he liked to feel like an interloper, that it made it more like a vacation spot.

Or like a spot perfect for hiding.

"I didn't know he still owned a place up here," I said.

"He comes up a few times a year. He enjoys the seclusion."

"I didn't know."

"He doesn't tell anyone."

"He tells you."

"Well," Mrs. Dinsmore said, as though that were the most obvious thing in the world. "He doesn't like company there. He needs to be alone so he can write and fish in peace and quiet."

"Yeah," I said. "Escape that hectic, jam-packed life at the gated community in Vero Beach."

"Funny."

"Thanks."

"You're on paid leave," she said. "So maybe you should, uh, leave."

"Mrs. Dinsmore?"

She looked up at me.

"You know all of the stuff I've been asking about lately?"

"You mean like murdered students and missing professors?"

"Yes."

"What about it?"

"I need you to give me the address of the lake house. I need to talk to Professor Hume in private."

CHAPTER 33

The life of a college professor, especially one who lives on a small campus, is pretty contained. You stay in the surreal world of so-called higher learning. You are comfortable there. You have very little reason to leave it. I owned a car, but probably drove it no more than once a week. I walked to all my classes. I walked into the town of Lanford to visit my favorite shops, haunts, cinema, restaurants, what have you. I worked out at the school's state-of-the-art weight room. It was an isolated world, not just for the students but also for those who have made such places our livelihood.

You tend to live in a snow globe of liberal-arts academia.

It alters your mind frame, of course, but on a purely physical level, I had probably done more traveling in the week-plus since seeing Todd Sanderson's obituary than I had done in the previous six years combined. That may be an exaggeration, but not much of one. The violent altercations, combined with the stiffness of sitting for hours in these car and plane rides, were sapping my energy. I'd been flying high on adrenaline, of course, but as I had learned the hard way, that resource was not unlimited.

As I turned off Route 202 and started climbing toward the rural area along the Massachusetts–New Hampshire border, my back started to seize up. I stopped at Lee's Hot Dog Stand to stretch a bit. A sign in the front promoted their fried haddock sandwich. I went instead with a hot dog, cheese fries, and a Coke. It all tasted wonderful, and for a second, heading up to this remote cabin, I thought about the notion of a last meal. That couldn't be a healthy mind frame. I ate ravenously, bought and downed another hot dog, and got back in the car. I felt strangely renewed.

I drove past Otter River State Forest. I was only about ten minutes from Malcolm Hume's house. I didn't have his cell phone number — I don't even know if he had one — but I wouldn't have called it anyway. I wanted to just show up and see what was what. I didn't want to give Professor Hume time to prepare. I wanted answers, and I suspected my old mentor had them.

I didn't really need to know it all. I knew enough. I only needed to be sure that Natalie was safe, that she understood some very bad people were back on her trail, and if possible, I wanted to see if I could run away and be with her. Yes, I had heard about Fresh Start's rules and oaths and all that, but the heart doesn't know from rules and oaths.

There had to be a way.

I almost missed the small sign for Attal Drive. I made a left onto the dirt road and started up the mountain. When I reached the top, Lake Canet was laid out below me, still as a mirror. People toss around the word *pristine,* but that word was taken to a new level of purity when I saw the water. I stopped the car and got out. The air had that kind of freshness that lets you know even one breath could nourish the lungs. The silence and stillness were almost devastating. I knew that if I called out, my shout would echo, would keep echoing, would never fully dissipate. The shout would live in these woods, growing dimmer and dimmer but never dying, joining the other past sounds that somehow still echoed into that low hum of the great outdoors.

I looked for a house on the lake. There

was none. I could see two docks. There were canoes tied to both of them. Nothing else. I got back in my car and drove to the left. The dirt road was not as well paved here. The car bounced on the rough terrain, testing the shocks and finding them wanting. I was glad I took the insurance out on the rental, which was a bizarre thing to think about at a time like this; but the mind goes where it goes. I remembered Professor Hume had owned a four-by-four pickup truck, not exactly standard liberal-arts driving fare. Now I knew why.

Up ahead I saw two pickup trucks parked side by side. I pulled my car behind them and got out. I couldn't help but notice that there were several sets of tire tracks in the dirt. Either Malcolm had gone back and forth repeatedly or he had company.

I wasn't sure what to make of that.

When I looked up the hill and saw the small cottage with the dark windows, I could feel my eyes start to well up.

There was no soft morning glow this time. There was no pinkness from the start of a new day. The sun was setting behind it, casting long shadows, turning what had appeared empty and abandoned into something more black and menacing.

It was the cottage from Natalie's painting.

I started up the hill toward the front door. There was something dream-like about this trek, something almost Alice in Wonderland-ish, as though I were leaving the real world and entering Natalie's painting. I reached the door. There was no bell to press. When I knocked, the sound ripped through the stillness like a gunshot.

I waited, but I heard no returning sound.

I knocked again. Still nothing. I debated my next move. I could walk down to the lake and see if Malcolm was on it, but that stillness I had witnessed earlier seemed to indicate that no one was down there. There was also the matter of all those tire tracks.

I put my hand on the knob. It turned. Not only was the door left unlocked, there was, I could see now, no actual lock on it — no hole in either the knob or the door to place a key. I pushed the door open and stepped inside. The room was dark. I flicked on the lights.

No one.

"Professor Hume?"

Once I'd graduated, he had insisted that I call him Malcolm. I never could.

I checked the kitchen. It was empty. There was only one bedroom. I headed toward it, tiptoeing for some odd reason across the floor.

When I stepped into the bedroom, my heart dropped like a stone.

Oh no . . .

Malcolm Hume was on the bed, lying on his back, dried foam on his face. His mouth was half open, his face twisted in a final, frozen scream of agony.

My knees buckled. I used the wall to support me. Memories rushed at me, nearly knocking me over: the first class I took with him freshman year (Hobbes, Locke, and Rousseau), the first time I met with him in that office I now called my own (we discussed depictions of law and violence in literature), the hours working on my thesis (subject: The Rule of Law), the way he bear-hugged me the day I graduated, with tears in his eyes.

A voice behind me said, "You couldn't leave it alone."

I spun around to see Jed pointing a gun at me.

"I didn't do this," I said.

"I know. He did it to himself." Jed stared at me. "Cyanide."

I remembered Benedict's pillbox now. All the members of Fresh Start, he said, carried one.

"We told you to leave it alone."

I shook my head, trying to keep it to-

431

gether, trying to tell the side of me that just wanted to collapse and grieve that there'd be time for that later. "This whole thing started before I got involved. I didn't know a damn thing about any of this until I saw Todd Sanderson's obituary."

Jed suddenly looked exhausted. "It doesn't matter. We asked you to stop in a million different ways. You wouldn't. It doesn't make a difference if you're guilty or innocent. You know about us. We took an oath."

"To kill me."

"In this case, yes." Jed looked again toward the bed. "If Malcolm was committed enough to do this to himself, shouldn't I be committed enough to kill you?"

But he didn't fire. Jed no longer relished shooting me. I could see that now. He had when he thought I'd been the one to kill Todd, but the idea of killing me just to keep me quiet was weighing on him. He looked back down at the body in the end.

"Malcolm loved you," Jed said. "He loved you like a son. He wouldn't want . . ." His voice just drifted off. The gun dropped to his side.

I took a tentative step toward him. "Jed?"

He turned to me.

"I think I know how Maxwell Minor's

men found Todd in the first place."

"How?"

"I need to ask you something first," I said. "Did Fresh Start begin with Todd Sanderson or Malcolm Hume or, well, you?"

"What does that have to do with anything?"

"Just . . . trust me for a second, okay?"

"Fresh Start began with Todd," Jed said. "His father was accused of a heinous crime."

"Pedophilia," I said.

"Yes."

"His father ended up killing himself over it," I said.

"You can't imagine what that did to Todd. I was his college roommate and best friend. I watched him fall apart. He railed against the unfairness of it all. If only his father could have moved away, we wondered. But of course, even if he had, that kind of accusation follows you. You can never escape it."

"Except," I said, "with a fresh start."

"Exactly. We realized that there were people who needed to be rescued — and the only way to rescue them was to give them a new life. Professor Hume understood too. He had a person in his life that could have used a fresh start."

I thought about that. I wondered whether

that "person" could very well have been Professor Aaron Kleiner.

"So we joined up," Jed continued. "We formed this group under the guise of a legitimate charity. My father was a federal marshal. He hid people in witness protection. I knew all the rules. I inherited that family farm from my grandfather. We made it into a retreat. We trained people how to act when they change identities. If you love gambling, for example, you don't go to Vegas or the track. We worked with them psychologically so they realized that disappearing was a form of suicide and renewal — you kill one being to create another. We created flawless new identities. We used misinformation to lead their stalkers down the wrong path. We added distracting tattoos and disguises. In certain instances, Todd performed cosmetic surgery to change a subject's appearance."

"So then what?" I asked. "Where did you relocate the people you rescued?"

Jed smiled. "That's the beauty. We didn't."

"I don't understand."

"You keep searching for Natalie, but you don't listen. None of us knows where she is. That's how it works. We couldn't tell you even if we wanted to. We give them all the tools and at some point, we drop them off

434

at a train station and have no idea where they end up. That's part of how we keep it safe."

I tried to push through what he was saying, the notion that there was absolutely no way I could find her, no way that we could ever be together. It was simply too crushing to think that all of this had been futile from the start.

"At some point," I said, "Natalie came to you guys for help."

Again Jed looked down at the bed. "She came to Malcolm."

"How did she know him?" I asked.

"I don't know."

But I did. Natalie's mother had told her daughter about Archer Minor's cheating scandal and how her father had been forced to vanish. She would have tried to track her father down, so naturally Malcolm Hume would be one of the first people she would visit. Malcolm would have befriended her, the daughter of the beloved colleague who had been forced to disappear. Had Malcolm helped her father run from Archer Minor's family? I don't know. I suspected that he probably did. Either way, Aaron Kleiner was Malcolm's impetus for joining Fresh Start. His daughter would be someone he'd immediately care about and take under his wing.

"Natalie came to you guys because she witnessed a murder," I said.

"Not just any murder. The murder of Archer Minor."

I nodded. "So she witnesses the murder. She goes to Malcolm. Malcolm brings her to your retreat."

"First he brought her here."

Of course, I thought. The painting. This place inspired it.

Jed was smiling.

"What?"

"You don't get it, do you?"

"Get what?"

"You were so close to Malcolm," he said. "Like I said. He loved you like a son."

"I'm not following."

"Six years ago, when you needed help writing your dissertation, Malcolm Hume was the one who suggested the Vermont retreat to you, didn't he?"

I felt a small coldness seep into my bones. "Yeah, so?"

"Fresh Start isn't just the three of us, of course. We have a committed staff. You met Cookie and some of the others. There aren't many, for obvious reasons. We have to trust each other completely. At one point, Malcolm thought that you'd be an asset to the organization."

"Me?"

"That was why he suggested that you attend that retreat. He hoped to show you what Fresh Start was doing so that you'd join us."

I didn't know what to say, so I went with the obvious: "Why didn't he?"

"He realized that you wouldn't be a good fit."

"I don't understand."

"We work in a murky world, Jake. Some of the things we do are illegal. We make our own rules. We decide who is deserving and who is not. The line between innocence and guilt isn't so clear with us."

I nodded, seeing it now. The black-and-white — and the grays. "Professor Eban Trainor."

"He broke a rule. You wanted him punished. You couldn't see the extenuating circumstances."

I thought about how Malcolm had defended Eban Trainor after the party where two students had been rushed to the hospital for alcohol poisoning. Now I saw the truth. Professor Hume's defense of Trainor had been, in part, a test — one that in Malcolm's mind I had failed. He was right

437

though. I believe in the rule of law. If you start down that slippery slope, you take all of what makes us civilized with you.

At least, that was how I felt before this week.

"Jake?"

"Yes?"

"Do you really know how the Minors found Todd Sanderson?"

"I think so," I said. "You keep some paperwork on Fresh Start, right?"

"Only on a web cloud. And you needed two of the three of us — Todd, Malcolm, or me — to access it." He blinked, looked away, blinked some more. "I just realized. I'm the only one left. The paperwork is gone forever."

"But there must be something physical you store, no?"

"Like what?" he asked.

"Like their last will and testament?"

"Well, yes, those, but they're kept someplace where no one can find them."

"You mean like a safety-deposit box on Canal Street?"

Jed's mouth dropped open. "How can you know that?"

"It was broken into. Someone got into the safety-deposit boxes. I can't say what happened for sure, but Natalie was still a huge

438

priority for the Minor family. If you found her, it could mean big bucks. So my guess is, someone — the thieves, a cop on the take, whatever — recognized her name. They reported it to the Minors. The Minors saw that the box was taken out by a guy named Todd Sanderson who lived in Palmetto Bluff, South Carolina."

"My God," Jed said. "So they paid him a visit."

"Yes."

"Todd was tortured," Jed said.

"I know."

"They made him talk. A man can only stand so much pain. But Todd didn't know where Natalie or anyone else was. See? He could only tell them what he knew."

"Like about you and the retreat in Vermont," I said.

Jed nodded. "That's why we had to close it down. That's why we had to run away and pretend that there was nothing there but a farm. Do you understand?"

"I do," I said.

He looked back down at Malcolm's body. "We need to bury him, Jake. You and me. Out here in this place he loved."

And then I realized something else that chilled me to the bone. Jed could see it on my face.

"What?"

"Todd never got the chance to take the cyanide pill."

"They probably surprised him."

"Right, and if they tortured him and he gave up your name, it stands to reason that he gave up Malcolm's name too. They probably sent men to Vero Beach. But Malcolm was already gone. He came up here to this cabin. The house would have been empty. But these guys don't quit easily. They'd just found their first clue in six years — they weren't about to just let it go. They would have asked questions and pored through personal records. Even if this land was still in his late wife's name, they may have found this place."

I thought about all those tire tracks outside.

"He's dead," I said, looking down at the bed. "He chose to kill himself, and judging by the lack of decay, he did it very recently. Why?"

"Oh God." Jed saw it now too. "Because Minor's guys found him."

As he said those words, I heard cars pull up. It was so clear now. Minor's men had been here already. Malcolm Hume had seen them coming and taken matters into his own hands.

So what would they do about that?

They'd have set a trap. They'd leave someone behind to stake out the house in case someone else showed up.

Jed and I both rushed to the window as the two black cars came to a stop. The doors opened. Five men with guns came out.

One of them was Danny Zuker.

CHAPTER 34

The men kept low and spread out.

Jed reached into his pocket and pulled out a pillbox. He opened it and tossed the pill inside to me.

"I don't want this," I said.

"I have the gun. I'll try to hold them. You try to find a way to escape. But if you can't . . ."

From outside we heard Danny call out. "Only one way out of this!" he shouted. "Come out with your hands up."

We had both ducked down to the floor.

"You believe him?" Jed asked me.

"No."

"Me neither. There's no way they're going to let us live. So all we're doing right now is giving them time to set up." He started to rise. "Find an escape route out the back, Jake. I'll keep them busy."

"What?"

"Just go!"

Without warning, Jed knocked out a windowpane and started to pull the trigger. Within seconds, return gunfire raked the side of the house and took out the rest of the window. Shards of glass fell on me.

"Go!" Jed shouted at me.

No reason to tell me a third time. I commando-crawled toward the back door. It was, I knew, my only chance. Jed started firing blindly, keeping his back against the wall. I headed into the kitchen, still moving low across the acrylic. I reached the back door.

I heard Jed let out a celebratory shout. "Nailed one!"

Great. Four to go. More gunfire. Heavier now. The walls were starting to give way, the bullets weakening and now penetrating the wood. From where I was, I saw Jed get hit once, then twice. I started back toward him.

"Don't!" he shouted at me.

"Jed . . ."

"Don't you dare! Get out now!"

I wanted to help him, but I could also see how foolhardy that would be. It wouldn't help him. It would just be suicide. Jed managed to stand. He was heading for the front door.

"Okay!" he shouted out. "I surrender."

Jed had the gun in his hand. He looked back at me, winked, gestured for me to keep going.

I glanced out the back window, preparing to make a break for it. The house was right up against a wooded area. I could go into those woods and just hope for the best. I didn't have another plan. At least nothing that would help immediately. I took out my iPhone and flipped it on. There was service. I dialed 911 as I looked out the window.

One of the men was in the back on the left, covering the door. Damn.

"Nine-one-one, what is your emergency?"

I told her quickly that there were shots being fired and at least two men hit. I gave her the address and put the phone down, keeping the line open. From behind me, I heard Danny Zuker shout, "Okay, throw the gun out first."

I thought that I saw a smile on Jed's face now. He was bleeding. I didn't know how badly he was hit, if his current injuries were mortal or not, but Jed knew. Jed knew that his life was over no matter what he did and with that, there seemed to come a strange sense of peace.

Jed opened the door and just started firing. I heard another man call out in pain — maybe another one of Jed's bullets had found its mark — and then I heard the hollow pop of automatic gunfire tearing into flesh. From my vantage point, I saw Jed's body fly backward, arms dangling overhead as though in a macabre dance. He fell back into the house. More bullets hit him, jerking his lifeless body.

It was over. For him and probably for me.

Even if Jed had managed to kill two of them, three would still be alive and armed. What chance did I have? I calculated the odds in nanoseconds. Almost zilch. I had one chance, really. Stall. Stall until the police could get there. I thought about how far out we were, about that drive up the dirt road, about not seeing any municipal-type buildings within miles of this place.

The cavalry wouldn't be arriving in time.

Still the Minors may want me alive.

I was their last chance to get information on Natalie. I could tap-dance a bit that way.

They were approaching the house. I looked for a place to hide.

Stall. Just stall.

But there was nowhere to go. I stood up and looked out the back door window. The man was there, just waiting for me. I sprinted across the kitchen and back into the bedroom. Malcolm hadn't moved, but then again I hadn't expected him to.

I could hear someone enter the cottage.

I threw open the bedroom window. What I was counting on here — and really it was my only shot — was that the man in back was watching the door. The bedroom window was on the side toward the right. From where the guy had been standing when I saw him from the kitchen, he wouldn't be able to see this window.

From the main room, I heard Danny Zuker say, "Professor Fisher? We know you're in here. It'll be worse for you if you make us wait."

The window shrieked when I opened it. Zuker and another henchman ran toward the sound. I saw them as I rolled out the window and started to sprint for the woods.

Gunfire erupted behind me.

So much for keeping me alive. I didn't know if it was my imagination or reality, but I could swear that I felt bullets nipping at my side. I kept running. I didn't turn around. I just kept . . .

Someone tackled me from the side.

It must have been the guy who'd been out back. He hit from the left, knocking us both down. I prepared a punch and delivered it hard to his face. He rocked back. I reeled back to deliver another one. Again it landed. He went slack.

But it was too late now.

Danny Zuker and the other henchman stood over us. They both pointed their guns down at me.

"You can live," Zuker said simply. "Just tell me where she is."

"I don't know."

"Then you're worthless to me."

It was over. I could see that now. The man who'd tackled me shook his head. He stood and grabbed his gun. There I was, lying on the ground, surrounded by three men, all with guns. There was no move I could make. There were no distant sirens coming to my rescue. One man stood on my left, the other — the one I had decked — stood on my right.

I looked up at Danny Zuker, who stayed a step back. I threw up one last Hail Mary: "You killed Archer Minor, didn't you?"

That caught him off guard. I could see the befuddlement on his face. "What?"

"Someone had to quiet him," I said, "and Maxwell Minor would never murder his own kid."

"You're crazy."

The other two men exchanged a glance.

"Why else would you try so hard to find her?" I asked. "It's been six years. You know she'd never testify."

Danny Zuker shook his head. There was something akin to sadness on his face. "You don't have a clue, do you?"

He raised the gun, almost reluctantly now. I had played my final card. I didn't want to die like this, on the ground beneath them. I stood up, wondering what my final move would be, when it was made for me.

There was a single gunshot. The head of the man on my left exploded like a tomato under a heavy boot.

The rest of us turned toward the sound of the gunshot. I recovered the fastest. Letting the lizard brain take over again, I dived straight toward the man I'd already punched. He was closest to me, and he'd be weakest from my earlier blow.

I could get his gun.

But the man reacted with greater speed than I anticipated. His lizard brain at work too, I guess. He stepped back and took aim. I was too far away to reach him in time.

And then his head exploded in another crimson haze.

The blood splashed me in the face. Danny Zuker didn't hesitate. He leapt behind me, using me as a shield. He wrapped his arm around my throat and put the gun against my head.

"Don't move," he whispered.

I didn't. There was silence now. He stayed close to me, moving us back toward the house to keep himself protected.

"Show yourself," Zuker shouted. "Show yourself or I'll blow his brains out!"

There was a rustling sound. Zuker jerked my head to the right, making sure to keep my body blocking his. He turned me more toward the right — to where the rustling had originated. I looked out into the clearing.

My heart stopped.

Coming down the hill, gun still in her hand and aimed at us, was Natalie.

CHAPTER 35

Danny Zuker spoke first. "Well, well, look who's here."

My body had gone numb at the sight of her. Our eyes met — Natalie's and mine — and the world exploded in a thousand different ways. It was one of the most powerful experiences of my life, this simple act of looking into the blue eyes of the woman I loved, and even now, even with a gun to my head, I felt oddly grateful. If he pulled the trigger, so be it. I had, in this single moment, been more alive than any time in the previous six years. If I were to die now — and, no, I didn't want to, in fact, more than anything else I wanted to live and be with that woman — I'd die a more complete person, have lived a more complete life, than if I had died just a few moments earlier.

With the gun still trained on us, Natalie said, "Let him go."

She never took her eyes off me.

450

"I don't think so, sweetheart," Zuker said.

"Let him go, and you can have me."

I shouted, "No!"

Zuker drove the muzzle of the gun into the side of my neck. "Shut up." Then to Natalie he said, "Why should I trust you?"

"If I cared more about myself than him," she said, "I wouldn't have revealed myself."

Natalie kept her eyes on me. I wanted to protest. There was no way I would allow this exchange, but something in her look told me to keep still, at least for now. I thought about it. She was almost willing me to obey, to just let this play out the way she wanted.

Maybe, I thought, she wasn't here alone. Maybe there were others. Maybe she had a plan.

"Okay then," Zuker said, still hiding behind my body. "Put your gun down and I'll let him go."

"I don't think so," she said.

"Oh?"

"We bring him out to his car. You put him in the driver's seat. The moment he pulls away, I put the gun down."

Zuker seemed to be thinking that over. "I put him in the car. You drop your weapon and he drives off."

Natalie nodded again, still looking directly

at me, almost willing me to obey. "Deal," she said.

We started toward the front of the house. Natalie kept her distance, staying about thirty yards back from us. I wondered whether Cookie or Benedict or some other member of Fresh Start was nearby. Maybe they were waiting by the car, armed, ready to take Zuker out with a single bullet.

When we reached the car, Zuker took an angle so that the vehicle and my body were still shielding him. "Open the door," he told me.

I hesitated.

He pressed the gun against my neck. "Open the door."

I looked back at Natalie. She gave me a confident smile that reached into my chest and crushed it like an eggshell. As I slipped into the driver's seat, I realized with mounting horror what she was doing.

There was no plan to save us both.

There were no other Fresh Start members who were going to intercede. There was no one hiding, waiting to pounce. Natalie had kept my attention, had offered up this hope in her eyes, so I wouldn't fight back, so I wouldn't make the sacrifice she was about to make for me.

To hell with that.

The car started up. Natalie began to lower her weapon. I had a second, no more, to make my move. It was suicide. I knew that. I knew that there was no way the two of us could survive this. That had been her thinking. One of us had to die. In the end, Jed and Benedict and Cookie had been right. I had messed up. I had stubbornly followed some love-conquers-all inner mantra, and now here we were, exactly where I was warned we would be, with Natalie facing death.

I wouldn't let that happen.

Once I was in the car, Natalie stopped walking and turned her attention to Danny Zuker. Zuker, understanding that it was his turn, moved the gun away from my neck. He changed hands so that the weapon was too far away from me, sitting as I was, to make any kind of foolish move.

"Your turn," Zuker said.

Natalie put her weapon on the ground.

Time was up. I had spent the seconds planning my exact move, the exact calculation, the element of surprise, all of it. Now I didn't hesitate. Zuker would have time, I was fairly sure, to take a shot at me. That didn't matter. He was going to have to defend himself. If he did that by shooting me, it would give Natalie the time to either run or, more likely, pick her own gun back off the ground and shoot.

No choice for me now. I wasn't driving off, that was for sure.

Without warning, my left hand shot up high. I don't think he expected that. Zuker had figured that if I did anything, I'd go for the gun. I grabbed his hair hard and pulled him toward me. As I predicted, Danny swung the gun in my direction.

With my left hand, I pulled his face closer to mine. He expected my right to go for the gun.

It didn't.

Instead, using the right hand, I jammed the cyanide pill Jed had given me into Zuker's mouth. His eyes widened in terror as he realized what I had done. That made him hesitate — the realization that there was cyanide in his mouth and that if he didn't get it out, he was a dead man. He tried to spit it out but my hand was there. He bit down hard, making me scream out, but my hand stayed still. At the same time he fired the gun at my head.

I ducked away.

The bullet hit my shoulder. More agony.

Danny started to convulse, taking aim for another shot. But he never got that one off. Natalie's first bullet caught him in the back of the head. She fired twice more, but there was no need.

I fell back, my hand on my throbbing shoulder, trying to stop the blood. I waited for her to come over to me.

But she didn't. She stayed where she was.

I had never seen anything more beautiful and crushing than the expression on her face. A tear ran down her cheek. She just slowly shook her head.

"Natalie?"

"I have to go," she said.

My eyes went wide. "No." Now, finally, I could hear the sirens. I was losing blood and feeling faint. None of that mattered. "Let me go with you. Please."

Natalie winced. Her tears came heavier now. "I can't live if something happens to you. Do you get that? It's why I ran the first time. I can live with you heartbroken. I can't live with you dead."

"I'm not alive without you."

The sirens were growing closer.

"I have to go," she said, through her tears.

"No . . ."

"I will always love you, Jake. Always."

"Then be with me." I could hear the plea in my voice.

"I can't. You know that. Don't follow me.

Don't look for me. Keep your promise this time."

I shook my head. "Not a chance," I said.

She turned and started back up the hill.

"Natalie!" I called out.

But the woman I loved just kept walking out of my life. Again.

CHAPTER 36

One year later

A student in the back of the room raises his hand. "Professor Weiss?"

"Yes, Kennedy?" I say.

That's my name now. Paul Weiss. I teach at a large university in New Mexico. I can't say the name of it for security reasons. With all the dead bodies at the lake, the powers that be realized that I'd be best off in witness protection. So here I am, out in the west. The altitude still gets to me sometimes, but overall I like it out here. That surprises me. I always thought I'd be an East Coast guy, but life is about making adjustments, I guess.

I miss Lanford, of course. I miss my old life. Benedict and I still stay in touch, even though we shouldn't. We use an e-mail drop box and never hit the send button. We created an e-mail account with AOL (old-school). We write each other messages and just leave them in the draft section. Periodically we go in and check it.

The big news in Benedict's life is that the drug cartel that was after him is gone. They were wiped out in some kind of turf battle. In short, he is free at last to return to Marie-Anne, but when he last checked her Facebook status, it had changed from "in a relationship" to "married." There were photographs of her wedding to Kevin all over both their Facebook pages.

I'm urging him to tell her the truth anyway. He says he won't. He says he doesn't want to mess up her life.

But life is messy, I told him.

Deep thought, right?

The rest of the pieces of the puzzle have finally come together for me. It took a long while. One of the Minor henchmen that Jed shot survived. His testimony confirmed what I had suspected. The bank robbers known as the Invisibles broke into the Canal Street bank. In Todd Sanderson's box, there were both last wills and testaments and passports. The Invisibles had taken the passports, figuring that they could be resold on the black market. One of them recognized Natalie's name — the Minors were still actively looking for her, even after six years — and reported it to them. The box was in Todd Sanderson's name, so Danny Zuker and Otto Devereaux paid him a visit.

You know where it went from there. Or you know most of it.

But a lot of things didn't add up. I had raised one with Danny Zuker right before his life ended: Why were the Minors so consumed with finding Natalie? She had made it pretty clear that she wouldn't testify. Why stir that up, flush her out, when the end result could very well be her running back to the police? I had at one point surmised that it was really Danny Zuker behind it all, that he had killed Archer Minor and wanted to make sure that the one person who could tell Maxwell Minor that fact was dead. But that didn't really add up either, especially when I saw the befuddlement on his face when I accused him of the crime.

"You don't have a clue, do you?"

That was what Danny Zuker had said. He'd been right. But I'd slowly started putting it together, especially when I started to wonder about the central question left here, the incident that started it all:

Where was Natalie's father?

I figured out the answer to that almost a year ago. Two days before they sent me to New Mexico, I visited Natalie's mother again at the Hyde Park Assisted Living facility. I wore a cheesy disguise. (Now my disguise is simpler: I've shaved my head. Gone are the unruly professorial locks of my youth. My dome gleams. If I wore a gold earring, you'd mistake me for Mr. Clean.)

"I need the truth this time," I said to Sylvia Avery.

"I told you."

I could see people needing new identities and vanishing because they'd been accused of pedophilia or had upset members of a drug cartel or had been battered by brutal husbands or had witnessed a mob hit. But I didn't see why a man involved in a college cheating scandal would have to vanish for life — even now, even after Archer Minor was dead.

"Natalie's dad never ran away, did he?"

She didn't reply.

"He was murdered," I said.

Sylvia Avery seemed too weak to protest anymore. She sat there, still as a stone.

"You told Natalie that her father would never, ever, abandon her."

"He wouldn't," she said. "He loved her so. He loved Julie too. And me. Aaron was such a good man."

"Too good," I said. "Always seeing just the black-and-white."

"Yes."

"When I told you that Archer Minor was dead, you said, 'Good riddance.' Was he the one who killed your husband?"

She lowered her head.

"There's no one who can hurt any of you anymore," I said, which was only partially true. "Did Archer Minor kill your husband, or was it someone his father sent?"

And then she said it: "It was Archer himself."

I nodded. I had figured that.

"He came to the house with a gun," Sylvia said. "He demanded that Aaron give him the papers that proved he'd cheated. You see, he really did want to escape his father's shadow and if word got out he cheated . . ."

"He'd be exactly like his father."

"Yes. I begged Aaron to listen to him. He wouldn't. He thought Archer was bluffing. So Archer put the gun against Aaron's head and . . ." She closed her eyes. "He smiled when he did it. That's what I remember most. Archer Minor was smiling. He told me to give him the papers or I'd be next. I gave them to him, of course. Then two men came by. Men who worked for his father. They took Aaron's body away. Then one of the men sat me down. He said if I ever told anyone about this, they'd do horrible things

461

to my girls. They wouldn't just kill them, he said. They'd do horrible things to them first. He kept stressing that. He told me to say that Aaron ran off. So I did. I kept the lie up for all those years to protect my girls. You understand that, don't you?"

"I do," I said sadly.

"I had to make my poor Aaron be the bad guy. So his daughters wouldn't keep asking about him."

"But Natalie wouldn't buy it."

"She kept pressing."

"And like you said, the lie had darkened her. The idea that her father had abandoned her."

"That's a horrible thing for a young girl to think. I should have come up with another way. But what?"

"So she pressed and she pressed," I said.

"She wouldn't leave it alone. She headed back to Lanford and talked to Professor Hume."

"But Hume didn't know either."

"No. But she kept asking questions."

"And that could have gotten her in trouble."

"Yes."

"So you decided to tell her the truth. Her father hadn't run away with a coed. He hadn't run away because he was afraid of the Minors. You finally told her the full story — that Archer Minor had murdered her father in cold blood while smiling."

Sylvia Avery didn't nod. She didn't have to. I said good-bye then and left.

So now I knew why Natalie was in that high-rise late that night. Now I knew why Natalie had gone to visit Archer Minor when no one else would be around. Now I knew why Maxwell Minor never stopped looking for Natalie. He isn't worried about her testifying.

He's a father who wants to avenge his son's murder.

I don't know this for sure. I don't know if Natalie shot Archer Minor with a smile on her face or if the gun went off accidentally or if Archer Minor made threats when she confronted him or if it was self-defense. I don't even ask.

The old me would have cared. The new me doesn't.

Class ends. I start across the commons. The Santa Fe sky is a blue like no other. I shade my eyes and keep walking.

That day a year ago, with the bullet still in my shoulder, I watched Natalie start to walk away. I shouted, "Not a chance" when she asked me to promise not to follow. She wouldn't listen to me or stop. So I got out of the car. The pain in my shoulder was nothing compared with the pain of her leaving me again. I ran toward her. I wrapped my arms, even the one aching from the bullet wound, around her and pulled her close. Our eyes squeezed shut. I hung on to her, wondering if I had ever felt such contentment before. She started to cry. I pulled her even closer. She lowered her head into my chest. For a moment, she tried to pull away. But only for a moment. She knew that this time I wouldn't let her go.

No matter what she might or might not have done.

I still haven't let her go.

Up ahead, a beautiful woman named Diana Weiss wears a wedding band that matches mine. She has decided to teach her art class outside on this glorious day. She moves from student to student, commenting on their work, offering guidance.

She knows that I know, even though we've never talked about it. I wonder whether that was part of her leaving the first time, if she felt as though I could never live with the truth about what she'd done. Maybe I couldn't back then.

I can now.

Diana Weiss looks up at me as I approach. Her smile shames the sun. Today my beautiful wife is glowing even more than normal. I may be thinking that about her because I'm biased. Or I may be thinking that because she is seven months pregnant with our child.

Her class ends. The students linger before slowly drifting away. She takes my hand when we're finally alone, looks into my eyes, and says, "I love you."

"I love you too," I say.

She smiles up at me. The gray has no chance against that smile. It vanishes in a wonderful haze of bright color.

ABOUT THE AUTHOR

Harlan Coben is the internationally best-selling author of more than twenty previous novels, including the #1 *New York Times* bestsellers *Stay Close, Live Wire, Caught, Long Lost,* and *Hold Tight,* as well as the popular Myron Bolitar series and more recently, a series aimed at young adults featuring Myron's nephew, Mickey Bolitar. Winner of the Edgar, Shamus, and Anthony awards, Coben lives in New Jersey.

The employees of Thorndike Press hope you have enjoyed this Large Print book. All our Thorndike, Wheeler, and Kennebec Large Print titles are designed for easy reading, and all our books are made to last. Other Thorndike Press Large Print books are available at your library, through selected bookstores, or directly from us.

For information about titles, please call:
(800) 223-1244

or visit our Web site at:
http://gale.cengage.com/thorndike

To share your comments, please write:
Publisher
Thorndike Press
10 Water St., Suite 310
Waterville, ME 04901